SUMMER AT LAST CHANCE BOOKSHOP

EVE

FROST WOLF

ISBN Paperback 978-1-910426-50-0

ISBN ebook 978-1-910426-49-4

PROLOGUE

What's past is prologue...
Shakespeare, 'The Tempest'

This is the story I don't want to tell.

Once upon a time, there was a girl who lived in a cottage in the woods. (You know how this goes, don't you? Nothing good ever happens to little girls in these kind of tales.) She thought it was a place of wonder. Magic creatures dwelt in the trees and her home was the court of a powerful wizard.

Except it wasn't.

When the curtain rose, she found it was home to thieves, liars and murderers.

All of which she became.

ACT 1

1

A thousand words leave not the same deep impression as does a single deed.

Henrik Ibsen

Even though I swore I would never come here, I find myself standing outside the bookshop, checking my phone again that I have the right address. Can this be it? The place looks like it might have gone out of business, along with the restaurant next door. The pandemic has cut a swathe through the already fragile high street. Someone has left rubbish sacks in the doorway and the windows are dusty. A little sign, 'Help Wanted', seemed more a plea than a job advertisement. Had the last theatrical bookshop in England taken its final bow already?

The doors flies open and a woman with a silver-pink pixie haircut framing her soft round face stands in the entrance.

'Bags, Vi!' she calls over her shoulder.

There is a pause.

'If they've mistaken us for a charity shop again, I'm going to complain,' a second female voice calls from further inside the shop. 'Tell whoever it is that we're not responsible for recycling all of London's copies of *Fifty Shades*!'

'Complain to whom, darling? The council? The police? E.L. James?' The pixie's voice is courteous and melodious, sounding sincerely interested in her partner's reply; she is in no hurry to shift the obstruction that prevents her from getting out her front door.

I wonder if I should pick a better moment. I really should. This was a bad idea.

'I told you we ought to get gates fitted. Everyone else around here has them; that's why people dump stuff on ours.' The second speaker approaches, more strident, a little bossy. Her looks match: a hollowed-out face with high cheekbones, hair chopped into a bob, currently scraped back by a fabric Alice band. Easter Island monolith in Central London. 'Ah. More books.'

'That's what I said, Viv. When did you stop listening to me?' says the pixie.

'In about 1975.'

'Oh you!'

But I've come a long way. It seems pathetic to lose confidence now.

'Excuse me?' I try tentatively.

The pixie woman turns to smile at me. There is a child-like innocence to her even though her cheeks sag to her neck like wax bending in a slow curl from an altar candle. Add a wimple and she could play the Reverend Mother in *The Sound of Music*.

'You're...open?' I manage at last.

'Good lord, no. It's only seven-thirty. We're going for our run,' says the strident one, Viv.

I had meant open as in 'not closed down for good' but that seems too difficult to explain. I register that the pixie lady is dressed in patterned leggings and long-sleeved sports top that says 'Fabulous at Fifty'. If I had to guess, the lady is actually more like fabulous at sixty-five.

'She's too early to be a customer, Bette.' The second woman speaks in a too-loud voice that tells me one of them is a little deaf. Her running gear is a serious all-black outfit with cropped leggings that don't hide a rope of varicose veins, and tank top that displays toned arms.

'Sorry. I'll come back later.' I pick up my tote, spilling out the rescued autobiography of Antony Sher—*Year of the Mad King*. Both women gaze at it in wonder as if I have just eviscerated a sacred goose and produced a favourable augury.

'Well, well. She likes dear Antony, may he rest in peace,' said Bette the Pixie in a hushed voice. 'Maybe she *is* a customer?'

'Then she'd better come in.' Viv is already plucking the book from the tiled step.

I back away in alarm. The two women remind me of the kind of pairings you get in Roald Dahl stories, elderly aunts who are short and tall, fat and thin, a little sinister. Bad things happen if you go anywhere with them. 'It's OK. Not a customer. I'll just...' I wave vaguely towards Shaftesbury Avenue. I'd wanted answers and thought this was the place to get them, but now I'm not sure.

'Nonsense,' says Viv. 'You're clearly here for a reason. Make yourself a cup of tea while we go for our run. We won't be long. We'll sort you out when we return.' Bette nods in agreement, standing back to let me pass.

Thoughts of wicked aunts fizzle out. The shop looks

dark and quiet, so much more inviting than the bustle of the commuting streets. I have so many questions and maybe I'd have a chance to find answers to a few here. 'Thanks. But I won't stay.'

'Oh do.' Bette smiles at me. Somehow I know she's seeing past the cropped hair and split lip. Who are these women? I know I look like a photo on a 'Wanted in Connection' poster, but they are giving me free run of the shop?

'Bette, we're getting behind schedule!' calls Viv, checking her Fitbit. 'We've only done two hundred steps!'

'Slave driver.' Bette rolls her eyes. 'Really, you are very welcome. Rough night?'

'Um, fell over. Unfamiliar bedroom.' I've relied on friends since my life went off course, couch surfing until I wore out my welcome. I'd banged into a clothes rail last night, waking the household.

'I know how that feels. Have some tea.'

Viv has already carried my tote inside, Antony Sher her prisoner. So I suppose that means I'm going in too.

'Sure. OK. Thanks.' Eloquence has gone the same way as my dignity. All that university education wasted. Not that I completed it.

Completion is not in you. Someone said that to me once. Can't remember who right now but they were important at the time.

I cross the threshold.

'Stand guard!' calls Viv, possibly to me. At least, I hope it is and not to some fierce Rottweiler. The door bangs and they're gone. Really gone. No guard dog. They've left me, a complete stranger, standing in the middle of the strangest shop I've ever seen.

. . .

THAT'S WHERE I START. Or finish, depending how you look at it. Standing on the doorstep of the last independent theatrical bookshop in the country. A snake with the tail in her mouth. I'm back sucking on the playwrights. The shop is called Last Chance Bookshop. I know the name, of course, like I know my own blotted family history. It's the place to dash to just before curtain up. Anyone who has anything to do with acting knows about it, which is why I'm here. Its archive is said to be unrivalled. When I'd seen the graffitied frontage, old bills on the closed metal shutters, I'd assumed that it had gone the way of most bookshops and become the fossilised imprint of its old existence. Maybe its spirit had been translated to some online afterlife of downloadable resources, but the creature itself had surely lumbered off into the digital sunset?

Still, it feels like a species under threat of extinction. Standing in the middle of the narrow shop, shelf upon shelf of scripts crowding me from under their swags of old curtain fringes, I experience a similar confusion to watching Punch and Judy at the Burford village fair years ago. Cosily funny but horribly violent. All those pages of love, anguish and evisceration. Wheels of words, shouting silences, vertiginous verbiage waiting to be unleashed. Biographies of vanity and vaingloriousness. Accounts of the shamans, shockers and charlatans.

I've come home.

BUT FIRST I go to the bathroom to wash my face and hands. The employees' W.C. is crammed in the back of the shop in a corner of the stockroom, small enough so you can reach out and balance when dizzy. That lip really does look bad. I should leave now but I'm exhausted by carrying so many questions. I feel a hundred years old.

I splash cold water on my face.

I've got to do something about myself.

Guessing that I have maybe twenty minutes before my absent hostesses return, I dry off with grey hand towels that cascade from the unit in clumps of six when I try to pull out one. It makes me want to cry and curse: a stupid overreaction to such a mundane malfunction. I wad them up and throw them in the bin.

Tea. They said to make tea.

A kettle stands on top of an old grey safe, the kind robbers haul out of banks in film about 1930s gangsters, pulled by a team of horses. Yee-hah—and away they gallop with the sheriff throwing his hat to the dust in frustration.

Lifting the kettle, I find it contains enough water for a single cup so I click it on. It roars with an unexpectedly loud noise, like it is angry at me for daring to make it heat. It clicks and huffs but then clunks off. I throw a teabag in a clean mug and gingerly pour in the boiled water. It spits and crackles but deigns to fill the cup. I prod the bag like a murderer trying to get rid of a body in a little brown sinkhole. I lift it out, squeeze against the side, and discard on top of the pile of teabag corpses. There's no milk in evidence so I drink it black, punishing myself with the hot, bitter taste.

Mine is not a life of milk and honey. It's a life of black tea and bitter pills. I've failed to launch myself, Jodie, one of my old university friends had said just last week as she sashayed off to start her training contract with a city firm. If she didn't have one of the best sofas, I would've been less willing to listen to her truths. It would be so good to walk away and audition for a new part. Maybe I could follow others of my generation, give up on England entirely. I could tag along as they shout YOLO, jumping from waterfalls, drink mojitos on a beach in Mexico, or sip green tea at a ceremony in Japan?

Impossible dreams. The problem with your real existence is you can't just dump it for another you'd prefer to play.

You never learned that, did you, Dad?

Maybe I should just abandon my quest for answers, shut the door on that dark cupboard containing unreliable memories?

The bell jangles. They can't be back already? I thought I could slip away before that.

'Viv, Bette?' It's another woman. Not my hosts. Only a little younger than me. Jarringly perky. I lumber from the back, a Calibanish creature from her lair.

'They're out.' Did I just growl? I've forgotten how to speak like a normal person, having had to bite my tongue for so long.

'Right.' A woman stands in the doorway, a flat cardboard box balanced on her hand like a waiter bearing a tray through a crowded cocktail bar. Dark hair is pulled high in a cheerleader's ponytail, still swinging from her entrance. 'I've got their pastries. Can you tell them Ayesha came by?'

'Um, I'm not staying. Just using the loo.'

'Oh. But the door isn't locked. What if...?' She gestured to the world beyond as if all sorts of pastry-stealing, book-thieving people could be waiting out there.

Another thought strikes. If I left, would I be inadvertently leaving their place to early morning looters? Maybe that's what the 'stand guard' meant? It would be a nice way to repay my Good Samaritans if I decamped early.

Manners: you never entirely grew out of them.

'OK then, I'll make sure they get them.'

'Thanks, um...?'

She's asking for my name—that's what civilised people do.

I scrape up some honesty from the bottom of my barrel of truths. 'Merle.'

'Thanks, Merle. Got to run. Lectures.' Ayesha shoulders her uncomfortable delivery bag. She zips back out to her bike to rejoin the other square-backed snails sent out by their employer to risk their lives on the roads for pastries and pizza.

I lift the lid on the box—I'm only human. Two perfect croissants, one with almonds, one with chocolate sprinkles, are nestled on white confectionary paper, cherished like antique tiaras. I find it somehow touching. The run makes more sense now. I'd bet that Viv has worked out how many steps they have to make before earning the calorific value of this indulgence. It's the new religion to replace that of sin and penitence through confession: one sin, so many Hail Marys; one croissant, five thousand steps. I dampen my fingertip and dust up just a little of the icing sugar from the edge of the paper. Sweetness swirls on my tongue, to the roof of my mouth, saliva pools.

The doorbell jangles again. I jump back as Bette jogs in, still looking fresh. Viv follows, face red as a bullfighter's cape.

'Good...' pants Viv. 'Still...here.' She presses a hand to her side. 'Shower, coffee and talk.' She goes upstairs.

Bette collects the box from the counter.

'Ayesha delivered it,' I say.

'I can see. She's early today. It was good you were here to take them in.' She glances down at the cup of tea. 'You found the kettle.'

'Thanks. I don't mean to, you know, impose?'

It's a classy word and I see that Bette registers it. She stands at the foot of the stairs. 'It's no imposition, my dear. Follow me.'

I follow, dragging my questions with me.

2

We were like two performers in a play, but we were divided, we were not acting with one another.

Daphne du Maurier, 'Rebecca'

Nineteen years ago

Dogberry Cottage wasn't a cottage at all. It was a HOUSE. I wrote the word in my diary in capitals to tell my future self just how big my new home was! So exciting! There were ten bedrooms, four floors, a terrace with pots, a tennis court, a rambling rose garden, a weedy vegetable garden, an empty swimming pool with an ants' nest, and...

I scrunched my face up, reliving the tour we'd been given today by Mrs Brampton.

An orchard with fifteen different kinds of apples. I'd ask her tomorrow for a list so I could note them down for POSTERITY. That was my word of the week, learned from Dad. He told me it meant 'the future' but it sounded like that big bottomed woman in a too small bikini, the one Dad laughed at on the beach in Southend.

Maybe I'd grow up to be that kind of posterity? At the moment I was a magic bean. Another of Dad's words. Small but full of potential. I could sprout and become a beanstalk leading to giants.

And thanks to him, I was living in what looked like a house from the most wonderful kind of story, the sort with wardrobes, talking rabbits or little white horses. I'd have to tell Mum all about it in my next letter. She liked Dad's stories too.

That's possibly what I loved most about my dad: his amazing tales and word spells. They just gushed out of him like spray from the firemen's hose. They showed us one last month in the playground. The officers let us feel the strength of the pipe, how it would thrash and spill if you let go. Dad was gushy like that. A magician of words. An engineer of sentence towers, he said. Never crude. 'Crudeness is for dolts!' he would declare when someone swore at him in the pub. That earned him a fist in the face but he claimed the Moral Victory.

I'd fetched a bag of peas from Iceland with the pound he'd given me. He'd laughed when I asked him what an Immoral Victory would be and said I'd find out when I was older.

I hated it when grownups did that. It probably meant it was something to do with S E X. About kissing boys and stuff. Adults got all funny talking about that.

Dad was lucky the black eye had gone down by the time he came for the interview for this job. Personal assistant to Sylvester Sligo—Uncle Sylvester as I'd been told to call him. The conversation to get the position had been very odd. I'd been there for one thing, holding Dad's hand. Children didn't normally go to job interviews, did they? We'd walked with Sylvester around the gardens. Paving stones tilted as we tripped over uneven steps. Dad told the playwright that he had a distinguished military career behind him and that we came as a package deal. Uncle Sylvester had glanced at me and frowned. He looked like an old white lion, all tufts of wild hair with a growly voice.

'Did you graduate?'

It took me a second to realise he was talking to my father and not me. Phew.

'No, sir. Though I have a first in the university of life.' One of my Dad's best lines. He sometimes added a 'boom-boom' but he didn't today.

Sylvester liked it. He chuckled, little tears gathering at the corner of his eyes. He mopped them with a silk spotted handkerchief, like the sort you tie bread in and put on the end of a stick to go Wandering.

'Her mother? Is she going to be a problem?' he asked once he'd caught his breath. 'Will she mind her living so far out in the countryside? Public transport is shocking around here.'

I had an image of shocked passengers on a bus with crosses for eyes and with hair up on end like cartoon people struck by lightning.

'Her mother went away,' said Dad.

'Mummy's dancing the tango in Buenos Aires,' I said. 'In a dress black as the night and spangled with stars.' That was what Dad had told me last week when we slept on a bench under the moon together after our Horrid Old Landlord changed the locks.

Sylvester's brown eyes softened at that. 'Is she indeed?' He glanced back at my father.

'In a manner of speaking,' said Dad. 'Merle, there're

some buttercups over there—and daisies. Make me a crown, will you?'

I nodded and ran off happily. I'd been eyeing those flowers for a little while now and he must've noticed. If I was good at something it was making daisy chains. I kept the nail on my right thumb a little long especially and didn't bite it like the others. The daisies had particularly fat stems, perfect for the task. There were so many I could tell no other children had come here to pick them.

Wondering if I'd been forgotten, I looked back at the two men talking together. It reminded me of the illustration of Aslan talking to the White Witch in *The Lion, the Witch and the Wardrobe,* Aslan up on his hind legs, paws behind his back, tail dangling behind him. That was Uncle Sylvester. My Dad wasn't in a dress and crown of course—don't be silly!—but he was tall with long black hair that he'd left loose today. He occasionally got wolf-whistled from behind and always enjoyed turning round to give the builders what he called 'a full gander' at his square jaw and man's chest. He told people he'd grown his hair after having to have it cut short in the army but I wasn't sure that was true because he also said to others that he'd been a vagabond and a gipsy king, a roadie and a folk singer. When I asked him which story was the right one he would say all-of-them-none-of-them just like that, all run together. I also asked him if he was really my dad then? He'd said 'yes, of course, pickle.'

But was he?

He'd once said I was found in a walnut shell. Another time the fairies brought me. Then I'd survived a shipwreck and been washed up on the shore where he slept on a beach in Borneo.

We didn't look much alike. I had fair hair, he had black. He was tall, I was short. He had brown eyes, I had blue-green. I had freckles and he had bristles. It was like we'd been dealt into two different piles with no 'snap!'.

He summoned me back with a whistle. I skipped over with a long necklace of daisies.

'Good news, little bean, we've got the job.'

Sylvester smiled at me. 'Would you like to live here, my dear?'

'Yes, please.' It would be far better than sleeping in Dad's tent in the woods where we had spent the night. I didn't like being cold and damp in the morning. I held out the daisy chain.

'For me?' Sylvester plucked the flowers from my fingers and wound them around his head in a double coronet. 'Splendid.'

My father smiled broadly so I knew I'd done the right thing. We had to charm people, he always said. Be what they want you to be. 'Stolen her away from me already, sir?'

'No fear of that, Evan. No one should come between a father and his daughter.'

So we moved in that same afternoon because there was nothing to stop us, not even school, according to Dad. I was used to moving so I wasn't bothered that it would mean a whole new set of children to get to know. After the tour by Mrs Brampton, the lady 'who does for Mr Sligo', I unpacked my rucksack. I had a little bedroom next to Dad's on the third floor. It used to belong to Sylvester's daughter. He had three children but they were all grown up with their own families. They didn't visit as they lived in other countries, Uncle Sylvester said, so Lucinda wouldn't mind that I now took it over. The wallpaper had horses, running at full gallop. There was a shelf with children's books. Looking at the backs at the descriptions I saw that some of the paperbacks were only 50p. Imagine books costing so little! They seemed very well read but with no bent pages. I liked that. Lucinda must've known to use bookmarks. Lots of them had illustrations. One was about children at a place called Green Knowe. I tried the name on my tongue. Green No-We. Green Ker-Now-E. Green No. I would ask Uncle Sylvester if he knew how to say it. Another was about a necklace of raindrops.

I chose that one and made a nest of my pillows on the bed, ready for my next adventure.

3

The theatre is certainly a place for learning about the brevity of human glory: oh all those wonderful glittering absolutely vanished pantomimes!

Iris Murdoch, 'The Sea, The Sea'

'Would you like a job?'

I put down my tea, this time with milk, and poured from a big brown pot on the rickety kitchen table upstairs.

'Sorry?'

The washing machine is whining as it cleanses their sports gear. It's either that or attempting to launch itself into space. I wonder if I misheard.

'A job,' repeats Bette. 'We need another assistant.'

I'm the passer-by they found standing on their doorstep just a couple of hours ago.

'You're joking?'

'Deadly serious, my dear. You look like you need a job and you were carrying *The Mad King* so you like books. What is your name, by the way?'

'Merle.'

'Like the blackbird?'

'Named for Merle Oberon, the actress,' I mumble.

Bette turns triumphantly to Viv. 'See. She absolutely has to be ours.' She refills my cup. 'I'm named after Bette Davis. She's named after Vivien Leigh. Parents!' She chuckles and shakes her head.

'Bette, we aren't collecting waifs and strays again,' says Viv, turning the page in The Times at the other end of the table from me.

'Oh, but we are.'

'We haven't even asked her why she's here. A job might be the last thing on her mind.'

True, but I wasn't against the idea.

Bette sized me up. 'She's our next project, I have a feeling for these things.'

Viv sighs, but doesn't contest the claim.

'Project?' I ask. When was I turned into a parrot? I can't seem to do anything but echo her.

'Our last assistant was a Lost Boy.' Bette says the description like a listing of the cast in *Peter Pan*.

'What happened to him?' Finally I got out of parrot mode!

'Ran off with the contents of the till,' says Viv sourly. She folds the page to leave the crossword face up. 'So much for our grand experiment.' She says this in an admirably snippy tone.

'There wasn't much in it,' says Bette happily and oblivious to Viv's reprimand. 'He said in his note that he had to get back for a family wedding in Romania. So you can see that you're an answer to our prayers.'

'Your prayers, not mine,' says Viv, pointing at Bette with a biro.

I can't quite work out what the relationship between these two is. They don't look much like each other and act like an old married couple so I decide that maybe they are together, rather than just business partners?

'I'm not sure I'm very reliable,' I say. Today I feel like the wooden garden furniture at Dogberry Cottage. Sit on it and risk falling through.

'Of course you are. You like Antony.' Bette cuts her croissant in half and puts a curl on my plate.

That wretched autobiography. It is getting me into more trouble than I thought when I picked it up from Oxfam.

Viv now cuts her almond pastry in two and gives me a second piece. That's what does it for me. I start to sniff, and swallow back tears.

'Allergic to nuts are you?' asks Viv, moving to take it back.

'No.' I blow my nose on an offered tissue.

'No need to make such a fuss then.' Viv pushes the plate closer to me. 'A bit of kindness makes the world go round.'

'I thought that was money.'

'The song is wrong. We all need kindness, not money.'

'But we'll pay you too,' says Bette. 'Not much but enough to keep the wolves from your door.'

'But no drinking on the job. No smoking on the premises. Those are our two conditions.' Viv fills in another clue.

'There's a third—no drugs. Do you do drugs, dear?' Bette said it like she was tip-toeing across a field of tulips, careful not to bruise a stem.

'No.' I notice they say nothing about not stealing the money from the till. Perhaps they just expect that now?

'Good. Where are you staying?'

'Um...' Jodie has asked me to find another sofa as she has

a party tonight. I haven't yet solved the issue of where I am going to go but I've definitely worn out my welcome. There is a limited tolerance for someone who can't get her act together. I understand it. From my friends' point of view, they can't see why I've stalled. I know they are talking about me behind my back.

'We'll have to find you somewhere to stay, of course,' Bette adds shrewdly. 'Close by so you can get here on time.'

'Not enough room here,' says Viv, nodding to the galley kitchen. We are crammed at the far end under the single window. Any spare space is used for stock overflow.

'But we'll get out the old camp bed for tonight. Who do you think would take her in?' Bette asks Viv, like I'm a stray cat. 'Larry? He has a spare room.'

'You surely jest?' Viv peers at Bette over her reading glasses. 'He isn't the type.'

Bette seems to agree. 'June then. I'll ask on Tuesday.'

'God help her,' mutters Viv. I'm not sure who she thinks needs help. June or me.

Worryingly, I think it might be me.

THE HOURS that follow are bizarre. I feel like I've been swept up by a pantomime genie and left in the hands of two mysterious and benevolent figures. They refill my cup and let me sit quietly in the sunshine spilling over the kitchen table as they potter around me, getting on with their tasks. I had come with questions, but now they've granted me time with them without asking why I am here, I find I can wait to for the answers I'm seeking.

'Why are you like this?' I murmur instead when Bette pats my shoulder in passing. 'I'm a stranger.'

She smiles. 'Viv and I have a pact: we accept what

fortune brings us if the signs are right. It's the path to blessing.'

'It's the path to being robbed,' calls out Viv, head down in a box of books.

'I suppose we should open,' says Bette with a sigh.

I look up at the clock. It's eleven.

'Oh we don't keep ordinary hours,' she explains, seeing where my gaze has gone. 'We serve the theatre crowd so no point opening up when everyone is sleeping off the night before. We stay open until seven-thirty instead, just as performances begin.'

'Can I watch you? See what you do?' I ask. My voice still sounds like I've gargled gravel. I've been fighting a tension headache but that has been reduced by two paracetamol.

'Of course,' says Bette. 'That's the idea of someone who now works here.' She is pleased at my interest. 'There won't be much to see. Most of our business is in licensing and hiring scripts—that comes in via the telephone or on the computer thingy.'

'Website,' supplies Viv. She tucks some bills under the fruit bowl on the table. 'I don't suppose you know anything about that, do you?'

My father would at this point claim he had worked for Google or gave Tim Cook his first break; instead I tell the truth. Maybe this is a new resolution for me? I've not said one lie yet. 'No, but I could learn.'

Bette beams at me. 'Could you? We're bright women, but we just aren't interested. Email is about all we can manage.'

'Larry might help with training,' says Viv.

'Larry?'

'Our brother. Head of Past is Prologue publishing.'

I remember the PiP logo on the spines of Sylvester's plays when they were printed. A fingerpost pointing ahead.

'Named after Laurence Olivier?' I guess.

'Yes. You're quick to catch on.'

I reconsider what I think I know about my hostesses. 'Are you sisters?'

'Of course!' Viv has a rather booming voice for this small space or someone with the ghost of a headache. 'What did you think we were?'

'Married—to each other?'

Viv laughs. 'Good lord! How frightfully modern of you. When we were young it used to be the other way round: lesbians would pose as sisters, now us sisters are mistaken for lesbians.'

Bette was also grinning. 'Even if we weren't related, she's not my type.'

'Sorry.' I'm reminded of how stupid I've become.

'No need to be sorry. You've brightened my day quite considerably.' Viv gets up. 'Come down to the shop and I'll give you the tour.'

The shop, which was originally two separate buildings on Old Compton Street, now spreads the full double width with a little room at the back for second hand books, mirror of the stockroom. They've arranged the scripts as a trip through time. At the front near the till are the works by living playwrights, plays that are in production in one of the London theatres, or have been until recently. Then the cases start to go back along the walls: twentieth century, Victorian, Romantic, Eighteenth Century, Restoration, Jacobean, Elizabethan, a slim case for Medieval mystery plays, then the Greeks and Romans. Shakespeare has his own bookcase in the centre of the shop floor, keeping an eye on all the goings-on around him. *All the world's a stage.* There is a biography and critical works section to match each division. All books are spine out. There are no buy-one-get-one-half-price tables or face-on promotions. It's the kind of arrangement with which George Bernard Shaw or Virginia Woolf would've been familiar from their perusing of bookshops in the nineteen twenties: you were expected to look for what you wanted, not have it shoved in your face by some best-sellers' list or publisher-bought slot. It has its downsides though: some books look as though they haven't been moved for years. I wondered how they kept the business afloat what with the pandemic and rising rents around here.

'What's with the swags?' I ask Viv, pointing to the curtain fringing that loops across the shelving. They look very sad and dusty.

Viv snorts. 'Bette's idea.'

'When?'

'Must've been in the eighties.' Viv stands next to me and frowns. 'I haven't noticed them in a while. I've always said they're dust traps. They look frightful, like rejects from *Phantom*.'

I don't say anything, but I agree. The shop doesn't need this whimsy. It has enough with the ass's head behind the till and the stuffed bear in the corner. There's theatre memorabilia in every nook and cranny.

Viv makes a decisive nod. 'I'll talk to her. We need to do a stocktake so that might be a good moment to change.'

The bell jangles and a sixty-something man with a pink silk scarf and ebony cane wafts in. I know the sort instantly from living with my father's cronies. He is the cliché thespian, a wannabe Ian McKellen. Viv's jaw tightens as she clenches her teeth.

'Vivien! Darling!'

'Robert.' Steeling herself for the encounter, she goes behind her till point to avoid his attempt to kiss her cheek. 'Up for a matinee?'

'Oh no: I've come to see you. The Bagwell Players are looking for something new—something challenging—for our autumn production. Have you got anything for me?'

I retreat a step into one of the chasms between shelving.

'Jez Butterworth's *The Ferryman* is very good,' says Viv.

Robert leans forward on his cane. 'Really? *The Ferryman*?'

'Set in Northern Ireland during the troubles. About the IRA.'

He sways back. 'Not about a ferryman then, but terrorists? And we'd need to do accents.' His own is distinctly RP.

'Everyone has an accent, Robert. Just as everyone is the hero of their own tale.'

Her profundity is lost on him. 'I'm not sure that is quite us. I'd manage, of course, having been to drama school, but we don't have the depth of talent it would require. Anything else?'

She loads him up with a selection of recent scripts and revivals. He stays talking to her as long as he can until she mentions that she had a delivery she really has to unbox. I can imagine he's told his friends down in Bagwell that he's on first name terms with someone 'in the business', making this expedition to town sound high-powered. He doesn't want to be brushed off like any old customer. Eventually he concedes defeat.

'Farewell, then. I'll be in touch and let you know which we want to do,' he calls, waving his cane jauntily as he departs.

As the ringing dies away, Bette creeps out of the stairwell.

Viv glares at her. 'Coward. You owe me.'

'But you're so much better at getting rid of him.'

I emerge from my spy-hole. Viv nods to the still swaying

bell. 'I suppose we should be thankful to customers like that —they keep us in business.'

'What'll he choose?' I ask. He'd gone off with some quite avant-garde pieces.

'It won't be one of those. He'll come back and ask for *An Ideal Husband* or *The Mousetrap* as usual.' Viv returns some of the rejected scripts to their place on the contemporary shelf. 'And they'll do a pretty good job of it for a local group, if the reviews online are to be believed, as long as the others can keep him under control.'

'Remember the year he tried to get them to do *Hair*?' says Bette. 'They made the national papers.'

'I certainly do. He's annoying but I have to remind myself there's something magnificent about him—like Bottom, the rude mechanical.'

'Not that I would want to see his bottom, in either sense.' Bette picked up the post from the mat. Robert had scuffed it aside with his cane on entering.

Their easy double act made me smile.

'*Let me play the lion too*,' I murmur.

I'm pinned again by their gazes. 'Exactly.' Viv gives me another of her affirming nods. I'm feeling quite drunk on the approbation they are giving me for the least sign of intelligence. It's a nice change. 'You might be right about this one, Bette.'

4

Bracing myself to meet a massive force...
Antony Sher, 'Year of the Mad King'

One Week Ago

Jodie had that look on her face as I rolled up my sleeping bag and tucked it behind the sofa. Dressed in black trousers, silky turquoise shirt, she had styled her spiralling hair back with silver grips. She always had a grip, did Jodie, even when we were in student hall together at eighteen. She was straightening the flat as it was the cleaner's day (paid for by an indulgent Mum and Dad) and I was expected to make myself scarce.

She plumped a cushion. 'Merle, it's been three weeks. You said you'd only stay a few days.'

She was right. I was in the wrong. 'I'm sorry. I'll sort something out.' This was a familiar stage in the Merle-on-the-sofa story.

'You said you were doing research.'

'I am.'

'I thought that meant you'd restarted your degree.'

And I let her think that.

'But you've not been to the library, not picked up a book as far as I can tell.'

'It's not that kind of research.'

She dropped the cushion. 'Then what kind?'

'Family history.' Even the words made me feel sick.

Disapproval was like a bad smell. She grabbed her messenger bag, checking she had everything for work. 'I don't understand you, Merle. You were one of the brightest in our year but you're wasting yourself on a...a hobby most people do when they retire.'

I crossed my arms over my stomach.

'I get that you had, you know, difficulties and had to drop out, but you need to get back in the saddle.' She laughed self-deprecatingly. 'That sounds terrible, and I'm no counsellor, but it's true.'

I felt even worse that she was such a kind friend and I was exploiting her generosity. 'I never really got into the saddle in the first place.'

She conceded the point with a look. 'You've done bar and restaurant work for the past few years when you could be building something, a career.'

That was the world according to Jodie: everyone on an escalator up. If you turned round and started walking down, you affected all around you.

Jodie picked up her phone from the charging station. 'We've been talking.'

That meant my long-suffering friends, from whom I hid so much.

'We were thinking you should see someone. We'll pay.

But you need to get yourself a job and start to...well...live a little.'

I nodded. 'I know. And I love you all for suggesting that. Just give me a few more days. There're things I need to sort out.'

'We all agree we have to stop giving you the excuse not to deal with things. We're doing you no favours letting you stay. Megan says you should see a psychiatrist, or a life coach, or someone.' Jodie wasn't really happy with any solution that wasn't purely practical.

A flutter of panic woke in my stomach. 'It is a favour and I really appreciate it.'

She sighed, but the call of the eight-ten train meant she had no longer to discuss it with me. 'I'll ask around for ideas as to who might be able to help you. Would you say you were depressed? Anxious?'

'Terrified.' I shot her a wavering smile. 'Of life.'

'I suppose I can understand that.' She gave me a brief hug. 'The world is a shocking place. But you've got to find a way of living in it.'

I really did.

With a nod, she went out, the front door banging behind her.

Now

Jodie is a little incredulous that I have found both a job and a place to stay without even formally applying for one. That doesn't stop her being relieved that the hot potato (what to do with me) had been passed on to someone else. She offers to drop off my stuff, gets on like a house on fire with Viv, and leaves my little bundle of belongings.

'I like your friend,' says Viv. 'You can tell she's going places.'

'They all are,' I murmur as I clean the bathroom in the staff room. My little group of friends from Uni were all flourishing. Megan was climbing the ladder at the BBC, Neil had a job as a researcher in Parliament, Harry had started training to be a police officer, much to our collective surprise. Only I am in beachball mode, circling on my screen of indecision.

The next stray Bette brings home is a dog—and only a few days after my own rescue. I'm beginning to realise I'm not such an extraordinary event—more a symptom of a habit. A kleptomania on Bette's part for needy animals and people. I wonder what's driving it. The dog in question has been run over by a bicycle messenger, hopefully not Ayesha, and Bette has already taken it to the vet to have its paw bound. Not microchipped, it looked destined for Battersea Dogs' Home until Bette intervened.

It's huge—somewhere between a Leonberger and a mastiff, great ruffs of chocolate and black fur, more ursine than canine. An Elizabethan hound down to the fluffy doublet and hose. My guess is that it's some homeless person's companion that's proved too expensive to maintain now the weather is getting warmer, or perhaps a lockdown puppy that grew too big for its owner to manage.

'You can't be serious,' says Viv.

'Oh don't go all John McEnroe on me, Viv! I had to bring him home—he's called Brutus!' She moves the metal tag on his collar so we can see that he is indeed called this. It's her clinching argument, so she makes a bed for Brutus in the stockroom next to my camp bed.

'He might have fleas,' calls Viv.

Good point, Viv. I'm keeping silent as I have no standing

here, but I'm not overjoyed to share my space with the Hound of the Baskervilles.

'No he doesn't. Brutus in an honourable hound,' says Bette, giving him a neck rub.

Viv snorts at the *Julius Caesar* echo. 'That might be, but honour does not deter fleas. Get him treated! I'll put a note in the window in case someone lost him and wants him back.'

I wonder if she had been tempted to put a similar notice about me. My questions about the past are still to be asked. It is not a subject for casual conversation, so I'm stuck how to proceed. One of them might know the answer, but I'm not sure which one. I just know he had dealings with Past is Prologue and a woman from here often visited us. I can't remember which one – I was a child. It might not even have been one of the sisters. I'm hoping that visitor has a clearer memory of events than I do. A cleverer person would've worked out a way on the first day. Can't I swap myself for someone better?

'So Merle, we'd better make a start on your training today, now you're rested,' says Viv, returning from tacking the notice up in the front. I'm a little confused for a moment, still thinking about dogs. 'Our website needs updating.'

Oh right. I rub my eyes. 'What system do you use?'

'The Internet.' She looks disappointed in me.

'I mean what's your website builder?'

'Oh. Er, not sure. The Romanian boy did it.' She turns the screen and shows me a login for the most popular website creator.

I can see I'm not going to get far asking her questions. 'I'll play with it—work out what you've got on there.' I close the window and call up the website as a visitor. I can immediately see there's bags of room for improvement and I find ideas edging in. 'You could, you know, link to the websites for current productions, particularly if they have videos about their rehearsal process and trailers?'

'We could?' asks Viv as if I'd suggested a quick trip to the moon. 'How?'

'Not sure. I'd have to work out how to do it, but I know it can be done.'

She taps the counter with the biro that's never far from her fingers. 'Training. I'm phoning Larry. He should meet you anyway.'

'He should?' I'm not sure I want to meet someone else. Two new people—plus Brutus and the steady stream of customers—is a lot for me. I've been on my own desert island, alone in a crowd, for so long now.

'Yes, we own Past is Prologue together, including the shop. Everything he does—everything we do—has to be approved by all three.'

I have to ask. 'Even the Romanian Lost Boy?'

Viv looks away. 'I'm not sure we had time to ask his opinion of Cristofor.'

'And how did Cristofor qualify for his position?'

'Christopher Marlowe, of course,' says Bette, coming in from the stockroom, Brutus padding along at her thigh. 'He even looked a bit like him. Don't worry. I'm sure Larry will like you.'

Viv purses her lips but says nothing.

VIV ESCORTS me like a prisoner under guard to the head office of PiP.

'You look very nice,' Viv says, sensing I need a morale boost.

'Thanks.' I'm in a summer dress that has a print of

seashells, boats and rope – some Seasalt cast-off that I found in a charity shop. My childish self would've adored it. It would've seemed to her like a Famous Five adventure in fabric.

'What colour's your hair naturally, dear?'

I keep it short and usually covered it with a hat or scarf. The colour has always attracted attention and people tended to treat me like doll, even reaching out to touch it to check the platinum was real. 'Mousey.'

'Hmm. You look like you might be naturally blonde. You can always tell.' She motions to the eyebrows.

Busted. I give her a vague smile but I doubt she is fooled.

PiP has found swanky lodging on the fifth floor of a modern office block set a little back from the Strand. I imagine a German bomb made way for this new building on one of London's oldest streets. The river has retreated behind the Embankment a hundred metres away but it still has the sense of a verge as the land falls steeply to water level.

'Just look at this place. Ghastly. It's the antithesis of the shop, isn't it?' says Viv, stabbing at the button in the lift to close the doors. She completely ignores the person running to squeeze in with us, just as she punished the doorman by refusing to state her business. If she could get her way, she'd probably find little torments for everyone who works here. I admire Viv. 'That's Larry for you. He wants us to look professional, God help us.'

The lift doors open. She clearly hasn't told Larry's PA that we are coming. The poor girl turns ashen as we approach. Viv is dressed like a gamekeeper—tweedy and brown—whereas the girl is wearing a silky white blouse and tailored trousers. I know immediately whom I'm putting my money on.

'Tell Larry I'm here, Joan.' That's Viv's first salvo from her shotgun. As her words echo around the office, I imagine rooks flying up and circling the rookery, cawing in alarm.

'I'm afraid Mr Bunter is in meetings all afternoon,' bleats Joan.

'Nonsense. He's probably just sleeping off his lunch. Larry, it's Viv! I've brought you a visitor!' The voice booms over the tapping of keyboards and hushed conversations. Heads turn, then quickly turn away.

'I'm sorry, but he said that he's really very busy today—'

'Ridiculous boy.'

'If you'd like to make an appointment...?'

'It's no good, Lambkin, I know you're in there!'

On the nickname, the door flies open and Larry appears in the entrance. He looks both appalled and resigned to seeing us there. 'Joan, hold my calls.'

Larry takes after his sister Bette, earning the lambkin for his soft features and wispy white hair. I can't imagine him having any other colour even when he was little. He looks about ten years younger. As I'm an only child, I can only imagine how difficult that was for him growing up as third in line.

Viv strides past him, kissing his cheek rather roughly in passing. 'You look tired, Larry. Not sleeping?'

'Do I?' He tugs his tie straight as his own version of an Ofsted inspection has arrived.

'This is Merle...Merle, what's your surname?'

I daren't invent a new lie. I give one of the names we used most often. It might even be my real one. 'Cardew.'

'She's updating our website and helping around at the shop.' Viv takes a seat on the sofa rather than by the desk, patting the place beside her. 'She's here for your blessing and some training.'

Larry blinks a few times, catching up. 'Joan, tea please, for three. Unless you prefer coffee?' This is addressed to me.

'Er, no. Tea's fine.'

He sits in the armchair opposite us and studies me. 'One of Bette's?' he asks his sister.

'Yes. One of her discoveries.' I give a little ironic smile: me and Brutus.

'She looks...small.' An odd choice, but maybe he meant fragile and couldn't quite say it in front of me? 'Do I want to know where she came from?'

'No.'

There's an awkward silence.

'Ms Cardew, if you hurt either of my sisters, then I'm warning you, I'll bring the full weight of PiP down on you.'

I look up in surprise. Lambkin is a lion. Maybe he does have more of Viv in him than I first thought? I approve. 'I've no intention of harming anyone, Mr Bunter.'

'We'll see.'

Viv bristles at the implied criticism, though she has said similar things herself. 'You can't blame Merle for Cristofor.'

He gives his sister a sardonic smile. 'Or, I suppose, for, who was it now? Rachel. William. And Randy—let's not forget that appalling American who lived up to his name.'

'Precisely. She's not them; she's Merle. And she likes the theatre.'

He raises a brow.

'We found her reading *Year of the Mad King* so we knew she was a keeper.'

Larry leans back in his chair. 'Well, I suppose, with that calling card, we should at least give her the benefit of the doubt.' He is as insane as his sisters.

'That's what we think.'

'What kind of training?'

Viv gestures to me, leaving this to me to answer.

I clear my throat. 'Website. I see that the last admin uploaded his own content?'

'That's right. The Romanian. A clever boy despite...well...you know...' He waves in a vague direction of Bucharest. 'It's a simple site, not cost effective to have changes farmed out to a web designer.'

'If someone here can teach me, I'll clear out the dead wood—get it up to scratch.'

Joan backs in with a tea tray.

'Thank you, Joan. Can you tell Ashley from marketing that I need a word?'

'Of course, Mr Bunter.'

'Have you looked at the main site—my site for the publishing wing?' At last someone is giving me a grilling, something Bette and Viv really should've done before they let me move in. 'That's where our main business lies. We really shouldn't keep the shop going.'

Viv snorts. 'Over my dead body.'

'Quite. So, as my sisters are adamant that the shop stays as part of our portfolio, it would please me if it could be brought more in line with the rest of the business. We're moving into publishing film scripts and books on screen-writing.'

'Froth!' says Viv. I'm not sure if she means all screen dramas or her brother's initiative.

'It's not froth, Viv. Screen performances are as worth our time as stage.'

'But there's no live audience—no need to master a whole part, not like playing Othello or Willy Loman straight for three hours. Film is Paint-by-Numbers acting.'

Larry turns to me with a 'see-what-I'm-dealing-with?'

expression. 'If you can make even a few changes to bring the twenty-first century into the shop then we'd be grateful.'

I push myself into trying a bit harder. 'I was thinking of, maybe, featuring current shows—reviews and videos? I could do the same for the screen dramas. You know, link things up?'

I sound such a fraud. Who am I fooling? I'm barely even here, functioning on the scraps of my old self before I failed.

It's not an impressive pitch but Larry still says as he pours our tea: 'This one might not be a complete disaster then?'

'We are optimistic,' says Viv, smiling at me. 'I have less hope for the dog.'

'Dog? What dog?' asks Larry.

5

Act well your part; there all the honour lies.
Alexander Pope, 'An Essay on Man'

Insomnia is an unpleasant side-effect of guilt. I've managed to stave off tiredness most of the day by keeping busy. Ashley from Marketing gave me a crash-course in WordPress and I've found the passwords for the shop system hidden in plain sight on a Post-it in the staff noticeboard, so I am theoretically good-to-go tomorrow. But action just seems beyond me.

I really need to pull myself together but I feel like candy floss, spun out and sticky.

It's surprisingly quiet in the stockroom bedsit even though we're in central London. Brutus, however, is restless. He's awake and chewing on the cardboard box Viv threw to him as a toy. I'd ignored his attempts to make friends earlier, pushing his head from my lap when I worked at the desktop, turning down the chance to feed or walk him. I've decided that he's Bette's responsibility, not mine. I've not had a good record with pets, having been forced to leave a trail of abandoned goldfish and gerbils with our frequent moves when I was little. Brutus has repaid the treatment by ignoring me for the last three hours.

Just one cigarette. I know I promised not to smoke but it is after hours even though I'm still very much in the workplace. Viv and Bette aren't anything to me—not family, not even friends, they're just...just Good Samaritans making themselves feel better by helping me. They wouldn't even know.

This arrangement isn't going to last long in any case. Nothing ever does.

I think of the packet of cigarettes still hidden in my bag. I've given up more times than I can remember and I always reach this point on a sleepless night.

Just one. Or maybe two.

Brutus crunches and the sweet scent of damp tobacco fills the air.

'What!' I shoot out of bed and grope for the switch. The strip-light hums on and I catch Brutus looking up at me from his mangled cigarette packet. His expression isn't even guilty. It's quizzical, as if to say, 'Why the light, dude?'

I want to wrestle him for the packet. But then I remember he's a dog and he's bigger than me. Not cool.

'Like Silk Cut, do you, hellhound?' I'm vertical so I decide I might as well clear up. I fill the angry kettle to make a herbal tea, grab a dustpan and brush, and clean up after Brutus. 'I can't even get angry with you, but you do know those things are bad for you?' I take my tea into the shop. Brutus follows, goes to the door and whines.

'Serves you right for stealing my smokes.' I switch off the alarm and let him out. I've got bare feet so I don't follow. If he wanders off, that's his lookout. He doesn't but it appears he's enjoying his sniff so I leave him to it. The door can stay ajar for a while. I sit in one of the battered armchairs placed for customers to dip into prospective purchases. The cup sits securely on the broad arm, steaming. I lay back my head and close my eyes.

Don't think about going in search of a twenty-four hour supermarket. Don't think at all.

Mind blank, I concentrate on my surroundings. The dusty smell of books blends with the cinnamon and apple of my tea. I actually feel...a little bit happy.

A wet nose nudges my thigh. I don't move, so Brutus gives one of his judgmental sighs, then flops down at my feet. I move my feet to rest on him—he's much warmer than the floor—and he doesn't seem to mind. He probably doesn't even notice. I need to get up and close the door but don't feel in a hurry. No one is passing and if they do, Brutus would make them think twice about coming in.

I study the shop in the darkness, only lit by street lamps and the light spilling from the stockroom. Twilight—such a pretty word. Is this place in its twilight like Larry thinks? Can it survive? To do so it will have to become so much more than a bookshop. And if I were the one to turn it around, I'd have to become so much more than I am. I don't have it in me.

Brutus grunts.

See, the dog agrees. All nature is against me.

Resting my head back and sipping my tea, I smile.

'MERLE? MERLE!'

I wake with a start. Bette in running gear is shaking my shoulder.

'Why is the front door open?'

'Ah. Damn.' Brutus stirs from under my feet. I've been sitting enthroned in the chair all night with him as my footstool, mug of cold tea on the arm. 'I had to let the dog out. I must've fallen asleep.'

'Clearly.' Bette takes a quick look around outside, then shuts it. 'I'm probably more trusting than I should be—Viv certainly thinks so—but this isn't the safest of areas, being a big city. You can't leave doors open—people tend to take that as an invitation to walk in. God knows what they'd steal in here but you never know.' She scratches Brutus under the chin in apology for curtailing his desire to roam. 'Grow up in the countryside, did you?'

The doors were never locked at Dogberry Cottage. It would've been better if they were. 'Some of the time.'

'We can't risk country behaviour here, I'm afraid, as it invalidates the insurance. I'd be grateful if you didn't do that again.' She clips a leash onto Brutus, her new running companion. 'At least Viv didn't see.'

'Didn't see what?' asks Viv as she comes down the stairs.

'Nothing!' Bette turns away.

Viv, naturally, is suspicious and does a quick round of the shop. She dips her head into the stockroom. 'Why does it smell like a tobacconist's in there?' Viv wheels round to point an accusing finger. 'Merle, we explained the rules.'

For once I am innocent. Saved by the hound. 'It was Brutus.'

'What?'

'He chewed up my cigarettes. The evidence is in the bin if you don't believe me.'

Viv doesn't take me at my word and checks the waste bin. She sniffs.

'It was the one I had with me when I arrived.' I sound pathetic. I *am* pathetic.

'We are strictly No Smoking in this establishment,' she says, rather grandly. 'Too many things that can catch fire. You can, naturally, smoke outside but away from our doorway. If you can't keep to the rules, then you'll have to go.'

'Viv.' Bette puts her hand on her sister's arm. 'It's fine.'

'It's not fine.'

Bette sighs. 'You don't have to always step in to protect me.'

Is she inferring...? 'I'm sorry. I didn't realise that it would be a particular problem for you.' I truly am contrite. I don't want to hurt Bette.

Bette smiles ruefully. 'Viv's outed me, as usual. Recovering chain smoker. In remission from lung cancer. But it's been years. If you want help kicking the habit, just ask. I was going to offer, but my big sister has preempted me, as usual.'

The sisters have surprised me again. If I had to pick one to have the habit, it would be Viv. Bette seems too fresh and clean living for a chain-smoker.

'I was tempted,' I admit, 'but, really, I didn't have time to smoke. Brutus snapped them up. I think he's addicted to nicotine.'

'It would be just like you to pick up a stray dog with a tobacco problem, Bette,' mutters Viv, retying a shoelace. 'Right, let's crack on. We're getting behind schedule.'

That signals the end of the inquisition. I like that about them: they don't let things fester. I've known too many people who bear grudges like it's an Olympic sport and they're gold medalists. The sisters go and I'm left to take in the daily croissant delivery, now increased to three. Ayesha stays to chat for a few minutes before zipping off to lectures. In these brief meetings, she's asked more about me than either Bette or Viv. It's beginning to confuse, this reticence my hostesses have. Aren't they curious? Not that I want questions. I shouldn't wish upon myself decisions between being economical with the truth and flagrant lying.

I go upstairs to shower and change—just a quick splash, making sure I don't use up the hot water. I leave the shower sparkling clean. This time I do look in the mirror and see that my hair is beginning to grown back. I run my palm over the baby soft fuzz. It hadn't been a good choice, hacking it all off. I'd half hoped for a shapely head, like the female characters in *Black Panther*, but instead mine just revealed that it should always be kept under wraps. I'm more skin-head Tinkerbell than Wakanda warrior.

Freshened up for the day, I get breakfast ready in the kitchen. It's the first morning I've done this. I'm remembering some domestic skills I'd forgotten I knew. Put out plates, butter and knives. Place the fruit bowl in the centre. Switch on the kettle. This one is of the happy variety and comes to the boil with only an excitable fizz and click, bubbles showcased in a little blue-lit window. I'm mesmerised until I hear quick footsteps on the stairs and the swish of showers. Viv is ready first. She says nothing, but gives me a nod as she takes her usual place with *The Times* crossword. I fill the teapot and put it on a mat to brew.

'Why haven't you asked me about myself?' I didn't realise I was going to say that. Sometimes my mouth has its own agenda.

'Because that's your business, not ours.' Viv frowns. 'Seven across: *Dislike Jude the Obscure's worthiness*.'

It's a peace offering. She's started including me on in her crossword ritual, her version of Bette's pats and smiles. Both want me to feel better about myself. They're extraordinary women: do they even realise that?

'How many letters?'

'Nine.'

Her question calls up memories of sitting with Sylvester Sligo on his cracked terrace on long summer afternoons as trails of ants marched to the sugar grains I'd scattered for them. Perhaps she'd done crosswords with him? He taught me many things, few of them welcome, but one useful skill he did pass on was how to do a cryptic clue. Read it once. Read it backwards. One part is the definition, the other is usually a play on words. Obscure Jude and a new word blinks back at you: price.

'Prejudice?'

'That's right.' She fills in the clue. I suspect she'd already guessed it. She peers at me over the top of reading glasses. 'You mustn't mistake lack of questions for lack of interest. Sometimes puzzles are more rewarding to work out than to be given the answers.'

I SPEND a desultory morning faffing around with the website. Perched on the high stool at the counter in front of the desktop, I monitor the comings and goings. At midday the shop is suddenly invaded by a party of visiting Korean students all come to see *Harry Potter and the Cursed Child.* They purchase the shop's entire stock of that work.

Bette and Viv should get some Hogwartish memorabilia, I think. Then I remember I'm not going to be the innovative person that is needed. But I make a note.

The afternoon assistant comes in at one. A drama student, Lillian is flamboyant and giggly, a waft of dead-straight black hair, a weft of caramel skin, a whiff of seductive perfume. She and I have made great circles around each other since we met a few days ago. I'm not sure who feels most threatened but we do both recognise that we are antipathetic to each other—Gryffindor and Slytherin, Montague and Capulet, or perhaps, more realistically, as I'm not worthy of such lofty comparisons, Tom and Jerry. She probably fears I'm going to take her job. And what do I fear? The usual thing. Being seen through, exposed like the villain at the end of Scooby Doo when the rubber mask is removed. I think someone of my own age is more likely to see me for what I am.

An hour into ignoring each other, the door opens again. I look up to find Lillian preening. A guy taps jokily on the counter bell even though she is standing right in front of him.

Ting-ting-ting. 'Hey, Lillian, is my mother in?'

Mother? One of my Good Samaritans is a parent? I quickly reassess the man: late twenties, pale blue eyes, light brown hair, strong jaw that you can draw with three lines down-across-up, accessorised by the suggestion of a dimple. The handsome strength of the face suggests Viv but...

'I'm afraid your mother and aunt have gone to the National matinee, Rupert,' says Lillian.

Am I being ungenerous or has her voice just dropped into sex chatline territory?

'Damn. I forgot. Mum did say.' He scans the shop, or at least pretends to do so. I can tell acting when I see it. 'And you must be...?'

He's come to check me out. As one of the sisters is his mother then I can't blame him. I'm lucky he hasn't brought pitchforks and peasants with flaming torches.

'I'm Merle.'

'Ah yes. Mum told me about you.'

I imagine two versions: found like Thumbelina cupped

in a flower (Bette), or dumped on a doorstep in a bin bag of builder's rubbish (Viv). What to reply?

'She's been very kind.'

His eye narrow. 'She always is.'

'Rupert, any news on Edgar?' says Lillian, nudging into the space between us.

A flash of pain registers but he covers it up with a sweeping gesture. 'Completely cocked up the call-back. Still, that's how the cookie crumbles.'

'God, yes. Rejection is to be expected. It totally sucks though when it happens. Every time.'

I work out they are talking about parts in *King Lear* rather than another relative.

Rupert shows he has the necessary resilience, though, as he's already chasing the next one. 'I have high hopes of the Bridge Theatre. They're auditioning for the October production. A revival of a piece that Uncle Larry commissioned when he first took over from my grandfather.'

'Any parts for a young drama student just waiting to be discovered?' Lillian says archly.

'Or a talented guy whose big break is yet to come? We can only hope.' They exchange the battle-weary smile of two people for whom the soul-destroying round of hope and dejection is becoming all too familiar.

Someone clears their throat beside me. I've been so caught up in listening in to the two actors, I've neglected to notice that one of the browsing customers has made it to the till.

'Can I help you?' I slide down from the stool, which has the ridiculous result of me ending up lower than when I was perched on high.

The customer bites back a smile. He'd never have this problem, being around six foot three. For all his height, there's something almost invisible about him, a slight hunch to the shoulders in deference to my lack of stature, a don't-look-too close shyness. That's a shame because, with his buzz-cut black hair framing a generous face, wide nose, dark eyes, he is very easy on the eyes. I discover I find gold-rimmed glasses on an earnest face really work for me. It's the first time I've had even a vaguely lascivious thought in an age. Another actor? He's certainly carrying enough texts to suggest that.

'I was wondering if Viv was able to find my special order for me?' he asks. And he has a nice voice too. Being an assistant has its moments.

The sisters have a book search service for rare editions of theatre-related books that have long been out of print. Being well-connected to old thespians, they are usually the first to be called in to evaluate the collections of those down-sizing or gone to the great audition in the sky.

'Name?' I ask, wanting to come across professional, an unexpected urge.

'George Appiah.'

I pause, wondering how to spell his surname. 'One p or two?'

'Two.'

I press return. 'There's nothing coming up on the system.' I frown. In fact, the reservation system is suspiciously empty.

Lillian pulls herself away from Rupert for a second. 'Viv's probably written it down. There's a notebook under the till. Look under "George".' She gives a little wave. 'Hi, George.'

George offers his hand and gives one of those long warm handshakes of someone who has time to pay attention to greeting you. 'Lillian.'

'How's the research going?'

'I'm getting there. Still have huge gaps to fill about the last years. Surprising really with someone so well known. So many people have died or disappeared—it's hard to find contemporaries who truly knew him beyond the public persona.'

Lillian is enjoying her role of being in charge of the shop, acting as hostess. 'George, have you met Rupert?'

All this is going on over my head—literally—as I flick through a battered old moleskin notebook. What was the point of having a computerised inventory and then not use it?

'Good to meet you. I'm Rupert Bunter-White. Bette's son.'

'I've heard a lot about you. Your mother is a wonderful lady—as is her sister.' George offers his hand again, which Rupert shakes.

'Yes, they are originals—both of them.'

'They've been very helpful to me with my research.'

'Oh? Are you writing a thesis?'

'Nothing like that. I've been commissioned by PiP—by your uncle in fact—to write the biography of—'

I find the entry and my heart sinks.

'—Of Sylvester Sligo,' George concludes.

Words continue to whirl around me but I now feel as though I'm hearing them through thick glass.

'How fascinating,' says Rupert. 'Love his work. I even met him a few times with my auntie when I was younger. I was just talking to Lillian about a revival of one of his at the Bridge.'

'Sligo?' asks Lillian. Really, a drama student should know him. He hasn't fallen so far out of fashion so fast, has he? He'd hate that.

'The eminent playwright,' explains George.

'Oh yeah.' She nods sagely as if to say *that* Sylvester Sligo.

'Larry would like the book to be ready for the Bridge run, but there's a lot still to deal with in his later life, I might miss my deadline.'

'Really?' Lillian is not covering herself in glory here.

'Darling rebel of the sixties, big name of the eighties, grand old man of the theatre in the two thousands. Went silent in the twenty tens for some reason – feeling his age maybe?—and died about three years ago.' George switches his attention back to me. 'Did you find the entry?'

I push the book over to Lillian. 'Got to go...somewhere.'

I walk out.

6

To enter was to be inducted into a space which was half-way between waking and dreaming, one in which something momentous seemed about to happen.

Simon Callow, 'My Life in Pieces'

Nineteen years ago

In the woods, the bluebells were in bloom and they were glorious.

I ran in my anorak, yellow wellies and green swimsuit down the path, over the stile and into the copse. The sky had fallen—Chicken Licken was at last right but it was nothing to be scared of. I had my kingdom to myself so I moved a log to make a throne in the middle of the flowers. I'd need a crown but bluebells aren't so easy to thread as daisies. After a little thought and scavenging, I solved the problem by making a ring of twisted ivy and winding the bluebells among the dark heart-shaped leaves. I undid my plaits and shook out my hip-length hair.

'I name thee, Queen Merle.' I imagined humming birds

lowering the crown on my head as my hands did the task. 'Once a queen of Bluebell, always a queen of Bluebell.' As soon as I spoke the words, I scrunched up my nose in disgust. I'd spoilt it. Bluebell was a rubbish name for an Elven kingdom, and I'd copied Narnia. Dad said it was OK to copy—an homage he called it, saying it like *fromage*, which I knew was French for cheese, so maybe the word was from France too? He said that homage was how we learned to be great artists. But I wanted to be a writer like Uncle Sylvester and make up my own stories, not steal from others.

I tried again. 'I name thee Queen Merle of Berrydoggia. May the light never leave this realm.' Oh, that was much better! Was light a kind of magic? Finding a patch of sunshine, I took off my anorak so I could lie on it and made a note in my exercise book. I imagined I was bathing in magic. The kingdom had pools like this where the elves went to recharge their powers. So that made darkness the enemy. But was that too much like other stories? Maybe too much light was the enemy? Maybe the enemy kingdom was scorched and bleached into a white desert?

'Oh look at that! Isn't she just the cutest!' The female guest who was walking with Uncle Sylvester had spotted me. Rats. It was too late to find a better hiding place. I sat up, crown sagging over one ear.

'Um, hello.' I waved, hoping they wouldn't come any closer. Adults didn't seem to know how to walk without crushing the flowers.

The woman waved back but Uncle Sylvester just looked, like he sometimes did, a really fixed stare. He and his companion had obviously chosen this morning to visit the bluebell woods too. Keira Fanning was a photographer from a magazine in New York, come to capture him *in situ*. (When they first said that, I'd thought Situ was maybe the name of a city? But it just meant in his normal place). Keira was wearing flared black trousers and a top that was really several spangled scarves sewn together. She wore a battered straw sunhat this morning so she looked like the Quangle Wangle in one of Lucinda's poetry books. Uncle Sylvester had a smaller version on his head: his disreputable, he called it. My dad said its proper name was a Panama and it could be squashed up and still come out that shape. That seemed the perfect magical power for a hat. Queen Merle would have a hat like that, bright blue, made of feathers.

'Isn't she darling!' Keira touched her host's elbow.

'Take her picture,' said Sylvester. It came out an order but he corrected himself. 'Please. There's something about this...something I want to remember. A Puckish moment. And you take such stunning portraits.'

I didn't want my picture taken. This was my kingdom. It didn't have cameras. Cameras were the enemy of make-believe. But how could I explain that?

'Oh, but shouldn't we ask her father?' murmured Keira.

'Evan's taken the car into Oxford. He won't mind.'

'Well...' I could tell she really wanted to take the picture even though she thought she shouldn't, because she was acting like I did with the last ice cream in the freezer. 'I suppose I could show him—get his approval to keep the images?'

'That's the ticket.' He called over to me. 'Merle, just carry on playing. Forget we're here.'

But how could I? I wanted to please him though—Dad said that was very important. I'd lose my lovely room with the horses and books if we upset Uncle Sylvester. I pretended to crown myself again but I just felt silly. The humming bird handmaidens had fled and my crown had begun to unravel. The children at school thought my make-believe games were lame and babyish as I didn't know the same characters as they did and hadn't watched many Disney movies. This felt the same: Keira had bleached out my kingdom.

That gave me an idea for my villain! I couldn't wait for them to leave so I could write it down.

'Would you lie on your tummy again, sweetheart?' asked Keira. 'Peek through the flowers at me.'

The photographer lay on her front too and we played peekaboo through the bluebells, except I was looking at a big black lens-eye, not a person. Maybe the enemies were huge bugs, like locusts? I'd had nightmares when we'd seen a glass box of locusts at the zoo. What if they escaped and bred and then ate everything in their path like they did on that nature films on TV? England would be just brown sticks. Oh, but that was a fabulous idea! Use what scares you, Uncle Sylvester had said.

'What a lovely smile,' crooned Keira. 'A little fairy princess lost in the woods.'

Her fantasy ideas were stupid. I wasn't little, nor a fairy, and definitely not a princess. I was the fearsome queen of Berrydoggia and Keira was the evil bug monster coming to destroy my land. It would be an age-long battle with great losses on both sides. My children, her armies—both would be sacrificed. I would have to think up a spell to destroy her. But I wouldn't use Latin as that would be copying *Harry Potter*. A rhyme then? Yes, I'd write a poem against her and all her kind.

When she showed no signs of stopping, I decided I'd played nice long enough so Dad wouldn't get cross with me. I stood up, rubbing at the red marks of the grass stalks and twigs on my bare limbs.

'I've got to go now,' I said. 'I'm going to play with a friend.' That wasn't true but there were children from my class in the village who I might go round to play with if they asked me.

'Dressed like that?' asked Keira, putting the cap back on the lens.

'They've got a swimming pool...' maybe that was going too far? 'A big paddling pool.'

'It's a bit cold to go swimming, isn't it? May in England is brisk to say the least.'

'Not swimming, just playing with water pistols.' I put my coat back on.

'Ah, now I understand. Good strategy having an anorak and a swimming costume. Have fun! Take no prisoners!'

Using that as permission to go, I ran off in the opposite direction to the one they were walking in and looped round to the stream. First checking they weren't going to jump out at me here too, I picked up the story where I had left it: the anointing of the queen. Water ran over my green-stained palms from the little stony fall. I lifted it overhead and let it trickle on my hair.

'With this water, I endow thee with the magic of Berry-doggia.' Julius, the Elven high priest and the queen's childhood companion, was doing the honours now—a tall, handsome elf who was doomed to die in the first attack and make all the kingdom weep. He didn't know this yet. 'Now go forth and defend the realm from all those who threaten our borders.'

'Yes, my Julius. I will do as you say,' I intoned solemnly, the water running down my face like the tears that soon I'd have to shed for him.

7

We should all have a curiosity about the profession, and what we have come from.

. Judi Dench, 'And Furthermore'

I come back many hours later, fully expecting to find my meagre belongings bundled up and waiting for me to collect. The walk helped though. The memories have come and gone like the tide and I feel like my inner self is scrubbed clean, only a few scoured twigs and empty shells left behind. Mercifully, only Viv and Bette are on duty, closing up for the night, so at least I don't have to face Lillian. I slide in and stand with my back to the door. Brutus approaches to sniff my fingers then retreats to his favourite spot by the armchair. No customer so far has refused to stroke him when he sits there.

'Where did you go?' asks Viv.

'I just walked.' I'd paced the circuits of Green Park and

St James Park until my inner turmoil went from Gale Force ten to a stiff breeze.

'Lillian said you walked out on a valued customer. Why? Are you racist?'

Her suggestion completely floors me. 'Come again?'

'The biographer, George Appiah.'

The hot scholar? 'God, no!' Trust Lillian to put the worst frame around my act.

'I didn't think so. Rupert thinks you were spooked by him, not George, what with him being Bette's son. Guilty conscience about something. Is that what happened?'

'Viv,' Bette places a hand on her sister's arm. 'Is this helping?'

Viv moves out of reach. 'We need to know we can rely on her if we leave her in the shop. Walking out for no reason is not reliable.'

'I get...get moments. I can't explain them.' I could, but I can't, not to these kind ladies.

'Remember how I was when I left William?' says Bette, still talking to Viv rather than me. 'I was a wreck. I had days when I couldn't cope and you were so patient with me.'

'This isn't the same at all!' Viv reaches over my head and I duck by instinct, but she's just turning over the sign to 'Closed'.

'Isn't it?' says Bette, giving me a speaking look. I get the message. She wants me to know that she understands what it's like to feel a victim. This makes me angry, though I'm not sure why. She's just being a decent human being.

'I'm sorry. I'll go if you want.' I don't wish to but it's going to end up that way sometime so I could just give in to the inevitable and leave now. Whose sofa have I not yet sampled?

Bette's hair stands out like a halo around her head. My

undeserved guardian angel. 'I don't want that—nor does Viv when she thinks about it. You had a moment and needed some fresh air. Very sensible. You didn't have your panic attack in front of a customer, you took it elsewhere. If my sister gets down off her high horse for a second, she'll see you actually coped quite well with your crisis.'

'Humph!' But it's not a totally hostile harrumph from Viv.

'However, I am concerned you've upset one of our customers. I'd like you to call George and tell him we've found his book—and apologise.'

'You've found...the book?'

'Yes. Viv did. She dug it out of the attic. House clearance from Richmond, wasn't it?'

Viv has moved behind the counter, a commander in her trench. 'Correct. Still working my way through what we brought back but I thought I'd spotted some of Sligo related works in there.' Viv checks the till receipts and grimaces.

My throat goes dry. 'You want me...to phone George?'

'Give the girl a gold star for attention. Yes, we do. Make this right and we can put it behind us.' She rips off the receipt printout. 'We're down on last month, Bette.'

'It's been very slow, hasn't it, boy?' Bette scratches Brutus' head. 'I'll cook supper.'

Viv looks up from her accounts. 'Aren't we expected at Larry's do?'

'Oh blow: you're right. Totally slipped my mind. No rest for the wicked.' Bette stands up and stretches, trying to drum up some enthusiasm for a night out. 'Merle, you can help yourself to anything you like from the fridge. We'll be seeing June at Larry's tonight so I'll ask her about the spare room. Hopefully, we'll come back with some good news.'

Am I ready for something as permanent as a place in someone's spare room? The thought is daunting.

'Before you ring George, look through the rest of the box to see if there's anything else he might want,' says Viv, powering down the till. 'It will soothe any hurt feelings if you go the extra mile for him. I've put it on the kitchen table.'

The prospect is as welcome as a cup of cold tea. But maybe it's better I do this when I have the shop all to myself? I can hardly walk out every time Sylvester is mentioned.

And I have come to ask questions, even if I don't like the answers they are unwittingly giving me.

'Sure. I can do that.'

'I've written his number on a Post-It. You can use the shop phone to make the call.'

'Fine.'

Viv's expression gives away that she isn't sure I'm going to carry out her wishes, but still, time is flying and she has to get ready to appear in her role as one of the PiP triumvirate.

'Which one is Pompey, which Crassus and which Julius Caesar in your empire?' I ask as they head for the stairs.

'I told you she was well educated,' says Bette. 'And I'm certainly not volunteering for the knife in my back.'

'Seeing how the others were killed in battle or assassinated, I'm not sure the comparison if flattering for any of us,' replies Viv sardonically. 'I think she's being funny. Is that allowed of an employee?'

Leaving that question hanging, the sisters go upstairs to put on what Bette calls 'their glad rags'. I know that the longer I leave the box, the worse it will be, so I go up to the kitchen. The book George wants is on the top: *Sligo's Right Hand: Memoirs of Decade with a Genius*, by Evan Carlisle. It's my dad's book, and I hate it with a consuming passion. It was published ten years ago by a small university press in America against all non-disclosure agreements and in the face of opposition from Sylvester but by then, of course, he didn't have a leg to stand on and my father prevailed. It's very familiar—Dad had been so proud of this, his first work of fiction posing as fact. I flick through to the photos. I don't feature in many—I hardly appear in the story at all, thank God—but you can catch me in the occasional one on my father's shoulders or Sylvester's lap, a tousled, grubby-looking urchin, inseparable from yellow boots for most of her years between nine and ten. I can remember them even now—the smell of earth they carried, the squeaky feel to the outside, the imprint of a bare foot inside as I rarely wore socks. Far the best footwear for rambling in the woods as they protected my ankles from brambles.

I turn to a page in the middle. He's still on the second summer spent at Dogberry. I was about eleven.

It was my privilege to wake up each day and be the very first to read his words. I used to get up and ask myself what wonder would he have dreamed up overnight? What scene of melancholy decline or loss of innocence would he turn to next? He was still celebrating the runaway success of the major work of his last years, 'A Walk in Bluebell Woods', and I had hopes he would find renewed inspiration in the countryside around Dogberry Cottage...

As usual, Dad is laying it on too thick. He was Sylvester's secretary, answered his business letters and emails, kept the office straight, did errands, but he wasn't the first audience on whom the playwright tried his material. Sylvester had picked me for that dubious honour.

Still, with Sylvester dead, there is no one to challenge my dad's version any longer. George will doubtless give at least a chapter to this falsely close relationship if he gets hold of this book. Dad will be thrilled.

I get out the other volumes in the box. Most are completely unrelated—collections of audition pieces, biographies of film stars I've never heard of. I even find one on Merle Oberon which I put aside, hoping to get a little more acquainted with my namesake. Then at the bottom I find three more works: *Plays 1966-1986* (a first edition), *Muse of Fire* (four lectures he gave at the Stratford Festival in 1995 which he turned into a book), and finally *Sligo in Situ: A Summer with Sylvester* by Keira Fanning. I hadn't known this book even existed. With growing dread, I flick through. Maybe she never got permission... Surely Dad would never've agreed...?

In the middle there's a wedge of green: candid shots and portraits of a girl she calls 'Sylvester's Fairy Muse'. I force myself to look. Now I'm an adult, I can see there's something wrong about these shots, like those images of the real Alice in her petticoats taken by Lewis Carroll. The person holding the camera just has too much power over the wide-eyed child lying among the bluebells in her green swim suit, wellies waving behind her to give her a rooting in reality. OK for a mother, but for a stranger to invade the girl's world? I... she...that girl looks angry, bored, and, in one shot, viciously happy. They are indeed Puckish rather than cute—Sylvester had it right.

But I was never asked if I wanted these out there, not by Keira, or Sylvester or even my father. I check the publication date—seventeen years ago. Cross-referencing online on Bette's tablet, I find it is still in print and gone through a number of editions. I'm tempted to send Keira an email demanding she remove my image, but how would that work? I'd have to prove I am who I say I am when I'm working under another name. And hasn't the damage already been done?

Perhaps it's best just to disown the child from the photo, lay her to rest alongside Julius, the poor doomed high priest of Berrydoggia, who had a most impressive funeral in the bluebell woods a week after the coronation. Queen Merle belongs there and not in my present.

Tempting though it is to hide all this from George, I know I can't. Viv is probably well aware of the box contents and has set this up as another test. I pick up the three books and go down to the phone.

'George?'

'Who is this?' There's a lot of background noise—a party of some kind. He's not at the PiP reception too, is he?

'It's Merle, the wandering assistant from Last Chance—the bookshop.'

'Oh, Merle.' From his tone, I can tell the sisters are right to suspect I'd offended him.

'Sorry for earlier. I had a...bad moment—I've got some... er...personal issues to work through. Nothing to do with anyone else.'

'Oh.' His tone is now much warmer. 'I'm sorry to hear that. Are you feeling better?'

'Much, thank you. Viv and Bette asked me to call you about the book you wanted.'

'There's news?'

'It's waiting for you in the shop. And we found two more that you might like so I've put those aside for you.'

'Which ones?'

I read off the details, trying to distance myself from the material like allergy desensitisation therapy: take it in little doses and maybe prevent another anaphylactic shock.

'I'm very interested in both. The photos, late period,

aren't they? I've only seen them referenced once or twice but not yet tracked down the actual book. Are they any good?'

Are they? They certainly evoke what it was like living in the court of King Sylvester, the entourage of acolytes, actors and scroungers that golden summer. 'They're pretty good.'

'Great. I must see if the photographer is contactable. What's her name again.'

'Keira Fanning.' That tastes like a paracetamol left too long in the mouth.

'Thanks, Merle. I'll be in tomorrow to pick those up.' He ends the call.

I do the same search on the computer he is doubtless making right now. Keira Fanning, my wicked witch of the woods, has a website which looks like it's updated frequently. I go to the events tab and then wish I hadn't. Keira is coming to London in the autumn for a new exhibition of her photos of living playwrights and actors. Fear blooms.

Don't be ridiculous, I tell myself. Even if on the off chance she comes in here, she won't recognise you from your nine-year-old self.

But that makes no difference. I just want all of that part of my life kept, far, far away from me. There's nothing good to be found in those memories. Because, between us, my dad and I, we killed Sylvester Sligo.

8

You're related by scandal.

Carrie Fisher, 'Wishful Drinking'

True to his word, George is waiting for the shop to open. Unbolting the door, Viv lets him in and gives me one of her stares to tell me I'm to complete my customer service repair by stepping up to help him.

Today he's in an open-necked shirt and pale trousers, radiating a fresh heartiness that's alien to my nature. He's a sparkling Oscar Wilde comedy to my Jacobean revenge tragedy and I wish I could change to fit in his world, go on a date in a piano bar, or to the theatre, making clever conversation. Instead, I'm left wading in blood and vengeance. I slide the three books across the counter to him. At least that will get them out of the shop. Being near him is like shoving splinters under my nails. Dad and I can't afford to have anyone unearthing the last days of Sylvester.

The Queen of Berrydoggia—that's who died in those woods. *Cover her face. Mine eyes dazzle. She died young.* John Webster had a way with words—not up to Shakespeare, but there's blood and sinew to them.

'Merle, thanks so much for digging these out for me.' George's smile could power a 100 watt bulb in the footlights.

'No problem.'

He doesn't just pay up as I hoped, but settles in for a chat, leaning with elbows on the counter. 'Do you know Sligo's work?' He caresses the top book—the first edition—like it's a cat purring under his fingertips.

'A little.' I reposition the pens in the holder, turning them all up the right way.

'I'm a big fan.'

'Really? I'd never've guessed.'

'His last major work, *A Walk in Bluebell Woods* has been called the *Lolita* of our times—or Lolita's revenge.' He mistakes my silence for ignorance. '*Lolita*? The Nabokov novel? About a man who falls in love with an underage girl? Very unsettling.'

'I know it.' I wish there was a way of hurrying him along without offending him but I can't think how just now.

'And Sligo's piece? It has this amazing confrontation between an old writer—some think it's an imagined Nabokov—and his victim, now grown up. She comes and challenges him for what he did—his hypocrisy—his trampling of her innocence to regain something youthful for himself.'

'Interesting.' This is the most boring and neutral response I can summon.

George still wants to convert me. 'It's amazing and contains many of the debates we're having now about constitutes appropriate behaviour.'

'I would've thought child abuse was never appropriate.'

He looks embarrassed. 'Sure—yes—I didn't mean...it's just the Lolita paradox: you can empathise while you condemn someone for what they do.'

'I hope you mean sympathise.'

'What?'

'Empathy means you're feeling along with them, like it's personal to you.'

'Oh, yeah, right. Sympathy. Pity.' He runs a hand over his head. 'It's hard for a guy to say anything right in this area. Sligo was very bold even to try.'

'Is that why you like him: because he's bold?'

I shouldn't have asked. It's just that if I could describe the anti-Sylvester it would be someone like George.

'No, not only that. He's a master of structure. The journey he puts the audience through—it moves like a thriller—is she going to shoot him right there in the woods? Would we cheer if she did?—while it's also a Chekhovian conversation about loss and family. And a fantasy. Look, you must come and see it with me.'

'I really don't think it's for me.'

'You can't reject something you know so little about; you've got to give it a chance. The Bridge are staging it in a few months. I'm sure Larry will get us complimentary tickets.'

I am very unlikely still to be here by then so I can promise him the moon. 'Free tickets? Never turn them down, that's my motto.'

He grins. 'Great, I can't wait until you see it in production. Nobody can see that play and not understand just how brilliant Sligo is at his best.' He picks up the books. 'Can I pay by card?'

'On the house!' calls Viv. 'Larry's orders. You'd only bill him anyway—for the research costs.'

'Thanks, Viv. I'd better make a start on these.'

He goes and the shop relaxes back into quietness. I ponder his invitation. I don't think it's because he likes me; how could he on such a slight acquaintance? It's more a mixture of awareness we got off on the wrong foot and a zealot's desire to bag another for the Sylvester appreciation society.

Been there. Done that.

Bette is out with Brutus, so it is just Viv and me. Lost in working out how to host videos on the site, I only look up when I hear a ripping noise—it's Viv taking down the red swags. Dust billows. She steps back to admire the newly exposed twentieth century shelf.

'I should've done that years ago!'

I bring the roll of clear plastic sacks that we use for recycling and hold one open. She bundles in the crimson velvet like we're disposing of a body.

'Leave that out tonight and I bet it'll be snapped up by some upcycler within the hour.' Viv blows her nose. 'What do you think? Better?'

I usually avoid looking at this shelf as Sylvester's works occupy half a row, multiple copies of his three most popular pieces: *Sea Dreams*, his first play, based on his experience as a child in World War Two; *Raven's Nest*, a satirical take on life in sixties London; and of course, *A Walk in Bluebell Woods*, my ravaged childhood.

I force myself to be impartial. 'It suits them better than velvet.'

'That's what I think. Curtains are a cliché.'

We spend the next hour taking down the swags and dusting. The customers who come in during that time joke about our enthusiastic Spring cleaning but all are complimentary (they wouldn't dare be anything else with Viv so clearly in favour). The shelves are revealed in their antique mahogany glory—they probably worth as much as the stock. We've run out of bags so I pile the last in the stockroom.

Bette returns an hour later with Brutus and a tall woman in tow. The latter is a very striking figure, with a tower of black hair arranged in an Amy Winehouse beehive and false eyelashes. As she has particularly large hands and feet, I wonder if she might be Trans. Not that it is any of my business, of course.

In that spirit, I try not to look too hard.

'Merle, this is June...what have you done to the shop!' Bette's friendly tone turns to peeved.

I'm tempted to say 'it wasn't me' and point at Viv like a kid caught out by teacher in the playground.

'Huge improvement, don't you think, June?' says Viv.

'I feel like I can breathe in here at long last.' June throws open her arms and takes a deep breath, like she's about to burst into 'Oklahoma!'.

'But where's the theatrical flavour gone?' wails Bette.

'It's in the plays themselves—and the props. Antigonus has survived the cull.' Viv gestures to the bear, still growling in his corner. He's an RSC retiree from *A Winter's Tale*, a little bald on his muzzle where he's been stroked by generations of children and actors who come to him for luck.

'I think...' But I remember I'd decided I wasn't *that* girl.

But the three women have turned to look at me.

'Think what, Merle?' asks Bette, clearly hoping for an ally.

Their silence forces me to say something. 'I was just thinking you could use the space you've gained.'

'And?' asks June, penciled eyebrow quirked.

'And sell some theatrical memorabilia, like Harry Potter merchandise, Roald Dahl or things related to the Disney musicals. Have a children's corner?' It comes out a mumble.

Bette sniffs, then regrets that as she immediately sneezes.

Viv seizes her chance. 'That's a good idea. Merle, sort it out and show us the plan. I imagine we have to get a licence to sell that merchandise but we're well positioned having been in business for a century. Our name is worth a lot. Any more ideas?'

I do in fact have more but I'm not ready to offer that level of involvement in the business. Just passing through. And it might anyway be offering fashion advice to prisoners in the tumbril if the shop is doomed. So I duck my head.

'This is your Merle?' June has turned her attention to me now. 'Who are you and why should I let you use my spare room?'

OK, so she's direct. 'I'm Merle Cardew.' Today at least. 'I'm sleeping in the stockroom and I think Viv and Bette want it back.'

'How did you end up in this predicament?'

I glance at Bette, hoping she'll head off the intrusive questions as she has done in the past but not today.

Not today, O Lord, O not today, think not upon the fault my father made... Poor Henry V. He had a shit father too.

'I dropped out.'

'Of university?'

'Of life.'

June smiles at that, but I'm not joking. 'Drink?'

I shrug.

'Drugs?'

I shake my head.

'Disreputable friends?'

'No!' barks Viv. 'Very respectable ones.' Jodie has made a favourable impression.

'Shame,' says June. 'Do you smoke?'

I shake again. It's almost the truth. 'Given up.'

'I'll give you a trial. Not rent-free. I expect you to pay your way.'

'She will. She's earning here. In fact, she's due her first pay cheque,' says Viv.

I mumble something about not having a bank account. I'd lost track of that some months ago.

'It'll be in cash then.'

'Can you give the rent directly to June?' I ask. I don't trust myself with money in my pockets.

That swings June definitively in my favour. 'I'll take you there now, if Viv can spare you? It's not far.' June doesn't wait for an answer. She's already striding out of the shop.

'Run along!' chides Bette when she sees I'm not moving.

Right, I'll do that then.

JUNE'S flat is above a Thai restaurant in narrow Bedfordbury Street, a stone's throw from Trafalgar Square and the English National Opera. In fact, from my room on the top floor, I can see the ball on the tower of the Coliseum theatre that is the ENO's home. It's funny imagining people living so central. I've always associated these streets with entertainment and tourists. The house dates from the Georgian period: brick frontage with sash windows from the first floor up, slate-tiled roof that you can also see from the dormer window in the attic. My bed is tucked in a corner among racks and trunks of costumes. When we entered there was still the pieces of a dress laid out on the white bedspread—a black gown with a feather-trimmed train. At the moment the place resembles a funeral parlour, with plumed bonnets and black clothes hanging on the racks. June is giving up part of her workroom to house me. 'Spare' room might be an overly generous description on Bette's part.

'I'll have to take your measurements,' June says, laying a folded towel on the pillow.

'What? For my coffin?' I rub my arms, wondering at the collection.

'Listen to her! So dramatic!' June opens the window to let in some air. 'No, for me, sunshine. I sometimes need people to try a costume on before I show it to the director. Everyone gets roped in.' She picks up the black silk swatch and takes it to a worktable. There's no room on that so she lays it over the back of her chair. 'Did you know that Viv has the exact same proportions as Gillian Anderson? And every Dame Judi costume gets tried first on Bette.'

I brush a finger over a lush piece of midnight velvet. 'What's with the mourning clothes?'

'Dickens,' says Viv, leaving me to guess which adaptation is being revived. I realise there is a funeral in almost every Dickens I can remember.

'We rather over-dosed on him in the 2012 season for the bicentenary, but his coming back now after a decent gap.' June looks down at me, strong-boned face pensive. 'Is this going to work?'

I like that she phrases it like that, rather than 'can I trust you?'.

'I don't know. But I'm going to try.' I was, wasn't I? This was my chance; life had stopped pissing on me and turned in my favour.

'That's all we can ask.' She sighs. 'I'm weak. I swore

never again after Cristofor. He slept here too. We all lost our hearts to him and look how he repaid us!'

She thought she was weak for taking in another stray but it would take a heart of stone to stand up to Bette who clearly meant so well.

'Well, I can promise you one thing: I don't have any family weddings to go to.'

She laughs at that, making a startling sound close to a human machine gun. 'Very well then. Let's see how this goes.'

That night I lie in bed, oddly missing the dream-driven grumbles and cardboard box chewing of my old room-mate. I feel like I'm in free-fall. Just over a week ago I had more or less given up. Sleeping on sofas had felt the last step in my descent and I was not thinking of any phoenix-like rise. Maybe I am not so much rising as being dragged up by the determination of my three fairy godmothers, like that moment when the ripcord pulls and the parachute jerks you back up for a few seconds? Yet it is a dangerous rescue in almost the worst place for me—only one better than trying this in Burford on the doorstep of Dogberry Cottage. Does anyone remember me still in that Cotswold town? Is there any danger that someone from my old life is going to walk in on this new one and spoil it for me? Or at least tell George enough so that he can join the dots? I could do without his unearthing of my rubbish, going about like some urban fox on bin day.

I stare at the ceiling until another thought lands.

Should I warn Dad?

9

I think very few people are completely normal really, deep down in their private lives.

Noel Coward, 'Private Lives'

Nineteen years earlier

When the summer holiday started, I began writing down the adventures of Queen Berry-doggia in an old school exercise book. Paying more attention than I did at school to my handwriting, I began her epic with a map that I illustrated in coloured pencils. The house and gardens became cities, farming country, lakes, and mountain ranges. The village where my school was became the enemy kingdom, a bit too much like Mirkwood. I crossed that out and tried to think of something I hadn't read before. An enemy kingdom full of people who were too normal—who killed magic by being too nice. They would suffocate the queen with their boring lives. I drew that kingdom as a series of little box houses and children marching in line to Maths and Literacy classes.

A shadow fell over my page.

'What are you up to, eh?'

Uncle Sylvester had come out onto the terrace and I hadn't even noticed. Normally I tracked his movements around the house and gardens with the devotion of a bird spotter with their favourite nesting species. I'd forgotten to keep track today as the queen's map was even more interesting. But I didn't want to share it with someone who wrote for a living. That made it feel so silly compared to what he did.

'No need to be shy!' he said in his growly voice, taking the seat next to me at the table. He dropped a heavy ring binder in front of himself. 'Are you keeping a diary?'

'No. A story.'

'Even better!' He opened his file and took out his ink pen. 'Then us writers should stick together. You write yours and I'll try to rescue mine from being utter drivel.'

I checked a few times from under my eyelashes that he was doing as promised—writing, not peeking at my book. I saw that he was engrossed in what he was reading, so I relaxed and went back to designing Berrydoggia. There would have to be a magnificent library with a lion-maned Keeper of the Books in charge. A wizard? Perhaps that needed a town all to itself? Bookford?

I lost count of how much time we spent on that sunny terrace. It must've been at least an hour because I'd coloured in my map and started my tale with the coronation. Then Uncle Sylvester spoke again.

'How's it going over there in your story?'

'Good, thanks.' I put my arm across the page so he couldn't sneak a look.

'Mine's pretty hard going, I have to admit.' He tapped the

papers. 'Merle, I was wondering: have you heard to C. S. Lewis—Narnia and so forth?'

'Yes.' I wondered what the catch was.

'Wonderful stories—read them to all my children. And *The Hobbit*? By Tolkien?'

I nodded. 'There was a copy on Lucinda's book shelf. I haven't finished it yet. I got confused in the battle bit.'

'Don't blame you. Too much story going on all of a sudden. But did you know that Tolkien and Lewis used to meet up every week and read each other their stories? No? They did. They called themselves—and their friends who came along to listen—the Inklings. Met in a pub in Oxford—grown men entertaining themselves over a pint with dragons, witches and elves. What do you make of that?'

I shrugged but I was wondering why it was only men.

'I mentioned it because it's given me an idea: if it helped them, why not give it a try?'

A rook cawed above us and headed for the tallest tree in the wood. 'Give what a try?'

'I'll read you my story and you can read me a little of yours and we can see if we can help each other out. How does that sound?'

It sounded terrifying. 'But mine's only make-believe.'

'My dear child, what do you think mine is? There's a good living to be made from make-believe if you dare. Look, I'll go first. Tell me what you think.' And without waiting for me to agree or disagree, he turned to his first page. 'Now this play starts in a wood, just like ours. It's bluebell time.'

That I could understand. 'Like a few months ago?'

'Exactly. Picture that. There's an old man sitting on a camp stool just staring at the bluebells.'

I closed my eyes. 'What's he like?'

'Bit like me—old and grizzled—best days behind him.'

He paused and I wondered if he wanted me to say something.

'Yes, I can imagine that.'

He gave a little huff of laughter. 'Out of the mouths of babes,' he murmured. 'Right, now a woman comes on stage —or into the wood in this case. She has a gun held so the audience can see, down by her side.'

'A gun?' This was getting interesting. 'Is she going to shoot someone?'

'Ah, that's what we're all wondering. Listen, she gets the first line: "Revisiting the scene of your old crimes, Edmund?" And off the play goes!'

He read the opening scene with the two people—old friends I realised after a few remarks—talking about something bad he had done in the past to her. She was very upset with him and had come to shoot him—or make him apologise—I wasn't very clear.

Uncle Sylvester put the ring binder down. 'What do you think?'

'Does she shoot him?'

'Do you think she should?' He waited as if the answer was important.

'Did he do something very bad?'

He nodded.

'Would she get away with shooting him if she did?'

His laughter surprised both of us. 'Now I hadn't thought of that! That's exactly what she'd be asking herself. I knew there was a reason I wanted to talk to you about it. Excellent.' He scribbled a note down in the margin.

'Did that help you?' Dad would be really pleased with me.

'Oh yes. That was precisely what I needed.' He closed the file. 'Now, let's hear yours.'

I put my arm back to cover it. 'Oh, mine's nothing. Not very good. I've done better ones at school.'

'Let me be the judge of that. I'm the professional here.' He winked at me.

Reluctantly, I turned the exercise book round so he could see the map. 'This is where my story happens —Berrydoggia.'

'Wonderful. How Italianate of you. And who is your main character?'

'Queen...um...Merle.'

'Good choice. Write what you know. What's this? A coronation. Another good choice. Start right in there with action.'

'Like the lady with the gun?' I was beginning to feel more comfortable discussing my story with him as he wasn't mocking me.

'That's right. Let me hear you reading it. Nothing like hearing the author read her work in her own voice.'

I began my coronation scene. I could see it playing out before my eyes as I narrated, the crowds of courtiers in the throne room, the clicking of the bug-eyed monsters threatening from without the walls, the warlike noises coming from the Kingdom of the Slamron.

Uncle Sylvester lifted up a finger. 'Slamron?'

'The normal people—the ones who don't believe in magic. It's "normals" backwards.'

'Ah. Just so. How do they fit with the bug-eyed Clickers?'

I bit my lip. 'Not sure yet. I only just had that idea this morning.'

'I see. It's a work in progress. Maybe they're allies?'

'But the Slamron wouldn't be able to see the Clickers as they don't believe in magic.'

'Good point. This is wonderful stuff, Merle.' He waved me on with a finger. 'Let's hear what happens next.'

I reached the end of the ceremony and the invasion of General Ariek, leader of the Clickers, when we heard my dad approaching with Miss Fanning. They were talking loudly, Miss Fanning's tone bouncing with a bubbling laugh. It sounded very much as if they'd become best friends over the last few days and I hadn't noticed. Miss Fanning kept trying to make friends with me too. I wondered what Mum would think when she got back from her trip to Argentina.

'I'm afraid, Merle, our revels now are ended. We are about to be overtaken by Slamrons,' said Sylvester. He gestured between our two stories. 'Let's keep this our secret, shall we?'

I nodded. It felt like great fun to keep a secret from my dad; he kept so many from me.

'And where have you two love birds been this morning?' asked Sylvester.

'Love birds?' Keira gave another merry laugh and threw her sunhat on an empty chair. She kissed his cheek. 'Hardly. Evan and I have been taking a tour of the local church—it's quite a gem, I have to say. I got some great pictures. I'd like to take some with you there.'

'Me in that place? Lightning would strike me down if I dared cross the threshold.'

'Shame. You're a dead ringer to one of the monuments in there. Sir Harold could be your twin.'

'I thought you were supposed to be photographing me in my natural habitat?'

Keira held up her hands in a sign of surrender. 'Fine, fine.'

My father looked at the papers on the table, then at me. 'I hope, sir, that Merle hasn't been pestering you?'

'Oh no, dear boy, nothing like that. It is rather I who has encroached on her morning, I'd say. Now you're back, Evan, let's go and tackle that pile of letters that came earlier.' He fanned himself with his disreputable hat. 'I rue the day I was ever put on the A level syllabus. Standard reply to most of them but we should put in a personal note to the teachers' conference woman.' He got up, chair creaking, scooped up his file and went back into the house, my father in attendance.

'Well, don't you look as fresh as a daisy!' Keira went to the chair he had just left and sat down. She reached for the lens cap. 'May I take your picture?'

I closed my exercise book and slipped it back into my unicorn bag. 'Yes.' I gave her my cheesy grin, teeth bared and no smile. She lifted the camera then put it back down.

'Never mind. Maybe later.'

'OK.' I got down from the table. 'Bye!' And I ran for my new hideout in the woods. No one had found that yet.

10

The truth of anything at all doesn't lie in someone's account of it. It lies in the small facts of the time. An advertisement in a paper. The sale of a house. The price of a ring.

Josephine Tey, 'The Daughter of Time'

For some unknown reason, George has taken it upon himself to keep me briefed about his discoveries in the books I gave him. Every time he comes into the shop, I try to hide but he waits for me to emerge.

'This Evan Carlisle character sounds quite a man,' he tells me on the third visit. 'According to him he slept with most of Sligo's female guests even as the author himself was indulging in his affairs with the same women.'

'Hmm.' I dust the shelf behind the till where we put orders waiting for collection. The duster makes the reservation slips bend like a passing breeze through corn.

'He sounds proud of it but he's probably bullshitting. He seems like the kind.'

'Hmm.'

'You know, the kinda guy whose always done one better than you?' The light catches George's strong neck and the curve of his shoulder and I have a momentary urge to touch it with my lips – a little homage to his male beauty. 'If you dated a model, he's been to bed with her and her sister. If you kissed Taylor Swift, he inspired her latest break-up album. If you met the Queen, he was–'

'I get the picture.'

Arms folded, George caresses his upper lip, mock detective pose. 'I'm thinking that half the things he says aren't true.'

'Only half?' *Stop, Merle; don't get involved.*

'OK, maybe nearly all the things he says, but there's a few that seem to be factual, like that he worked in close proximity to Sligo all those years. I've seen the bank accounts that confirm it.'

'Hmm?'

'The statements were in the cache of papers Larry handed over.'

There is more evidence than I've expected. My heart flutters. I've come for answers but I haven't expected for it to be in such a courtroom-worthy form. I'd wanted to check my memories against those with more reliable recalls but bank statements…! The shelf is so completely dust-free I must find another task for me to play-act distraction. I start sorting out the flyers for the latest shows that we have in a rack by the front door. He follows me.

'There's one strange coincidence.'

'Hmm.'

'There's a little girl in the account. She's got the same name as you.'

'Hmm?'

'Not a common name, is it?'

I shrug. 'Maybe it was in the year I was born?'

'I don't think so. I've never met another one. Have you?'

'There were three of us in my year at university,' I lie.

'You went to university? Really? Which?' George steps in front of me, intercepting a sheaf of Aladdin flyers in Cadbury's chocolate purple.

'UCL.'

He grows even more inquisitive. 'Which course—which years?'

'Why?'

'I went to UCL too. Maybe we met?'

He probably knows my friends. I stuff the flyers next to the caramel bar colours of *The Lion King*—the West End's candy shop for kids. 'And you've forgotten me already?'

'Oh. Right. When was this? Maybe we didn't overlap?

'I dropped out. I had some health issues.' I feel more at home with the scarlets and black of Beckett and Pinter. I put them at the front.

'I didn't meet any Merles that I remember.' He's like Brutus with a cardboard box. 'Which years again? You look around my age?' He makes it a question.

I've no intention of sharing any more with him. It's bad enough I've handed over one little nugget of truth. 'I wasn't there long.'

'OK. I get the hint. Sorry about the...' He stops, not knowing what the hell he's apologising for and I don't enlighten him. 'I wonder what became of that little girl at Sylvester's?'

My hands still over *Hansel and Gretel* open air production. 'Why wouldn't she still be with her father?'

'Not likely. She must be in her mid to late twenties by now. Hardly still with Carlisle at that age unless there's something wrong with her. It's just interesting that she's so present but hardly mentioned—like a ghost flitting around at the edge of the story. A fairy. I think she might've been Sligo's inspiration for the bluebell girl—it fits with the photos, which are magnificent, by the way.'

'Hmm.'

'That Evan Carlisle character barely mentions he's the father. I wonder if he's contactable?'

'I'd better refill *Mama Mia*.' I gesture to an empty slot on the rack of flyers, trying not to show my racing pulse. 'Need to go to the stockroom.'

It's only when I'm in the back and out of his sight, re-running our conversation, that I realise he'd never said Merle was Evan's daughter but I'd inferred I knew. Had he noticed?

I don't leave the stockroom until I'm certain he's gone. I have to be more careful and stop letting a handsome face distract me.

IT'S June's birthday and she is in ecstasy. Not because of the night out she has planned—though she's pretty revved about that—but because she's been asked to dress a touring production of *Priscilla, Queen of the Desert*. This means that, after a long day in the shop, I find myself standing on a stool—I'm far too short for any of the actors cast in this Australian comedy—being pinned into a variety of outrageous costumes. Gone are Dickensian funeral plumes; in are sequins and Vegas showgirl feathers. June has invited over two friends from the drag queen community to give their verdict. Ru Paul, eat your heart out.

'Gorgeous,' says Ray. He's just come from work so is in civvies, as he calls his business suit. He makes a glamorous blonde in the Marilyn Monroe line when dressed up—at least, that's what June has told me, but I'm finding it hard to picture.

'Needs a bit more on the bust—some sparkles,' suggests Simon. His alter ego is Lady Netta, a slinky red head. He's come to get changed for the night out so is half way through his butterfly transformation—make up done but wig yet to be donned.

June takes the last pins from her mouth. 'The actor's planning to wear some spectacular dangling earrings. I don't want to upstage them.'

'Then I'd say it's about right. And who's the sweetie?' Lady Netta flutters her eyelashes at me (with her wig on, I feel I should change pronoun).

'A Bette waif.' June lifts the dress over my head, leaving me standing in bra and leggings. None of them are the least bit interested in me in that way so I don't find this too excruciating.

Lady Netta helps me down from the stool. 'What's your story, honey child? Fall off a rainbow?'

'Something like that.' She's making me feel tiny, looming over me. I quickly pull a hoodie over my head.

She plucks at it in disgust. 'June, tell the girl that those things do nothing for anyone. Might as well wear a sack.'

'I rather think that's her aim,' says June.

Mood turning melancholy, Lady Netta cups my cheek gently, an oddly maternal gesture. 'You poor thing. Are you Pisces?'

Startled, I shake my head.

'You have the look about you. Capricorn?'

'Gemini,' I whisper.

She nods as if she expected that answer all along. 'Come

out with us, sweetie. Let your very short hair down for a night. We'll protect you.'

I can't help but laugh at the idea of me in a drag club. 'You don't want me with you. I'll cramp your style.'

'Not if we let June get to work on you. You can go in disguise. Pretend to be a boy pretending to be a woman while actually being one—the most fiendish of triple bluffs.'

I reach for my trackies. 'This is getting positively Shakespearean.'

Trousers are whisked from my hand and a sequin mini dress is put in its place.

'Come on, Merle. It's my birthday and we can't leave you here all on your own. Everyone will be there. What's the worst that can happen if you do go out with us?' asks June with a definite challenge in her voice.

I try a last ditch defence. 'This is madness.'

Ray is unbuttoning his plain white shirt. 'That's the attraction. You only live once.'

June gives me a look that makes me feel I'll ruin her day if I don't agree. I still have this annoying part of me that likes to please people to whom I'm in debt. So I hand myself over to her and her friends. The mini dress is tacked to fit. My features are exaggerated with false eyelashes and a cupid bow mouth. They offer me a platinum blonde wig which I very fiercely refuse. A long blue wig is added instead. We almost come unstuck on my feet, which are far too small for any of their heels, until June remembers a box of Cinderella shoes from last year's pantomime season. I end up looking like a jazzed-up fairy and my new friends are delighted.

'She's like a little doll—the sort I was never allowed to play with! We'll definitely have to keep an eye on this one. They'll love her,' crows Regan, the Monroe version of Ray.

We are to start the night by meeting the rest of the

birthday celebrants at a karaoke club near Piccadilly—another first for me. I knew such clubs existed but didn't really believe in them. What entertainment is there in hearing inexpertly sung hits? As far as I can tell, the person having the most fun is the one inflicting their voice on the rest of us. And to make the nightmare worse, June has also invited Larry, Bette and Viv. They've brought Rupert and George, along with a big birthday balloon which bobs over our table, dancing in the flashing lights to the beat of the booming music. I'm not sure who has invited whom but it seems there are links here that go way back. George is Larry's protégé, I've deduced that much. And June went to school with Larry, or so she tells me as the publisher goes with Lady Netta to fetch the first round of drinks.

'June, what have you done to Merle!' exclaims Bette holding me at arm's length to admire my transformation.

Rupert does a double take. 'That's your little assistant? I would never've guessed!'

George grins. 'So she's finally out of her shell.'

Not so. I'm even deeper inside it. This outer package is a ridiculous wrapper, a conch hiding the slug-like sea creature curled within.

Lady Netta returns with drinks, including a sparkling water for me. She must've noticed my bemused expression as a man finishes 'I will survive' to enthusiastic applause. 'You've not drunk enough yet to make this fun. A couple of vodka shots will set you to rights.'

That's probably true, but I'm not comfortable enough to risk dropping my inhibitions under the influence of alcohol. Who knows what I will say and later regret? I slide into the back of the booth we've reserved and nurse my tall glass, wondering when I can get myself out of this. It's not too far to walk home.

June has bagged a spot on stage and is now bringing the house down with her rendition of 'Stand by your man'.

'What do you sing?' Regan asks. She's freaking Rupert out by trying to put her arm around him—on purpose from the glint in her eye. He's trying to act cool but I get the sense he's not sure what the right way to react.

I shake my head. 'Nothing.'

'What would be your song if you had one?'

'"Good Girl Gone Bad".' I bite into the lemon slice, letting the sour taste hurt my mouth.

She looks puzzled.

'Rhianna,' says George from across the table.

I nod. Not my favourite song but I'd listened to it on loop one summer.

'Ah. My musical education stops at the millennium,' admits Regan.

Lady Netta is checking the music list. 'They don't have that one on the karaoke machine but they do have "Umbrella". We'll put you down for that.'

I try to grab it from her. 'Hey! No.' I only sing when drunk.

She holds it above her head. 'Everyone has to sing—that's the rule. Even Larry is going to do a turn and it kills him every year. That's partly why June picks it.'

'Not "Wonderwall" again?' groans Rupert.

Larry raises his glass in an ironic toast.

I've wandered into some friends and family ritual. I should know better.

'No one told me the rules,' I protest.

Lady Netta nudges George. 'Hey, first-timer: did you know the rules?'

George shrugs. 'No. But it's a karaoke bar.' He says it with a 'duh!' intonation. I'm tempted to step on his foot. 'If you do

"Umbrella", I'll do the JAY Z part. Then at least the humiliation is shared.'

That's sweet of him but they are all living in a fantasy world if they seriously think I'm performing up there.

'I'm going to sing "Bring him home",' says Rupert. And no one is surprised.

'I could've picked a show tune? Not fair,' I say.

'Too late. I've entered your number,' says Lady Netta.

Regan bumps me with her shoulder. 'Don't worry about it. We're nearly all awful. I'm bound to get booed. Anyway, you're in disguise, remember? You're not you; you're your Gemini twin.'

As there is no way am I going to do this, and I'm far down the list, I decide not to worry. Viv and Bette are up next, doing a dodgy version of 'Let's call the whole thing off'. Rupert is looking pained but leads the clapping at the end.

'I don't know why they do that every year,' he confides. 'They always forget the words and won't wear their glasses to read the autocue.'

A girl then gets up to do a surprisingly good cover of 'Castle on the Hill' as the sisters come back triumphant to our table.

'Mum, you were excellent,' says Rupert, kissing her cheek.

'No, darling, I was awful.' She beams at us. 'If any of us were any good, we'd be getting paid to sing rather than paying for the privilege.'

With our numbers increased, the table breaks up into many conversations. I don't join them but listen in on the one George is having mainly with Rupert and Lady Netta. He's naturally reverted to his favourite topic. I can manage a little of Sligo now. Maybe the small doses therapy is working?

When Rupert asks how the research is going, George is leaning forward, earnest, like a revolutionary from *Les Mis* recruiting for his cause. 'I find it fascinating how Sligo gets into the fantasy world of the child. He was what? Seventy-three when *A Walk in Bluebell Woods* was first staged?'

'Honey, we all stay fifteen in our heads,' says Lady Netta.

'But this is a little girl's private world.'

Exactly! I want to crow.

'You can sense the unevenness. It's not the idea of a child's world made up by an adult, not like Peter Pan, you know, with a nod and a wink to the adult? It has the freshness mixed with derivativeness that strikes just the right note. I can remember making up stories like that.'

'See: that was the writer in the making right there,' says Rupert, pointing to George. 'There were always too many authors around me growing up, I didn't dare add my own stories to the mix—just acted them out.'

George gets in first with what I'm thinking. 'See: actor in the making right there.'

'Guilty as charged.' Rupert smiles and gives a little bow, hand on heart.

'Ham,' says Viv affectionately from her end of the table as she catches him in the act.

'Auntie Viv, mind your language!' Rupert exclaims with mock-indignation.

'Quite right, Rupert. That's on the list of proscribed words in our family,' adds Larry.

'What are the others?' asks George.

'Wooden—such a cruel insult.'

'We don't much like actorly lies either,' says Viv.

'Such as?' asks George.

She leans in and takes his hand, looking into his face with a saccharine smile. 'Darling, you were wonderful.'

'Don't forget "I never read my reviews"—always a stinker,' says Larry.

'See what I had to cope with growing up?' laments Rupert to all us non-family members. 'It's a wonder I'm not in therapy.'

'Therapy? You don't know what you're missing,' slips in June. 'Captive audience of one.'

At this point, an acquaintance comes over to greet her and wish her 'happy birthday' so the table divides again into separate conversations.

'But going back to Sligo's piece, I think the child's fantasy is part of its appeal to directors,' says Rupert. 'The sections when the fantasy plays out, morphing in and out of the "real" characters is a challenge—brilliant if got right.'

'I like that there's the third level of this being all acted out for us so there's no "real" for us to hold onto,' says George, 'just as we never know how much the girl Anna imagined of the abuse. Memories can be false.'

I swallow against a constriction in my throat.

'Have you seen it staged?' asks Rupert.

George nods. 'One of my favourites.'

'I'm hoping to be cast in the Bridge production as Karl who doubles as Julius the High Priest. That's why I'm brushing up on it. I got a call back.'

Bette reveals that she has been silently listening in to her son all along by giving a whoop. 'Oh, Rupert, that's marvellous! You'd be just perfect as Julius. Not so sure about the Karl part—your gardening skills aren't stellar.'

'Thanks, Mum. I don't think Karl actually does any gardening. Rather he wanders around like...who's that character from D.H. Lawrence?'

'Mellors,' I murmur.

Rupert gives me a nod. 'Yes, the gamekeeper. He's the

natural sex guy in the piece, as opposed to the messed-up bastard Edmund who stole Anna's childhood.

'It's a wonderful dramatic juxtaposition,' says George, 'Julius getting killed off in the fantasy as that avenue is closed to the child by the actions of the adult. It's a mark of his genius that Sligo came up with that.'

Suddenly, I have to get out but I'm trapped in the corner of the booth. Unable to stand this any longer, I wriggle under the table.

'Hey! Merle, what are you doing?' asks George.

Escaping. 'Loo.' The floor is horribly sticky down here, but I've known worse.

'Mind the dress!' calls June. 'I need that for *Dreamgirls*.'

I emerge somewhere near Viv's chair. She picks a scrap of tissue out from the blue strands I've dangled on the floor. Larry offers a hand to help me up. I brush off my knees, embarrassed I'd actually emerged rather too close to his crotch.

'That really wasn't necessary,' he says. 'They would've moved to let you out.' He's still not a fan of my presence in the family business.

'Are you all right?' asks Bette. 'Want one of us to come with you?'

I give her one of my practised smiles. 'I'm fine.'

I leave them arguing the merits of the onscreen Mellors they've seen in various adaptations. At least they've shifted topic.

I spend a long time gathering my thoughts in the Ladies, doing a Lady Macbeth at the sink as I wash my hands repeatedly. The crud seems to stick no matter how many times I soap. When had I first realised Sylvester had stolen my fantasy world for his play? Not till far too late. He never read those scenes to me for obvious reasons. I can remember, though, the child's inarticulacy, struggling to explain to my dad what had been done to me when I did find out months later. My rage, my cries of 'not fair', being sent to my room for 'my tantrum' as Dad liked to characterise it—it still rankles. He told me not to make such a fuss, that great men found their inspiration all around them, that I was honoured that Sylvester had found a seed of an idea in my childish games.

Dad just didn't get it. It wasn't an honour. It wasn't even so much about the theft. It was that Sylvester had cut me out of my skin, put it on, and walked around in it on the stage. I was dispossessed. From then on, I was at war with Sylvester and he knew it. He understood what he'd done but was prepared to sacrifice me for his craft like a latter-day Agamemnon and Iphigenia.

For the first time, I'm glad he's dead.

I emerge from the Ladies to find Rupert is doing a pretty good rendition of his *Les Mis* song. Even though it's the wrong pick for this Friday night crowd, who are more in the mood for power ballads, he's winning them over. I don't feel like going back to my table and there's no way I'm going to be up on stage after Rupert's just shown everyone why he might have a future in musical theatre. I decide to stay away until my slot on the list has passed. There have been a couple of other no-shows and they don't hang around if no one comes forward when their solo is called. I go instead to the bar, joining at the end of the press of people. Thanks to my wage packet, I have actual money on me for once, contained in a little silver purse. Just ten pounds, but that's ten pounds more than I usually carry.

'What'll it be?' asks the barman, getting to me eventually. He's got the full hipster vibe going: thick beard and a little bun at the back of his neck.

I can't face more fizzy water. 'Mango juice.'

He saunters to the bar, singing along to Rupert's soaring crescendo. I dig in my purse.

'Let me get that for you.' A stranger has come up behind me and reaches over my head with a note held out to the barman.

Normally I'm fine with charity, but not in a bar with someone I don't know. 'It's fine.'

'No, no, I've got this. Just add it to my order. I'll have two pints of Fosters, two house whites, and a gin and tonic, no ice.' The guy looks down at me and grins. He's nice looking, auburn hair, freckles, with a few lines that puts him in his thirties. 'See, one little mango juice isn't going to break the bank.'

The bartender looks at me for permission. I put my money away. It seems simpler that way. 'Thanks.'

'Are you here on your own? Because if you are, you can join my table. We're over there.' He gestures to a group who are contemplating the music menu—another guy and three girls. Yeah, they'll really love me to come over and unbalance the gender split even further.

'Thanks but I'm with friends too,' I say.

'Oh?'

'By the stage.' I gesture to the booth where Rupert is returning to receive his due praise. I feel a surge of affection for our loony, larger-than-life, mismatched gathering.

'Right. I noticed your party earlier. Colourful. Like you. Except...I take it you're all girl?' Regan has got up to smother Rupert in kisses.

'Would it bother you if I weren't?'

'Only in that it would suggest I need to go to Specsavers. Thanks, mate.' He leans round me to collect the first drinks from the bartender, brushing against me. Alarm bells ring. I move a step over but there's not much room; instead of backing off, he closes the gap. OK, so he's a creep. I was already heading that way with my verdict but that decides it.

'Thanks for the drink.' I take the mango juice as soon as it's placed on the bar with the rest of the order.

'Hey, don't rush off!' He puts the two wines down so he can bracket me with his arms. 'We were just getting to know each other. We haven't even got to names. I'm Mike.'

He's waiting for me to reciprocate but I've no intention of encouraging him. 'Nice to have met you, Mike. And thanks. But I've got to get back to my party.'

'Really? You look great in that dress, but...' *Don't say it: it's such a cliché.* He says it, mouth by my ear. 'I bet you look even better out of it.'

I can't help it. I laugh. 'Where did you learn that line, Mike? Cheesy Chat Up dot com?' Then, to my utter amazement, I feel his palm under my skirt, right on my butt cheek. 'Hey!' I slap his arm down. 'Not cool, Mike!'

'You know, you're really hot.' He hasn't moved his hand but has closed the remaining millimetres between us so I'm crowded back against the bar. I'm being sexually assaulted in a room of people yet no one can see us. The bartender has moved down the line to serve someone else. The next singer is beginning a rowdy version of 'Bat out of Hell' so my protests go unheard.

'Get off me!'

He's undeterred. 'Come on, bluebell.' The chance nickname makes me freeze. In my mind, he is all those who have cornered me – touched me without permission. 'Let's slip out the back. With this little skirt flipped up, I can be in there in no time and send you to paradise—just give me ten seconds to change your mind.'

I'm not a victim. I throw the mango juice over him—and

over myself as he's so close. June is going to be pissed off about her mini dress but it's worth it to see his face shift from lust to shock. 'I said, hands off!'

We're finally attracting attention. He's furious but he has to step away. 'Christ, you can't take a joke, can you?' he says for the benefit of our audience. He looks down at himself and glares at the damage to his suit. 'You'd better pay for my dry cleaning!'

George arrives and steps between us. 'What's going on?'

'That mad bitch threw the drink I bought her all over me!' splutters Mike.

George, bless him, doesn't take any notice of him. 'Merle, are you OK?'

'I was only flirting with her. What do us men have to do these days? Apologise for breathing?' Mike continues in his self-righteous defence.

'Flirting? Touching me up under my skirt is not flirting!' I manage at last to find some words among my rage.

'He did what?' George doesn't need me to repeat it. He's looking round for the CCTV. 'Tell me they have a camera.'

Except we're in a dark corner and Mike was crowding me back against the bar the whole time. I shake my head.

Mike's mates have worked out that something is seriously delaying their drinks order. The other man in the party comes over. High forehead, reddened face, tie askew, he looks as though he's a few ahead of the rest of his party in the drinks stakes.

'What's going on?' he asks.

Mike passes the guy one of the beers, attempting to make it seem like the whole thing has blown over. 'She took something I said the wrong way. I only tried to buy the chick a drink!'

'Merle, do you want to make a complaint?' George persists.

For what outcome? A session with a police officer for a 'he said she said' statement? I want to stay off any official radar.

I fold my arms. 'Your friend's a prick,' I tell the man. 'Watch him in bars. He'll be arrested one day.'

'What, Mike? No way. Fuck, Mike, look what she's done to your shirt! You should sue the bitch!'

'Make that two pricks. George, can we get out of here?'

George gives me a look, opens his mouth to argue, but then thinks better of it. 'Yeah. I'll text Larry to let him know I'm walking you home.'

I poke my attacker in the chest to push him out of my way. 'Mike, you're a sick man. Get yourself some help.'

'Last time I buy a girl a drink!' he says.

'Good, because you're confusing agreement to having a drink bought with consent to a quick shag out the back. They are so not the same thing.'

As we force our way through the crowd, I feel George's hand brush down my thigh. In shock, I slap it away. 'Hey!' Is everyone trying to feel me up tonight?

'Sorry but your skirt was rucked up,' he mutters in embarrassment. 'He really did touch you?'

'Of course he did!' I'm offended he doubted my word, but then, why should he side with the female in the dispute? Didn't life teach me that men tend to stick together?

Not this one, it appears. 'Let's go back. I think you should report him.' George is such a Boy Scout.

'Too much hassle. I just want to go home.'

'I could find him and punch him for you.'

'You would?'

He pauses. 'No, probably not. I'd go over to him and end up saying something really lame.'

'My hero.'

'Hah! I'm nobody's hero.'

I pull the wig from my head as we emerge onto the street. Eros on his plinth is aiming over our heads at the neon sign board showing an advert for the latest superhero film. 'In my experience, heroes are overrated. They often take the wrong side. I prefer friends.'

George tucks the wig in his jacket pocket. 'Then I'll do what friends do, and walk you home.'

11

Actors use and subsume their personalities in the identities of figments. They want both to hide behind someone else and to show off.

Michael Coveney, 'Maggie Smith: A biography'

Rupert gets the part.

This is big news in the PiP world. Larry is adamant, when he comes to congratulate Bette, that it was talent not connections that got the heir to the empire his break, but you have to wonder. There are so many skilled actors and a suspicious number who break through have a surname you recognise. Royalty, American politics, and acting share a love of dynasties.

Whatever the truth, I wish Rupert well in his career—I really do—but I would be happier without the resurrection of yet another link between me and my past. He talks about the play every single time he comes into the shop, joining George in his 'all Sligo did was fascinating' fan club. They love to explore the play's depths together and both assume I'm as fascinated by the subject as they are, despite my signals to the contrary. I definitely need to improve my emoting skills as I'm giving off all the wrong vibes.

Perhaps they mistake stricken dread for rapt enthusiasm? It would be so much easier if I could just tell them why I hate what they're talking about, but I can't. I'm left with staying or going and, after my last wobble, I daren't walk out on either of them. For much of the time, I can be happy here and I don't want to risk that. Sylvester Sligo has already taken too much from me. I'd come here to ask my questions from someone who knew us both back then to help with the dizzying mix of reality and fantasy that made up my memories but have found myself unable to broach the subject because everyone else is obsessed by digging up the very same history. Ironic really.

I should leave but I've grown to love the mahogany shelves, which I polish with furniture wax when the shop is quiet. The beeswax links to feelings of safety and contentment, a new addiction. Here I don't need to be anything other than this person without a past, this Merle who started on a doorstep like some over-sized foundling from a fairy tale. Enjoying this new version of myself, I do the ordering for the Potter and Disney merchandise and organise a children's corner. It's actually fun to put a little imagination into something; I haven't built a bower since I played in the woods. Rigging up the fairy lights and arranging moss green cushions under a reading lamp shaped like a tree appeals to some old instinct. Word quickly gets around that if you're looking for a break when up in town with the children for a show, that there's a new place to which you can retreat before curtain up. I like to sit there and read to some of our younger customers while their parents browse the adult shelves. Most of the books are theatre-related classics, and I send quite a few families away with Pamela Brown's *The Swish of the Curtain*, Dahl's *Matilda* and Noel Streatfeild's *Ballet Shoes*, ones I'd read as a child, thanks to Sylvester's Lucinda. I'd been soured towards all those memories but now I am regaining some of my love for the world from which I'd been ejected. Not all of it was bad.

George comes to sit cross-legged beside me once my latest listener has carried her pick to her mum. I never tire of looking at him. I think it's the air of goodness to him, a 'you'll be fine with me' feeling that I'm beginning to trust. He'd've made a wonderful doctor if he hadn't been lured into studying English literature.

'You really like children?' he asks.

'Is that a problem?' I slot the displaced books back in their places on the shelf.

'No, of course not. Just unexpected.' His voice ripples through me like swirls of caramel and chocolate. I try not to think about pulling him down into my bower, but if there weren't customers and if I could somehow lock the door... 'Most people pretend with other people's kids, getting bored really quickly. Haven't you noticed that?'

Oh, right, we were having a conversation. 'I like children because they don't pretend. If they like something they'll listen; if they don't, they walk away.'

'I was hoping you'd notice that I'm not walking away.' He waits for me to work out what he means: a little segue to his next words. 'I wanted to ask you out—on a kind of date.'

'A date, or just a kind of date? Like 1st March or 1066?' I smile at the pile of books I'm shelving.

'A definite date. Well, more of a mercy mission on your part because I can't find anyone else to go with me.' His awkwardness is touching. I've already decided I'll go just to put him out of his misery, but he needs to try a little harder to earn my agreement. It'll do him good.

'You're not selling this very well, George.'

He gets up, goes to Antigonus to rub his nose for luck, then sits back down. 'Start again. Please, Merle, would you come with me to see the new Marvel film? All my friends claim they're too highbrow for Hollywood popcorn movies but I've invested so many hours of my teenager years in following the superhero movies from 'Iron Man' onwards, I have to see how it carries on.'

I run a hand over my silky scalp which has reached otter fur length. I'd stopped covering it when Bette let slip that my scarves reminded her too much of her time as a chemo patient. 'Confession time: I haven't seen any of them.'

'That won't matter—much,' he self-corrects for honesty's sake. 'It'll be a true test of how good the storytelling is to see if you can follow. And I'll pay for your ticket.'

'But—'

'Least I can do as, clearly, from the sound of it, you wouldn't be going otherwise.'

The film holds no attraction but the company does. 'A definite date, to see a superhero movie where actors dress up as comic book characters and stuff blows up?'

'I've been avoiding all spoilers but I think I can guarantee that there will be costumes and explosions. And possibly banter.'

'OK.'

'I'm overwhelmed by your enthusiasm.'

We grin at each other.

. . .

WE GO to the film and I spend a very confusing few hours trying to untangle the plot. It's like watching something in a language in which you haven't quite achieved fluency. But George buys me pizza afterwards, puts up with my questions about what the heck happened, and tries to explain that, yes, the time travel plot does really make sense (it doesn't). We both enjoy arguing about it because we can hold passionately differing opinions without it mattering in the real world. And a certain playwright is not mentioned once. It's reassuring that George swims in mainstream culture as comfortably as high end.

At the end of the evening, when George drops me off at June's, he kisses me—a light but lingering kiss on the lips that tells me he had been serious about the date part of the invitation.

I look up at him. 'Does this mean that we're…' Feeling I'm in uncharted territory, I play with the zip on his jacket.

'Dating? Going out?' He runs a hand over my head, warm palm shaping my scalp like a sculptor admiring a finished piece. 'I've been wanting to do that for weeks. I'd say so. Are you OK with that?'

'You're a bit of a geek.'

'Is that a strike for or against me?'

'Good question. I'll let you know.'

'Tomorrow?'

'And tomorrow, and tomorrow. Goodnight.' I go up on tiptoes and kiss him.

He chuckles. 'Goodnight, Merle.'

'DON'T you have a library you can go to?' I tease George as for the fifth time this week I find him sitting in the shop armchair, Brutus flopped at his feet, laptop open, book balanced on the arm.

'Hmm?' He looks up, pencil in his mouth.

'I hope that's your own copy and not one of ours.'

He's annotating a play. I don't have to look at the cover to know who it's by.

'It can't be easy, setting up here. Don't you want a big table to spread out your notes? You know, the kind of thing they provide—in libraries?'

He catches my hand and presses a kiss to my fingers. 'I like it here: it's got an atmosphere, Brutus, and you—not necessarily in that order of importance.'

'Wow, you smooth-talker, you.'

Lillian comes by with a stack of books to shelve. 'Hi, George. Got everything you need?' Lillian didn't get a call back for the Bridge production but shows no sign of holding it against Rupert when she sees him. She says there's a moment for every actor and hers just hasn't come yet—an admirable if overly rosy view of rejection.

'You know the chair is for customers, don't you?' I say with mock-severity, squeezing George's shoulder in passing.

'Oh, come on, Merle: I must be one of your best customers.'

'And the last time you paid for a book was when exactly?'

He looks indignant. 'I bought my niece that book about the cat you recommended for her birthday just last week.'

'True. I forgot that. Then the chair is yours, sir.'

'I wouldn't mind a cup of coffee,' he says to Lillian, knowing better than to try sweet-talking me.

'We're not one of those bookshops,' I remind him. But maybe we should be? Not a fully-fledged cafe but one with a little coffee point?

'I'll make you one,' she says, giving him her best smile.

I wonder if she's making a play for him or if she does that to everyone a part of her act of charming shop assistant. I, of course, play the grouchy one. I've always thought that if you need to be jealous about other girls around a guy you're seeing then he's not really yours, so I decide not to worry. He either likes me or he doesn't. It's not as if we've reached the stage where we're picking out curtains together.

She brings him back a mug filled from the staff coffee pot.

'White, no sugar,' she says.

'Thanks. You're an angel.' George balances it on the other arm, a king with his staff and sceptre, for which read, book and coffee mug.

I give myself little devil horns and he smirks.

'Nearly finished?' Lillian indicates his screen.

'Pretty much, thanks to those last books Merle dug out for me. The editorial deadline is next week. I've got one major interview left to do on the last years, footnotes and references to check, but otherwise I think I'll manage to hand it in on time.'

'That's great, George. You should be so proud of yourself. I've been reading up on Sligo since you and Rupert first mentioned him, for the audition, you know? He went through lots of stylistic changes, didn't he?' I can see the hands-up schoolgirl in Lillian as she ventures her opinion to the expert. She wants to show she's done her homework.

'That's what the book is charting.' George beams at his prize pupil while I grouch away in the background. 'Larry's editing it himself and he's already seen the earlier drafts. Sligo's estate has also been very cooperative—we're the first researchers they've let look through his papers.'

I wonder who's in control of his things? One of his children, I suppose. I never met them, despite living at the cottage for years. I have no idea what his relationship with them was like as it must've happened away from home on his many trips abroad – that was all part of the confused memory problem. I could ask George but that would be encouraging him to tell me more than the 'too much' he does already. I want to speak to someone who really knows, who was there.

'Between Larry and me, we should be able to get it out in time for the Sligo season,' George concludes.

The world tilts again into an unpleasant angle. 'Sligo *season*?' I ask. This is the first I've heard of it.

'My idea.' *George, how could you?* I want to wail. 'There were so many things coming together I suggested to Larry he folds them into one big Autumn season. It's easier to pitch that way for marketing purposes: biography, play and the Keira Fanning photographic exhibition.'

I hug my arms to myself. Not her too. This is a nightmare. 'I thought she was exhibiting her images of living playwrights?'

He's not looking at me as he's absorbed in what he's reading onscreen, missing the signals that I am shaken. 'Thanks to the season idea, she's stretched the definition to include those who have died since 2000, which means she can include Pinter and her Sligo work. She jumped at the chance actually. Nice lady.'

'That's…' Unutterably awful? The worst news I've had all year?

He doesn't wait for me to finish. 'I know: it's amazing. It'll get my biography much more attention. My debut could not be happening in better circumstances.' He checks a quote from the play against his manuscript. 'It's a dream come true.'

'I'm so pleased for you, George.' Lillian said the exact same words to Rupert when she heard about his casting. Unlike my boyfriend, she's noticed my body language and tone. I can't tell if she's covering for me, or wishing to make the most of my failure to celebrate his achievement and ingratiate herself. What I do know is that I wish I could echo her, and sound the kind of person who rejoices in another's good fortune, but all I can think is how awful the autumn is going to be.

'How long a season?' I ask.

'A couple of months—for the run of the play,' says George, distracted. 'Oh, by the way, there's someone coming to meet me here this afternoon. He said he knew the shop, so I thought it was a good place to connect up. He might ask for me at the till.'

'Barista and now your receptionist too?' I say, trying to regain some of my jokey tone. 'I'd better warn Viv and Bette that you're moving in. They can charge you rent for our services.'

I retreat behind the counter and busy myself with making some tweaks to the new website. I try to get lost in cyber space, a relief from the world that contains Sylvester's admirers. But inside I'm kicking myself. Have I lost all sense of self-preservation? What on earth am I doing dating someone whose whole life revolves around the man I most detest? I correct myself. Second most detest. The prize for Most Detested goes to my father. I suppose I've been waiting for the day—and it will come—when George hands in this book on Sligo and moves on to a theme that doesn't rub me raw. A study of Noel Coward or Alan Ayckbourn? He did postgrad studies in Twentieth century drama so is well qualified to spread his wings further. He's talked about both writers and they would be entirely safe areas for me. But it seems this Sligo weed in my life just keeps on growing and spreading out tendrils.

Despite all the ties I'm beginning to develop here, I might have to move after all. The thought sickens me.

And then something happens that is beyond anything I could imagine—something so terrible that I want to laugh at the horrible hand that fate has just dealt me.

The bell above the door rings and I look up, half-expecting Robert from the Bagwell Players to be in to collect his order of *She Stoops to Conquer*.

But no, it's no one as harmless as that.

'George? George Appiah?' the man asks, coming to a stop by George's armchair office.

George almost spills his coffee as he gets to his feet. 'That's right. Mr Carlisle?'

My father bows. 'The very same.'

12

Comedy, as they say, is all about pain.
Ian Kelly, 'Mr Foote's Other Leg'

Nineteen years earlier

Banished from the breakfast table to my room, I was only now realising how big a mistake I had made. Appealing to my dad about my story when he was with Keira Fanning had never been going to work. Miss Fanning was Sylvester's friend and my enemy so obviously, idiot, she wasn't going to side with me! Dad still wanted to impress her because they were having sex, kissing and stuff. Fury had driven all thinking out of my head. I should've waited until he didn't have an audience.

I screamed into my pillow but that didn't help. I thumped the mattress—no comfort there either.

Frustration mounting, I went to the window with some half-baked idea of climbing out. I was reminded by the view that the drop was too far and that I wasn't the kind of story-book child who could scale a drainpipe. Besides, there weren't any near my window. I could see that Dogberry Cottage was full of Sylvester's friends who had gathered for the after-party to celebrate the first night of *A Walk in Bluebell Woods*. Miss Fanning, Dad and Sylvester's girlfriend, had even flown back from New York for the show and to take more photos. The party had ended in the middle of the night but the visitors' cars remained lined up on the gravel drive like piglets suckling on the house. That meant there'd be strangers downstairs and in spare rooms. Had any of them heard my outburst? I wasn't sure I'd even made any sense in my protests. Maybe only Dad, who knew me well, would be able to make head or tail of my jumble of upset about the Queen and Julius and Berrydoggia.

Grownups were stinky toads. I hated them!

I hated myself too because I'd let myself be fooled. I'd had this fantasy that I was Uncle Sylvester's chosen writing friend, that I was special, Luke to his Obi Wan Kenobi. Now I had to face the fact that our secret sessions had been a lie. He'd been using me. I should've suspected something. I was so stupid!

Tugging on the curtain cords, I twisted them into knots. I should've started asking questions when I found out that I'd not been invited to the first night—because the material was too adult, Dad had said. That had struck me as wrong because Sylvester had read me so much of the play when he was writing it. I had imagined I'd be a guest of honour. What didn't I know about it?

At least I'd had time to think this through while they were all out at the theatre. I'd become suspicious something was going on, or maybe just curious what might be so shocking in the play that I was too young to watch. Did they all run around showing their willies or something like in that film on TV that Dad had switched off when it got to the icky bit? Determined not to be left in the dark, I had launched my investigation when Sylvester and his supporters got back. If I hadn't, I wouldn't have known even now what he'd done. A veteran of many a theatre visit, I knew where to go for answers. I looked for the first opportunity to read one of the programmes they'd brought back from the Chichester festival. Many of the playgoers had one tucked inside their handbags so it was easy enough to lift a programme out when the guests were gathered in the living room, laughing and playing loud music. I took it up to my room with a bowl of cereal for a late night snack and began reading. First quivers of doubt struck when I saw the production photos. I let the Rice Krispies go soggy as I scanned the pages. Quivers turned to quakes when I saw one actress had an ivy crown, another a shiny black trouser suit with great lens eyes. I flipped forward to the cast list in the centre. My made-up names were there: the key court figures and their enemies. It couldn't be!

I flipped back to the plot summary, skipping ahead to the bits that mentioned my people. The only change he'd made was that my queen was now called Anna. But it was me—my character!

But what could I do about it then? Dad was in the middle of a party; he'd hate me if I messed that up for him. I made myself go to bed. But I woke up the next morning fuming. That was why I'd burst into the dining room like a rocket firework. Only Dad and Miss Fanning were at the breakfast table. Among my hissing and spitting protests, Dad had quickly grasped the spark to my outrage. He then acted to dowse it with flat phrases like 'lucky girl', 'compliment', 'live for all time'. That just made it worse. I wanted—no, I *demanded* that he be as angry as me. Instead he made me feel...

What? I leant my head against the cool pane of glass, imagining hurtling through it. Would he even be sad if I did?

He had made me feel small and silly.

I'd called Sylvester a thief and a sneak. Guilty of child abuse—those were the most powerful words I knew, like saying 'Avada Kedavra', the killing curse. I wanted to ring the number they told us about at school and report his theft.

'Go to your room,' Dad had thundered, relishing the role play of strict dad, one he rarely bothered with. 'And don't come out until you're prepared to apologise to Keira for your behaviour.'

What had she got to do with anything? I hadn't said any bad words about her even though she'd done nothing but spoil things since her first visit in the summer with her fake smile and 'let's be friends' phoney talk. Her photographs. I didn't want to speak to her, get near her, or apologise. It looked like I'd have to stay in my bedroom for ever. Till I starved.

Or I could run away.

I got as far as packing a bag before I gave up. They'd just fetch me back.

Not if Mum were here.

That was the answer! I'd get hold of Mum and beg her to come for me. I didn't mind living in Argentina if necessary. I was prepared to go anywhere, do anything, to get away from Dogberry Cottage. I just needed to find her address. I'd been writing letters to her which Dad had posted so he must know how to contact her. Maybe he even had a phone number so I could speak to her right now?

I went into Dad's room. A woman's silky nightdress lay on the floor. Miss Fanning's. I stomped on it. Would I tell Mum about that? Dad had said they weren't divorced but maybe Mum left him because he was in love with another woman? That would explain so much, like why she was too angry to get in touch.

But forget that for now: I had to get the address. I could worry about exactly what I would say later. Where would he keep it? He'd once told me—and I thought it was probably the truth—that he kept really important things in a box at the bank, things like his passport and any official documents. He didn't want anyone to unearth items in his real name, he'd said, explaining that if I was going to be as successful as him at covering my tracks, I should do the same when I was older. But an address book wouldn't count, would it? It only had other people's names in. He'd need that for sending letters and keeping in touch with his brother who lived in New Zealand. Uncle Neil. I believed there really was an Uncle Neil because I'd seen the old blue airmail letters.

I turned up nothing in the chest of drawers or in the desk under the window. Everything smelled of Dad—a little bit smoky as he still had the occasional cigarette even when he claimed to have kicked the habit. There were some colourful square things in his side table. I read a label and dropped them back quickly. I wasn't a baby. I knew what a condom was. I felt scared to see one in Dad's drawer. I slammed it closed.

Under the bed? I hid things under mine.

I went on hands and knees and saw our suitcase. I pulled it out. It felt pretty empty. Opening it, I found nothing but a bundle of letters. Not Uncle Neil's but mine. Every single one of them, including the ones I'd illustrated in coloured pencil, drawing Dogberry Cottage and the fire engine visit at my old school. Dad hadn't sent any of them to

Argentina. No wonder Mum hadn't written to me. She must've thought I'd given up on her!

'Merle, what are you doing in here?' asked Dad. He was standing in the doorway with Miss Fanning.

'Dad, why didn't you post my letters to Mum?' I asked, holding them out to him so he couldn't deny it.

He looked up at the ceiling briefly, then back at me. 'I sent her scanned copies. Do you realise how expensive it is to post things to South America?'

Was that true? 'Did she like them?'

'Of course she did.'

'Can I see her replies?'

'Oh, I didn't keep them.'

'But you said you have to be careful on computers, that nothing's ever really deleted. You can get them back.'

'Evan?' asked Miss Fanning, taking a step back from him. 'Are you still married?'

'I...' He looked at me, for once appearing a bit desperate as he's skewered between two incompatible truths.

'He and Mum aren't divorced,' I said quickly. 'They still love each other.'

'Bastard! I don't steal another woman's man!' Miss Fanning said bitterly. 'I told you I know what that feels like and I'd never do it to another person. I just won't. It's a red line.'

'You're not...I'm not...' Dad was making a really bad show of pretending. He was normally much smoother than this. That pleased me.

'Damn you, Evan. I'll call a cab. I think I'll head to Heathrow early and see if I can get a cancellation.' Miss Fanning grabbed her nightdress off the floor.

'No, Keira, look, that's not necessary. Her mother and I aren't together any longer. We can't be because...'

'Because what? You'd better have a really good excuse!' There was a moment of stillness as she waited for him to confess.

'Because Amanda is gone. She's dead.'

Outrage boiled over. Of all his lies, this was the worst. 'My mum is not dead! How dare you say that! She's in Argentina!'

Dad rubbed his face. 'Jesus, God, I told her the worst possible way, didn't I?' He was looking to Keira for sympathy. 'Merle love, I'm so sorry. I should've told you before you found out. Your mum's gone. I'm so, so sorry.'

I refused to believe it. I'd believed the stories about her dancing the tango in a spangled dress, but not this horrible dull nothing. 'You're lying. You're just saying that because you want to have sex with her. Tell her you're lying!' I crushed my letters in my fists—my never-sent-never-scanned letters.

He crossed the room and tried to hug me but I ducked, scrambled over the bed, and jumped down the far side. 'Merle, don't be like that. You had to find out one day but I'm sorry it came out all wrong.'

'I hate you—and I don't believe you! You're always lying to me—always! I want Mum. I want to live with Mum, not with you. Tell me where she is! Tell me!'

He was actually crying now but I couldn't tell if he meant it or if this was just another of his acts. 'Merle, your mum's gone. She was cremated at Southend Crematorium and I scattered her ashes from the end of the pier as she wanted. I'm sorry.'

Keira put a hand on his back, her eyes glistening too like our pain was her pain.

I was beginning to panic. Terror like nothing I've ever

known before ripped through me. 'No, she's in Argentina. Dancing.'

'Merle, think, why would she be there when you're here?' asked Dad.

'Because...because you said she wanted to trip over the light fantastic. You said it—you did!'

'I told you that because I wanted you to not miss her—to think she was having a marvellous adventure.'

'My mother. Is not. Dead!' I bellowed the last word and ran from the room. I ran and ran, down the stairs, out of the back door, through the garden and into the woods. But I hated the woods now. Everyone knew about Queen Merle and Julius the High Priest. They were rubbish too. Everything I did was stupid. I was stupid. I'd believed my dad when I knew—I *knew*—he was proud of his ability to lie. Mum had died and I hadn't even realised!

I splashed into the stream and lay face down into the water, sobbing. I had some idea of drowning myself but it was only a few centimetres deep so I just got cold.

I kicked my feet. 'I hate you, I hate you, I hate you!' I lay there punishing myself with the kiss of freezing water.

'Hey, hey, hey, what's all this?' It was Sylvester. 'Do you know that your dad has everyone out looking for you?'

I wanted to shout that I hated him too, that I wanted to kill him, but all I could do was shudder and sob.

A warm hand circled my wrist and pulled me up. Uncle Sylvester hugged me to his chest. I didn't want to like it but he felt warm after the stream. 'Whatever's the matter can't be worth all this.'

'My mum's...dead.'

'Ah. Then maybe it can. I know, sweetheart. She's been dead a while.' He pushed the wet hair off my face. 'Your father told me what happened to her when you first arrived. She died years ago.'

'He scattered her from a pier. I can't even see her. She's ju...just gone!'

His hand rubbed my back. 'It's cruel what death does—to all of us eventually.'

Nothing was ever going to be right again. 'I want to d...die.'

He was silent for a while. 'Sometimes, so do I.'

13

I don't like myself very much. I'd much rather be someone else.'
Maggie Smith

We have a protocol, my dad and I. If we meet by accident and don't know the scam being played, we pretend not to know each other. So that's what we do. I can tell Dad has registered my presence behind the till by the slight widening of his eyes and the fact that he then never looks my way again while talking to George. This gives me time to recover from the shock of seeing him and take in this current version of himself. What does Evan Carlisle look like now he's no longer tethered to his old employer? Hair is cut to the collar, dark with distinguished silver wings over the ears. Brown eyes alert and crinkling easily into crow's feet when he smiles. He worked out long ago that people will assume you are charming if you do the broad smile that makes your eyes nearly disappear. If I didn't know better, I'd like him too. A white open-necked shirt sets off a tanned throat, folded up at the sleeves to display strong brown forearms. Smart jeans, not Dad ones. So he's settled into the good-looking intellectual role, a shadow of the kind that speaks at books festivals and on arts programmes. People in the past he himself has mocked as professional bullshitters.

I should've suspected then that he was just insulting them because he wanted to be one. That's been his whole existence, hovering on the edge of the circle of which he desires to be the centre.

Seeing him so close to George is like watching a plague carrier infect my boyfriend. I know already that I'm not going to feel the same way about George after this contact. The one good thing in my life has been sullied.

'Mr Carlisle, so good of you come to meet me.' George shakes his hand. 'Have you had to come far? Your American publisher didn't give me your address—only the email.'

Of course, my father would keep in touch with them as he'd want what little royalties might still be coming his way.

'I'm living in Bath. Got a flat near the Royal Crescent.' He pats the bear. 'Splendid place this: so pleased to see it's still in business.'

I would've snorted at the blatant lie about his living arrangements—Dad could never afford such a prime location—but I don't want to draw attention to myself. I open up the website and begin the mechanical task of listing recent rare book acquisitions. I only fumble a little on the keyboard.

'Please, give me the receipt for your travel costs. I have a budget for that kind of thing,' says George.

My dad waves that off. 'Really, it's no problem.'

So he has fare dodged. He's a master of that, knowing all the weak spots on the lines he uses, the turnstile you can jump without being seen, the unguarded entrance at a rural station, where to go on the train when the ticket inspector does his rounds.

'Can I take you somewhere for a coffee?' George packs his stuff away. 'For an interview? I've got so many questions. You won't mind if I record our conversation?'

'Of course not. I doubt I have anything very interesting to say.'

I remember the lessons: self-deprecation invites praise from the mark.

'Oh no, you're wrong. To me, anything you have to say about Sylvester Sligo is of utmost interest. He was a fascinating man and you are one of the few who spent any time with him at the end.'

My dad looks down modestly. 'I suppose I was invited in to the Holy of Holies so to speak.'

George carries his messenger bag laden with books to the till. 'Merle, would you mind looking after this for me? I'll come back for it tomorrow.'

My dad gazes into the middle distance, artfully disengaged.

'Fun fact: Merle here has the same name as your daughter,' says George brightly, expectantly. I wonder for a flickering second if he knows but he doesn't go on to ask the question of either of us.

I'm getting paranoid.

'Hmm?' Dad turns but his eyes are directed somewhere to my left. 'Oh, yes. Pretty name. Quite fashionable a couple of decades ago when my daughter was born.'

'Really? I've not met many in my generation,' says George.

'In my circle there were two or three—these things have a way of catching on.'

'I see. Thanks, Merle.' George gives me a goodbye kiss, waves to Lillian, and heads out. Dad gives me a backward glance as he goes through the door. I know that that means.

WHEN THE SHOP closes and I'm walking home to June's, I keep my eyes and ears open. Sure enough, Dad falls into step with me when I reach the corner.

'How've you been, bean?'

I can't believe he's used that old joke as his opener. As a child, I used to laugh each time he said it, but no longer. 'Fine.'

Dad keeps a little distance between us, as suits two chance-met people, no hint of father-daughter relationship. 'You've been keeping well?'

'Not great.'

A normal parent would ask a follow up, but not Evan Carlisle. 'What's going on—with the shop?'

'I've got a job.'

He smiles at that, not believing me. He thinks I must have some long game I don't want to share with him because that's what he'd do. 'Not sure I like the hair. A girl with long blonde hair has so many options.'

'Yeah, life's a real pick-and-mix counter for a blonde. Such fun on the streets.' Every building site a trial by wolf whistle.

'You've been on the streets?' He sounds genuinely shocked.

I can see how he's misunderstood my remark. 'Just out and about, not prostitution.' My father has no idea who I am, does he?

'So you cut off your lovely hair – your best feature!' His

distress is for my failure to exploit my assets rather than my fate.

'Well, you weren't there to pitch the tent or find a safe park bench, Dad.'

He digs his hands in his jeans' pockets. 'And whose fault is that, Merle?'

'Yeah, yeah.' I'm tired of this old argument. We both know each other's lines in this dispute. He never understood why I objected to what we'd done. He always thought it the greatest scam of his whole career and I spoiled it for him. 'Can we just imagine we had that whole discussion and move on?'

'It's still not too late,' he says as we wait at a crossing for the green man to show.

I knew he was going to say that. 'Yes, Dad, it is. I'm not coming back.'

'But it's just sitting there, waiting for you to claim it.'

'Let it sit then.'

His fists clench at his sides while his face keeps his sunny expression. If you want to know what my dad really thinks about something, watch his hands. 'I don't understand you.'

That's the first genuine thing he's said to me for years. 'I know you don't.' We are approaching Trafalgar Square. I'm going to have to get rid of him soon. 'Don't you ever get tired of all this?'

'All what?'

'Living a lie?'

He gives a world-weary sigh. 'I thought you would understand by now that it's just the way things works.'

'Survival of the most devious?'

He shrugs but it is what he means.

'Survival for what end? What kind of life does it lead to?'

He's silent for a moment. 'Ah. I see what you're doing. Very good. The repentant sinner—that's a great play for sympathy, better than the offended innocent you used to do so well.'

Anger rose as he turned my very real trauma into yet another pose. Not being allowed to be genuine is exhausting. Had he ever believed me? I reach the turning to my street but I don't want to show him where I live. 'No.'

'No, what?'

'Sometimes the pretending has to stop. I'm not trying to be anything other than myself.' It's why I'd finally turned back to ask questions but he is absolutely the worst person to go to for the truth.

'That's the greatest deceit of them all. I'm proud of you.' Tapping his forehead in salute, he heads off.

Dad always makes sure he gets the last line.

AFTER MAKING it upstairs to the empty flat, I spend a long time lying on my bed, a puppet with her strings cut. I can't even summon the energy to throw a few things in a bag and leave as I should. Why is he like this? He's a human hall of mirrors: every time you think you've reached the real thing, it's yet another surface you slide off. I've wondered often enough if he ever feels any genuine feelings or always behaves like an actor inhabiting a role, separate from the person he plays. I've never been able to find out.

He told me once that we were from a line of con artists. His parents had started a cult in the sixties, some lentil and flower-power retreat in the wilds of Devon. From the specifics he'd given, I'd decided on balance that this wasn't made up. It was certainly plausible so if not the full truth, maybe something like it actually happened? They'd got on quite well until they'd scammed the wrong business man and they'd ended up in jail for a short while. That's when he and Neil had been thrown on their own devices. After their release, his parents decided Spain would be a better place for their activities—then Greece—and finally India. Dad had lost touch after that until he got notice of their deaths from Neil. They'd died a few months apart, living quite well in Pondicherry running a meditation centre. Dad had shown me a photo Neil had sent, depicting an elderly couple with long grey hair, red dots on their foreheads and flower garlands. They seemed quietly radiant in the picture so maybe they'd fallen for their own spiel in the end and found the peace they promised others?

In his letter, Uncle Neil said they left only debts. Dad believed him because he described Neil as his opposite: the one who played everything with a straight bat and emigrated for an honest life as a Maths teacher in Wellington. Dad had thought that hilarious: the family white sheep in a flock of black.

I'd not thought about this as a child, but I wonder now if Neil would want to meet his niece? With Dad back in my life, however briefly, maybe I could get the contact details from him and ask? Neil might even understand and invite me to put enough distance between myself and what we've done here? It might be the only solution for me.

But I'd need a passport—and money for a ticket—and money in a bank account. Could I risk going official again?

The bell rings downstairs. June is in Birmingham doing the final touches to the *Priscilla* costumes so I go down to answer. It's George.

'Oh.' I hold on to the door, not opening it fully.

'Hi.'

'I left your bag at the shop.'

'No problem. I came for you.' He holds up a shopping bag. 'I've brought us a celebratory supper.'

'Right.' I stand back and let him in. He kisses me in passing, friendly rather than passionate, and heads for the kitchen where he knows his way around. Before I can quite get my feet under me again, he's already plating up a couscous salad and cold salmon with a slice from a loaf of fresh bread. He knows I don't drink so has brought a bottle of elderflower pressé which he pours into two wine glasses. I pull up a stool to sit at the breakfast bar. 'Thanks. This looks great.'

'I felt like treating myself. I think I've got the last piece of the puzzle.'

'You can finish your book now?' I'm not going to escape without some conversation on this subject, am I? I have to go through the motions.

'Yes, I think so. Evan explained how Sligo was losing some of his faculties towards the end—couldn't rise to the challenge of coming up with anything as good as *A Walk* so preferred not to try.'

'I see.'

'It's such a shame to see such genius clouded over so quickly. It's like his imagination fell off a cliff.' He puts the plate in front of me. The colours seem garish, like a meal painted by Toulouse-Lautrec. I pick up a fork and play cancan with a piece of lettuce.

'I'm not surprised that Evan can afford to live just off the Royal Crescent. His daughter was left the house, did you know that?'

I shake my head, not looking up.

'Sligo's children didn't even challenge it. They left the management of the estate to the lawyers.'

I have to say something. 'What did happen to them—the children?'

The daughter's in America and the sons are in Australia. She's an architect, the eldest boy's a lawyer and the youngest a film director.'

'So they've done OK?'

'Yeah, very well. Probably don't even need the money. All right for some.'

'Hmm.'

'Evan described the life at Dogberry Cottage as a kind of idyll. Do you know what he meant by that?'

'Doesn't that mean something like a dream?'

'I suppose.' George has cleared half his plate while I've barely started mine. 'That's what the photos suggest too—long afternoons in an English country garden. I've found a great one for the front cover. Would you like to see?'

I nod automatically. Any other response would invite more questions.

'I've been corresponding with Keira—Keira Fanning?—and she sent me some that she's not published.'

I put my fork down, stomach rebelling.

'Here. What do you think?'

It's a shot of Sylvester sitting on the terrace with me at the table next to him. It's from before I knew about the betrayal. We're looking at each other with a smile, like we're sharing a most delicious secret. She must have taken the picture without me knowing.

'Evan said his daughter wouldn't mind me using it. It shows a side of Sligo that no one else has seen—and that's the point of my book.'

'I don't think so.' I get up and go to the sink to fill a glass with water.

'Really? You don't like it?' He tilts it, trying to see what's wrong with it.

'Not much. A head shot, just him—that would be better. One of the younger man. He was good-looking in the nineteen sixties. Use one of the David Bailey's.'

George is frowning at the photo now. 'I think he's a fine looking man even in his later years. And the girl is adorable. It's magical.'

I make a small sound of distress in my throat but he doesn't hear it.

'I envy her—imagine the opportunity to know such a genius! I bet she never realised how lucky she was until she grew up—took it all for granted. You really don't like the picture?'

I can't keep talking about this. 'Ask Larry's marketing department. They'll have a view, won't they, on how they're selling the book?'

'Yes. I'll do that.' He puts the photo away. 'Sorry, you must be getting bored of all my talk about Sligo. Tell me when you've had enough, OK?'

I take my water back to the breakfast bar. 'Enough.'

He laughs and shakes his head. 'OK, I'm a Sligo bore. I'll try to do better. How was your day?'

Apart from the reunion with my long-lost father? 'Fine. Good actually. I found an old collection of plays put on in Drury Lane in the 1790s in one of the junk boxes—Viv was really pleased with me. It would've been sent to the dump if I hadn't got curious about the moth-eaten book at the bottom.'

He kisses my cheek. 'I salute my sleuth!'

'Thanks, George.'

He refills our glasses. 'You're getting good at this book hunting—you've got an eye for detail.'

I was trained to pay attention so I suppose I have one thing to thank Dad for. 'I like it. Satisfies some treasure seeking instinct.'

'Then let's toast that—to turning up treasures!'

I chink my glass against his. As I sip, I silently add another wish to keeping things hidden. There are some things that should stay buried no matter how deep people dig.

14

The play's the thing...
Shakespeare, 'Hamlet'

Eighteen years earlier

I'd stopped talking to anyone. It was easier than I thought as girls are excused: we're shy, or quiet, even a good girl for being undemanding in class. Perhaps something would've been done, some attention paid to the reasons why I'd gone radio silent, but it wasn't a blanket ban on speech: I still said 'please', 'thank you' and 'here, Miss' when my name on the register was called. I just didn't want to have anything to do with real people anymore.

I disappeared into books. My classmates got so used to seeing me at break time, head down over a story, that they learned to keep their distance. There was no point teasing me or snatching it from my hands; I just didn't respond and went and got another. I read so many that the class library, Lucinda's collection, and even the local library couldn't keep pace. Dad saw that the only thing that brought any spark to my eyes was a visit to a bookshop, especially secondhand ones where I could find rare stories that hadn't survived more than one generation of children. He occasionally indulged me with a special trip. I became a child out of time, more at home with the manners of the Edwardian nursery than my era a century later.

And I made up my own when I couldn't find any new stories to distract me. Kingdoms were born as I spurned the spoiled world of Berrydoggia: cities on distant planets, countries through gateways, magic enclaves in our own world. I was really excited when I discovered I wasn't the only child to go this way; the Brontës had been here before, living intensely in their little worlds of Angria and Gondal. C. S. Lewis and his brother Warnie with the land of Boxen. That made me feel I'd found my own kind of normal. There were many more of us that history didn't know about, hiding away in our own fantasies.

Dad was annoyed with me though. He wanted me to carry on charming Sylvester but instead the playwright and I were at a silent standoff. I unnerved Sylvester. Silence is a powerful weapon for someone who only knows how to fight with words. Dogberry Cottage became a house under a perpetual thundercloud with only my dad pretending the sun was shining.

Then one day in the third summer, I overheard Sylvester and Dad talking on the terrace as they finished up the paperwork. I was crouched inside in Sylvester's study, raiding the lower shelves for collections of plays he wouldn't miss, sipping on the dessert wine I'd stolen from the pantry. His George Bernard Shaw were dusty so I decided to take *Pygmalion*.

'End of the school year now,' said Sylvester, stating the obvious.

'Yes, sir.' Dad tapped the pile of letters together for posting.

'Merle will be going on to big school?' Sylvester was sitting back in his chair, legs stretched out in front of him, disreputable hat on his head.

'Of course. She's got a place at the local one. She'll be able to cycle there.'

I rolled my eyes. Only if Dad bought me a bike and taught me how to cycle. He always had these plans for others without providing us with the means to do them.

Sylvester caressed the little goatee beard he'd grown that spring. 'I've been thinking, Evan... You've been working for me for a few years now?'

I went still—so did my dad.

'Yes, sir. I hope I've fulfilled my duties to your satisfaction.' My dad's tone was defensive.

'You have. Absolutely. You'll hear no grumbles from me. But I've been thinking that maybe I don't need an assistant full time. Not live-in. In fact, I'm thinking of taking up a writer's residency at Yale for a year and closing up the house. Naturally, I'll give you good references—put the word around that you're going to be available.'

My dad took a second, but then recovered. 'Is this just an idea—or should I start looking?'

'I think it's best you start looking—for Merle's sake, choose somewhere she can come out of her shell a little. London maybe. Somewhere busy.'

'She's still grieving, sir.'

'I know. It's only natural. But it's damned uncomfortable to live with full time.'

And then I understood what this conversation was really about: Sylvester wanted to get rid of me. Everything else was just sugar coating.

'I'll...I'll start looking,' said Dad.

I ran upstairs to my room, leaving *Pygmalion* on the floor. My room! I couldn't bear to leave it. My books—my treasures on the windowsill—my big bed with the soft pillows. I couldn't go back to sleeping in a tent again. Spinning in circles, not sure how to stop the grownups doing this to me, I had mad plans of barricading myself inside and refusing to come out.

But that wouldn't work. That never worked. I'd have to get ready to move.

The most important thing to take were my stories. I pulled the shoebox of exercise books out from under the bed. Would they fit in my backpack? I couldn't risk Dad deciding to do what he called 'a midnight flit', not leaving me time to get my things together. I had to keep my bag ready.

Dad stormed in, not bothering to be Charming Evan with me.

'Well that's just wonderful, isn't it? You bloody well spoiled everything for me!'

I looked up.

'Oh don't give me that wide-eyed look. I know you were listening—I saw you. Do you understand what you've done?'

I shook my head.

'This is the best place we've ever been in and you have to go and muck it up. I told you to be nice to him; instead you walk round like a little Banquo, haunting his steps. You need to get out of your head and pay attention for once!' He took me by the shoulders and shook me. 'Wake up, Merle. You've made us homeless. Are you satisfied?'

Seeing the tears in my eyes, he pushed me aside, disgusted with me and himself. He looked at my exercise books and picked them up in a stack with a sneer. He read the titles, dropping them back on the bed as he did so.

'*Legend of the Lost City*, *Six Go to Sea*, *Voyage Round the Moon*, *Queen of Berrydoggia*...' His eyes narrowed and he picked up that discarded title and flipped it open. 'Wait... you wrote this all down? The story Sylvester used?' He scans the pages. 'Oh my sacred aunt, and you dated it—look a little copyright sign like it's a real book!'

I flushed. I'd done that in anger when I saw the play, found the symbol in the front of all my books and copied it.

He hugged the story to his chest for a second, wheels turning in his mind. 'I think...I think you might just have... but would it work? It's a big risk...'

I rescued the discarded stories and stuffed them in my backpack. I put it on.

My dad looked down at me and frowned. He looped a finger through the tab on the top of the bag and pulled it off me. 'You won't be needing to do that. Merle, you may have just saved us both.'

I snatched the backpack away from him, not trusting him in this mood. Not that I ever trusted him since Mum.

He sat down on the edge of the bed and patted the place beside him. I remained standing.

'Do you remember what you told me the day after the play was first put on?'

I nodded.

'That he took your story without asking—that he abused you?'

I nodded again, but cautiously. I'd said the bad powerful words—my Avada Kedavra.

'Good. Just remember what you said and leave the rest to me.' He winked at me.

I swallowed, afraid like I'd never been before. 'What are you going to do, Dad?'

'Never you mind, magic bean. I'll take care of everything.' He got up and kissed the top of my head, one of his rare expressions of affection when no one else was watching him play father. 'Sorry I got so angry. Forgive me?'

'Yes,' I whispered. 'Can I have my story back?'

'Not just yet. I need it.' Dad leafed through the pages, his smile growing. 'You're right: he stole this lock, stock and barrel, didn't he?'

'Why do you need it?'

'Call it—insurance.'

'What's insurance?'

Dad went to the door. 'Something adults need to stop bad things happening. Go back to playing. You've got the whole summer here to enjoy it.'

15

We're only as sick as our secrets.
Carrie Fisher, 'Wishful Drinking'

Of course, my dad isn't going to leave me alone, not with a house in the Cotswolds to be claimed. I'm almost tempted just to give Dogberry Cottage to him if that buys him off, but I can't stomach the idea of rewarding his scheme. He—we'd—made Sylvester suffer those last years, two sprouts of honey fungus battening on his oak trunk until we killed the thing that supported us. Sylvester was in an impossible position. He'd been caught by his own play. If he threw us out, Dad would go public with my exercise book, prove the playwright stole the fantasy from a little girl, and by implication, stole something much worse. Sylvester had written about it, after all. What was the theme of the play but a working out in public of a private guilt? How the outraged father, whose scales had just fallen from his eyes, could storm and weep for the press!

He would've milked that role. I think he was almost disappointed Sylvester chose silence and to put up with our continued presence as his half of the devil's bargain.

And did my dad really think that Sylvester had abused more than my trust? No normal father would leave his child in that circumstance with the least doubt but we aren't dealing in 'normal' here. Dad watched me—watched us—whenever Sylvester and I were together, which wasn't often. I think he thought that, while there may be no smoke without a fire, the whiff he caught didn't push it into the category of something he had to make a decision about. No need to ring the alarm. If it remained a possibility, a maybe, then he could ignore it.

And he never asked me. I just escaped into my books. There was plenty around and no one noticed. I got good at hiding.

And now there's a house sitting empty in one of the most expensive parts of the country. It has to be worth millions and that just kills him.

'Bette, you're looking very well this morning,' my dad says with a twinkle in his eye as he bends over her hand with old fashioned gallantry not seen since the nineteenth century. Dad knows a romantic when one crosses his path.

'Here again, Mr Carlisle?' says Bette, with a flustered smile.

Oh God, don't pretend you like her, please. She's been messed about by one abusive man; she doesn't need another. Whatever her husband did to her, is nothing to the psychological pain my father can inflict.

But I keep my mouth shut.

'I just love it here.' He sweeps an arm to the shelves. 'It reminds me of Sylvester's study. I do miss him so much.'

'George told me about your daughter inheriting his

house. That was so sweet of him—to remember her like that. And generous.'

'I know. Sylvester really did love her. She became like a daughter to him—a grandchild—as he never saw his own. So sad.'

'Why was that?' asks Bette.

'Some coolness after his divorce, I think. He didn't get to see his own offspring enough as they were growing up and they all grew apart. It can happen when a father doesn't see his sons—or daughter.' Dad shoots a glance at me.

Come on, Dad, you'll have to do better than that. I'm not going to fall for such cheap plays for sympathy.

I can't bear being near him.

'Bette, if it's OK with you, can I pop home this lunchtime? I promised June I'd be in to accept a delivery.' I slide from my stool.

'Of course, my dear. We should work out a proper schedule for you—holidays and so on. I don't think you've had a day off since you started.'

'Good worker, is she?' asks Dad. 'Your new assistant?'

'The best. So imaginative. The children's corner is all her work.' Bette points to the scatter cushions, currently occupied by three book-devouring tots. Actually, one of them is really devouring a book. I hope the parents pay for the damage. 'Merle, would you mind taking Brutus with you? He could do with the walk.'

'Sure.' Brutus and I have reached an understanding: I pretend not to like him and he pretends to ignore me, until we are on our own when we are allowed to show each other affection.

'Brutus!' calls Bette.

He heaves himself up from the children's corner, unseating one of the kids, and pads over hopefully.

'Walk?'

He heads into the stockroom and returns with his lead in his mouth.

'Aw, that's so cute!' says the children's mother. She has the book-eater on her hip. 'I think I owe you.'

'Don't worry about it,' says Bette at the same time as I say:

'Five ninety-nine.'

The mum grins and hands me the cash. If Bette had her way she'd dole books out for free to all customers. She hasn't a commercial bone in her body.

She's now glaring at me.

'What? It's a good book. The baby'll enjoy hearing it and eating the corner. That's worth at least six pounds.'

Brutus nudges my leg.

'I'll walk with you,' says my dad. 'Keep an eye on the great gallumphing Brute.'

'No need.' I knew he'd offer. I'd been hoping he'd leave before I had to ask for the time off but he's been sticking close waiting for his chance.

'We're going the same way. It would be my pleasure.'

At least it will get him away from Bette.

'Fine.' I clip on the leash and head out, stuffing a few dog bags in my pocket. Once I'm on the pavement, I add, 'But you do the scoop.'

He just smiles and falls into step with me. The thought of my dad actually stooping to do anything so mundane slash gross as pick up dog poo is laughable. No, he'd con a passerby into doing it—claim he's partially sighted and it's a service dog or something.

'I went to have a look at the house last month, before I knew where you were,' says Dad as we weave through the lunchtime crowds on Shaftesbury Avenue.

I don't say anything. No need to throw any fuel on his fire. He's going to tell me what he wants.

'The garden's a wilderness. It was heading that way, of course, but now you'd hardly know there's any structure under the brambles.'

'Good for wildlife, I bet.' A pigeon lands on the pavement in front of us, takes one look at Brutus and flaps off in alarm.

'So this is all some grand plan to run your own wilderness sanctuary? Congratulations, you've achieved it. Wildlife would probably have moved into the house too if I hadn't insisted the lawyers keep it sound until you come forward to claim it.'

'I told you to tell them I was dead.'

'I did think of doing that, as it would come to me then, wouldn't it?'

Flipping heck, it would.

'But I thought you'd probably wait for me to do so, then come back and accuse me of fraud. I do not want to spend a decade in jail, thank you very much.'

It is a better plan than I would've come up with. He is crediting me with more deviousness than I possess.

'There's a small amount left in the will for upkeep. They're using that, topped up with your share of the royalties.'

Sylvester had left all the proceeds of *A Walk in Bluebell Woods* to me, aside from the cut that went to his agent who managed his literary estate.

Dad is right about one thing: I can't leave the house like this. It keeps the wound open. 'I'll do something about the cottage—when I'm ready.'

He heaves a put-upon sigh. 'Just don't throw it away on some ridiculous whim.'

'Like what?'

'Home to...to abandoned dogs.'

I touch my lips as if the idea had just struck me. 'What a great idea!'

'Merle!'

I turn the finger from my lips to him, not touching him but pointing. 'No, you don't get to do that.'

'Do what?'

'Sound...' I circle my hand in the air, 'parental. That ship sailed when I was about nine—if not before.'

'I didn't raise you to bear a grudge.'

'But that's how I turned out. Sucks to be you, hey?'

'Or use such foolish slang.'

'Whatever.'

'Merle!'

This is almost fun. I now have a new weapon with which to wound him. I hadn't realised.

'Soz, Evan.' I grin. He doesn't even know what that means. I think I'll start calling him Evan from now on. He's never been much of a dad and there's probably some psychologist somewhere saying this would be a good way for me to get distance. 'This is where you go your way and I go mine.' The open stretch of Trafalgar Square lay before us. I wanted to push him into one of the fountains but, hey, you don't get everything you wish for.

'You can't blame me for worrying about you!' he protests, making no sign that he is moving on.

'Really? Is that what this is about?'

'You're showing too many indications that you're going to same way as your mother.'

That makes me go cold. Brutus whines, sensing my distress.

'Like what?'

'The self-harm,' he gestures to the hacked-off hair, 'the aimlessness, the depression.'

'You've diagnosed me on the strength of...what exactly? A haircut and a couple of days reacquaintance?'

'No, on years of experience. Why did you leave university if not because of that? I'd got a great deal for you—the fees and living costs paid by my employer. You were rolling in clover but you threw it all away.'

I hold up a hand. 'Stop. You extorted that from your victim—say it like it is.' And it had been a bed of nails, not clover. Try rolling on that.

'I worked for what we got, right until Sylvester died. I was the one who closed his eyes.'

I shudder at the thought. He's the last person I'd want at my deathbed. 'Yeah, what a nightmare for him. I bet he was pleased to finally escape. What were his last words? "Rot in Hell, Evan"?'

My father shakes his head, eyes meeting mine. 'No. They were "say sorry to Merle for me".'

I don't believe him. That's exactly the kind of bunk he would make up. 'Shog off, Evan.'

He doesn't react to my Shakespearian dismissal except by grabbing my elbow. 'What did he do to you, Merle? Was it just the story?'

'Too late to ask, Dad. You should be asking what did you do to me.'

With a tug on Brutus's lead, I head away towards the Strand, determined to lose him in the crowds if he dare follow.

16

People are being born and dying at this minute; we're just doing a play, that's all we're doing.

Judi Dench, 'And Furthermore'

Eighteen years earlier

I decided to become a detective. Children did it all the time in the stories I'd read or seen on TV—Famous Five, Emil, Nancy Drew, Scooby Doo—though he was a dog and didn't do much sleuthing. He usually tripped over the answer.

I could do that, I decided, stumble over the truth if I couldn't find it by following clues. I was up against my arch nemesis: Dad. He was a master of disguise and subterfuge. So I had to be better. The first mystery I wanted to solve was whether or not my mother was dead.

I knew she had once existed because I remembered her. She had blonde hair—not as blonde as mine—but it had been pretty, like a mermaid. She'd also been small like me. Dad's nickname for her had been 'pixie'. They'd met at a concert, he'd said, or a festival—the story changed, but I guessed that it was an entertainment involving music. She'd had a nice voice and sang me folk songs while playing her guitar. That instrument had stickers on it—hearts and an 'I love New York' sticker. Had she gone there? I would prefer it if she'd headed off to that city rather than died. I'd even forgive her for leaving me behind as I knew what it was like to really *really* want to be somewhere else.

But how to find out the truth? Dad had to have something of hers left, some way of reaching her if she was alive as he never completely stopped any game he played, even marriage. He always said you didn't know when a new opportunity would come around again and make it a useful part of your life to revive.

Mum hadn't been old or sick. She'd just gone away when I was in Year 2. I concluded that it was much more likely that she was still alive and he had just been lying so he could go on sleeping with Wicked Witch Keira. It would be a grand revenge on them both if I could find proof that he'd been making it all up to get her sympathy.

Thankfully, his girlfriend wasn't with us this summer so I had a chance. I knew he was still in contact with Keira though. She was talking about coming back in the autumn. I could bide my time.

I liked the sound of it: 'bide my time'. Definitely the kind of plan detectives in books made up. Wait until you could gather all the suspects in the same room and spring the surprise.

But I had to know what the surprise was first. And that involved digging.

Dad went with Sylvester to the Edinburgh Festival, leaving me in the care of Mrs Brampton. There was tension between my father and Sylvester now. The playwright would look at my dad, then at me, and actually seem scared, which was so odd. One thing I'd never seen before was a grownup who was frightened of me. They left, taking a chauffeured car to Scotland, Sylvester like a prisoner under guard. I was free of both of them for a week.

I made full use of it. I searched every inch of my dad's room—but there was nothing I hadn't already found. He'd got rid of my letters from the suitcase, which came a relief. I didn't want a reminder of the hours I'd spent on them, the care I'd taken to use my best handwriting and get the pencil colouring-in even. I'd start again if I found Mum. I shook my head. *When* I found Mum. She wasn't dead until I had word on that from someone other than my father.

I searched again, trying all the tactics that book detectives used: looking for anything that was out of place, or missing. I checked the back of drawers and under flat surfaces. I scooted under the bed with a torch to check the bottom of the mattress. There was nothing that felt like a clue, only some photos of him, Mum and me in a pouch from Boots that hadn't even been hidden. It had been in the second drawer down in the bedside table. I took one, just to remind myself that she had really been as I remembered.

On the third day, I found Sylvester's stash of spirits. I'd seen him, my dad and his friends all drinking heavily together and they seemed to like it, though they usually complained the next morning. I tried a sip of each to find out why they enjoyed it. Most tasted horrid but I quite liked the sweet sherry. It made my head go funny. I started going back from time to time like a bee to nectar. He'd never notice. No one noticed what I did.

It was only on the fifth day of Sylvester and Dad's time in Edinburgh that I thought to search for Mum online. Dad had taken his laptop with him so I couldn't sneak a look at his emails, but I could do a general search, couldn't I? If I could remember what name we last used when with her. It was quite a few years ago now. Mrs Radley's class. It hadn't been Carlisle. Cardew? Yes, Cardew.

I went downstairs and found Mrs Brampton snoozing in a chair in the kitchen, radio on.

'Mrs Brampton?'

'Yes, pet?' She sat up and picked up the recipe book that lay face down across her knee, trying to look as though she hadn't been sleeping on the job. Not that it mattered. I liked her. She could take a nap if she needed it; I was never going to tell anyone.

I twisted a lock of hair around my finger, a nervous habit I couldn't shake. 'Um, would it be OK if I played some games online?'

'What's that?' Mrs Brampton's children had all grown up before everyone had computers.

'My friends told me about some cool new sites.' I wondered how to sell it to her. 'Educational ones. From museums. Very safe.'

She smiled and sighed. 'I'm getting left behind by all this technology. Yes, pet, you do that. Do you know how to use the desktop?'

I nodded. 'I use it all the time for my homework.'

She suddenly remembered she should be keeping an eye on me. 'Only those games from the safe sites, Merle. Don't start...er...chatting to strangers online. Be careful what you click on.'

'I will, Mrs Brampton.'

Satisfied now she'd given me her online safety lecture, she settled back with her book. Adults were funny sometimes. They hadn't a clue what was out there.

I went into Sylvester's study and woke up his computer.

It hummed a little as it opened up windows to welcome me. He never changed his password. I liked the computer: it was interesting and could tell me things no one else did. How to begin? Simple really. I decided to do a search of my mum's name in the web browser.

Amanda Cardew.

A few links to women who weren't my mother popped up. I was lucky she didn't have a really common name because I could check these out really quickly. Of all of them, I decided I liked the sound of the realtor in America best, but then remembered I wasn't shopping for a new mother, but trying to find my missing one. She liked to be called Mandy so I tried that. Nothing came up that looked right. Then I recalled that she usually spelt it with an i at the end, a little circle for the dot. I changed the entry and tapped 'return'. One of the early results had a single line leading to a Southend newspaper. The article—'Fatal Accident at Level Crossing'—was from three years ago.

Woman recovered from railway tracks identified as Mandi Cardew, aged 30.

She'd been recovered. That was good, wasn't it? That meant rescued. Maybe she had been injured? Perhaps she was in hospital still, recovering? That sounded bad but maybe I could visit?

I tapped on the article and read on.

17

You start with a vision, and you deliver a compromise.
Nicholas Hytner, 'Balancing Acts'

George disappears for two days. When he comes back, he's bursting to tell someone about his trip but is wary of raising the subject with me. And that's not suspicious? I overhear him talking with Lillian, so it's easy enough to work out what he's been doing. He's been to Dogberry Cottage—at least, he's trespassed in the grounds. Having worked on Sligo for so long, of course, he wants to see where he came from—I should've seen this coming. However, even my father couldn't get him the key to enter, despite a phone call to the lawyers. They are taking a strict line on people entering the property.

I must remember to thank them when I eventually contact them.

'I took this one through the window. Evan said no one would mind,' says George.

I find I do mind.

'You can tell it's a magical place,' he says to Lillian while I pretend not to listen. 'Like something out of *Sleeping Beauty*, gone to sleep for what, the last two or three years?'

That is hardly a period of time worthy of a fairy tale. Has nature taken over so quickly? It's a reminder that the world really didn't need us and would be better off if we all just vanished.

He shows her photos on his phone, but quickly pockets the handset when I approach, like a teenager hiding pot from his mum. 'Everything OK, Merle?'

'That would be impossible because it would mean I'd stopped climate change, cured cancer and solved world poverty.' I rub his back in passing to show I don't mean to be abrasive. Look, I'm smoothing him down, aren't I?

He catches hold of my hand. 'Stop a moment. I came to say I've turned in my manuscript. You should be happy: no more Sligo.'

'Congratulations.' I feel as though a weight has lifted from my shoulders as well as his. 'So what next?'

He laughs. 'I'm not quite ready to move on as there's revisions, publicity and so on. Larry has me writing the catalogue for Keira's show.'

I drop my hand. 'Oh.'

'But...' He stretches the word out, teasing me. 'I'm thinking...my next project is...'

'Don't make me give you a drum roll.' I put my fists on my hips.

'Noel Coward.'

Absolutely no danger zones with Coward. Delighted, I bop on my feet and kiss him. '"I'm Mad about the Boy"!'

'Do I get "A room with a view—and you"?'

Lillian is looking at us as if we have lost our minds.

'Noel Coward songs?' prompts George.

'Sorry?' She is genuinely flummoxed. How can she work here and not notice? I grab a booklet of Noel Coward's sheet music from the musical section and point to the Bryll-creamed dapper gent with receding hairline on the front.

'Noel Coward? Only one of the twentieth century's most famous singer-songwriters-playwright and actor,' I say triumphantly. '"Mad Dogs and Englishmen"?'

'Oh. He looks like a vampire.'

'Think a musical Stephen Fry, but of your grandmother's time,' says George generously.

'Great-grandmother,' I correct him. I expect Lillian's grandmother is a child of the sixties.

'Do you think he's too obscure to be worth a biography?' George asks, a little crestfallen by her vacant expression.

'I've never heard of him,' says Lillian.

But she'd never heard of Sligo so that isn't a very high bar.

'You can bring him back into fashion.' I dance the sheet music over to its slot next to Leonard Bernstein, feeling happier than the situation requires. 'He's due a revival. You can't keep following the herd. He's like Lin-Manuel Miranda, only in a dinner jacket. Think about it: even some of his lyrics are like raps.'

'You're right. I'll pitch that to Larry. He already loves the subject. I think he met Coward when he was younger.'

Of course he did. Noel Coward was a fixture in the theatre scene for decades if actors' biographies are anything to go by, drifting through parties in a cloud of fragrant cigarette smoke, tinkling on the ivories, dropping the *bon mot*. I think I was born to live in the wrong century. I would've loved to have draped myself over the grand in a dress by Chanel and traded witty repartee.

'I can help you with the research,' I say eagerly.

'You'd do that?' I can't blame George for his sceptical tone. I'd blanked everything to do with Sligo.

'Of course. I do have half a degree in English. I know my way round a library.' It's the only place on earth I can navigate with ease.

George catches my enthusiasm and perks up again. 'You should finish your degree—I'm sure Bette and Vi would support you doing that. Wouldn't they, Lillian?'

She looks up from the page of the magazine she's been flipping through. 'Hmm? Oh yeah. They let me work round my lectures. As long as we don't have too many clashes, you'd probably be able to do that too.'

'I can't afford it,' I say automatically. But I have a house. What better use could I have for it than to pay my way through university and then hand the rest over to the dog's home to spite my dad. I can just about stretch my conscience that far.

'Get a loan then. That's what everyone else does,' says Lillian.

'I'll think about it.' But I'm smiling. There's this tiny unfamiliar thing budding inside me—hope.

George considers his job done. He gives me a hug and moves in to kiss me. No one but an artfully disinterested Lillian is in the shop so he lingers, making it one of our kisses, not a social one. He rests his forehead on mine. 'I'd love to work on this with you. I'll start scoping out the subject, work out where the archives are, plan a research programme.'

He is so gorgeous, with just enough assertiveness to add spice to our kisses.

'I love it when you sweet-talk me like this,' I say Marilyn-Monroe breathily, but spoil it by grinning.

'This geek has some moves, hey?'

'You had me at scoping.'

With a laugh, he gives a final kiss and heads out. Leave Sligo for Coward. Yes, I can do that.

ENCOURAGED by the change of focus in George's life, I decide it is time I alter mine. The house is only dragging me down to the past, like a concrete boot on a gangster dropped from Brooklyn Bridge. I have to be free of it so I can breathe easily. Cut loose from the past. Then I realise that I can do what an ordinary person would in this circumstance: I can go and inspect my property, find out what it is worth, and then decide how best to announce myself to the lawyers. They're used to being confidential with client information, aren't they? It's not the same as announcing it to the world.

Not that I have to make all my decisions in one go. A quick visit to Dogberry Cottage is the first, necessary step.

Agreeing with the ever-generous Bette that it is time I had some holiday, I take Monday off and head into the Cotswolds by train, going as far as Oxford then negotiating the last leg by bus. Burford is a town that expects you to drive and doesn't make many concessions for the less affluent. I wonder how George got here. Does he have a car? I've never thought to ask. I walk the last couple of miles down lanes filled with cow parsley. The sun is hot on the back of my head and I strip down to my t-shirt, wishing I'd thought ahead and brought some water.

As I approach the houses of the little hamlet in which Dogberry is the main property, it becomes all too familiar. There are a few cosmetic changes—a trampoline in one garden, a camper van in another—but otherwise it could be my younger self walking home from school. The bike never materialised. That would've involved Dad actually thinking about me.

I reach the gates. They are latched but not padlocked. I should probably do something about that. My footsteps crunch on the gravel. Weeds have invaded the edges, creeping further across the stones. How long would it take the drive to completely disappear? Dogberry Cottage itself peeps through the trees: built from honeyed sandstone, it is comfortable in its double-fronted facade and portico-ed splendour. It looks like something out of an E M Forster novel, *Howards End* maybe. The slates look a little mossy. Is the roof letting in water yet? Am I actually having a responsible thought? Such a house doesn't feel like it belongs to me. In fact, the idea feels ridiculous.

I don't bother to try the front door. It'll be locked. But no one knows a house like a child who has lived there. I go around the north side to the pantry. The small window is latched but I'm the owner. If I want to break my own window, I will. I grab a rock and smash out the glass, a strangely satisfying procedure. I should break more things. No worries surface about what I'm doing as I have worked out that I can secure the house by locking the pantry door when I leave and then instruct the lawyers to mend the glass. Putting my denim jacket over the ledge so I don't cut myself, I climb on a water butt and clamber in as I did so many times before. Fortunately I still fit or this would be embarrassing. I drop down onto the old butler's sink and then step to the floor.

Easy. Or easy-ish. Despite my best efforts, I've cut the heel of my hand. I let the water run in the sink, waiting for it to freshen, then rinse off the wound. Not too bad but the blood is still seeping. I then remember the ever-efficient Mrs Brampton kept a first aid box in here. Sure enough, it is still in its place on a high shelf. I turn a bucket over and use it as a stepladder. Inside are some ageing but still useable sticking plasters. I cover the injury. All better.

Mrs Brampton used to kiss my injuries when I was little —it was a jokey thing between us. In her honour, I kiss my plaster. I hope she's enjoying her retirement.

Bracing myself, I open the door of the pantry. The house is in twilight. Blinds and curtains are closed. George must've hunted to find one that would give him a shot of the interior. Probably through the glass in the front door? There was never any curtain for that.

Each step feels like a journey further back in time. I check the kitchen first. The chair is still in its spot by the radio. The smaller contents have been cleared from the dresser but the big items of furniture and equipment are still here. The cord and plug for the fridge hangs over the half open door like a ball dress train resting over a lady's wrist, waiting for her dance card to be marked. The inside is spotless. Mrs Brampton was conscientious to the end. This has always been one of my favourite rooms. Nothing to upset me here.

I head along the corridor to the dining room. This has French windows out on to the terrace. I pull back the curtains. Dust has settled on the oak surfaces. I draw an M on the table, then rub it out. The paintings have gone, leaving shadows on the wall, William Morris' 'Strawberry Thief' wallpaper slightly darker where they once were. I wonder if they were left to me too? Had the will included contents? If it did, I would lay money on my father having removed and flogged them. He had the 'what's yours is mine' attitude to family. He'd've made up some excuse, or used the confusion after Sylvester's death to rearrange things to his advantage. I'd liked those paintings. There had been a Cornish seascape and a portrait of the Reverend Bartholomew Hawking, a clergyman from the eighteenth century that Sylvester referred to as his Old Dad.

'What do you think of this scene, Old Dad?' he'd ask when he read out a piece of new writing. Or 'My Old Dad wouldn't like this newfangled nonsense,' he'd say when an *avant-garde* piece was presented to him for a review. Listening to him, I'd enjoyed the proof that adults had imaginary friends too. It made my own behaviour normal. I don't think Bartholomew was actually anything to do with him as the playwright had roots back in Ireland, but Sylvester has enjoyed the make-believe that he had some Jane Austen-esque clergy family behind him.

I bypass the study. Not yet.

I go upstairs to my old room. I turn the handle and immediately get hit by a wave of memories, some happy, many sad. Oh my word, the bookcase is still here! I rush to kneel in front of it, a little household shrine. All my old favourites, unchanged except for the layer of dust. I take out *The Children of Green Knowe*. A couple of pages fall out, proof I'd literally loved this to pieces. *The Swish of the Curtain* is there too in a long extinct edition with a photo from some BBC children's drama. There's an *Alice in Wonderland*. I'd not liked it much as a story but I'd been fascinated by it. With adult hindsight, maybe that was because the randomness and cruelty it showed seemed anything but fantasy.

So many doorways. So many friends.

I'm not usually a sentimental person but I allow myself to take a book away with me. It is hard to choose but in the end I pick *Green Knowe* as it is the one that is forever mingled with the best imaginary games I played here, none of those shadowed by adult intrusion.

Another thought strikes. I wonder...?

I open the top drawer of the chest and find that, as anticipated, no one has thought to clear out my things. Mrs Brampton would've expected me to come back at some point now I own the place and it simply would not have crossed Dad's mind. I select some socks, t-shirts and jeans that still fit me. If anything, they've become a bit loose. The clothes have survived surprisingly well, apart from an old school cardigan which is moth-eaten and needs to be chucked but I leave it for now. I stuff the clothes I'm taking in the canvas tote I brought with me from the shop. It's emblazoned with the perky slogan 'All's Well That Ends Well'.

Sorry to disagree, Shakespeare, but I'm not sure that is proved either by the play or by life.

There is nothing else of interest for me here on the upper floors. Dad's room is stripped, as is Sylvester's. There's no sign of damp coming in from the roof so I have to assume the moss is not doing any harm as yet. The next owner can sort it out.

I pause on the landing and look down onto the foyer entrance. I can almost summon the ghost of Sylvester striding through with leonine confidence and then the later hesitant shuffle that was the man under my father's thumb. I'd read accounts of spouses who are mentally abused by gaslighting partners; Sylvester was in an odd couple relationship with my dad very much like that. Black was white, up was down, what he remembered was false. All confidence flew away, replaced by the cuckoo of second guessing and approval seeking. It is little wonder he never wrote anything again.

Or did he?

OK, it is time. I have to face the study.

I almost knock on the door, as I might've done when I

was a teenager. It opens without a sound, even my footfalls are muffled. Crossing to the windows, I pull back the curtains. One is hanging off at one end as a brittle plastic curtain hook has snapped. I can see the hook end lying on the floor by the window like a fallen comma. I open the French doors to let in some air. This room mirrors the dining room and gives out onto the terrace. A geranium is still struggling in one of the pots, a splash of blood against the brick. Grass has seized every crack, as has chickweed and forget-me-not. The table is a mosaic of bird droppings and lichen.

Turning back to the study, I see that it too has been left almost unchanged. One painting is missing—the most valuable one—a gift to Sylvester by a director of one of his plays in the eighties. It had been by John Piper, the twentieth century artist. I'd loved the blues and golds of the abbey ruin against a stormy sky. It was often in the background to my stories about knights and dragons. I make a mental note to see if it has mysteriously cropped up in any auction houses recently because, if it belongs to me, I would be damned if I'd let my father reap the benefit. If ever I got to the stage of having a place of my own, I'd maybe like it on the wall.

The desk top computer is still there, last of Sylvester's tech updates. It doesn't matter that I'd gone off to university by the time he'd installed this as he always used the same password. Odd that no one had cleared this away, not even the efficient lawyers. I press the 'on' switch and am a little surprised when it hums into life. Less surprising is the length of time it takes to boot up from computer deep freeze so I prowl the rest of the room. Sylvester has two shelves devoted to his own works, the rest he has arranged by period and then alphabetically, very much like we do in Last

Chance. What had he thought at the end of his life, sitting here looking at this record of his own achievement? I can see how people find *A Walk in Bluebell Woods* a great play. I read it finally in full just before I dropped out of university and even with my close association with the piece I had to recognise the craftsmanship. Did he decide it was no bad thing to go out at the top of his game, or had he had more things he wished to say?

The computer might tell me.

Dusting the screen with the bottom of my t-shirt, I sit down in his chair. It creaks and for a fraction of a second I feel as if he's here with me. O heavens, that takes me back. Would he mind? I decide I can't answer that. Our relationship had been so off-kilter, so much unsaid, so many secrets. I pause for a moment to adjust, then type in the password. As anticipated, he'd stuck to the one he could remember. He used the same word on all his accounts, completely against all advice, but I'm with him there: life is far too complicated to keep setting quizzes for yourself. It's the modern equivalent of locking yourself out of your own house by leaving the key and then forgetting the cunning hiding place.

The desktop lights up and I'm jolted by the picture he has chosen as a backdrop. It is the one George showed me: Sylvester sitting next to the nine-year-old Merle with us both looking as if we share a wonderful secret. I had no idea he had this. I'd never seen it before George turned the phone screen to face me.

Or had my father put it up? It was the kind of mind game he would play with Sylvester.

That does give me an idea though. I had been going to look at documents first, but I decide to dip into the photo collection. It takes a while to load but when it does I see that he has over three thousand images from 2005 onwards.

Before then, he probably used film. The thumbnails bear out the version of Dogberry that is in the public imagination: groups of good-looking or famous people lounging about in deckchairs, playing croquet on a bumpy pitch, gathered around a Christmas tree with champagne flutes. I notice though that the pictures get rapidly less joyous as my father's reign begins. Sylvester looks older. What I hadn't seen before is how he now sits at the edge of gatherings and my father has moved into the middle. In the Christmas shot, my father is there with Keira Fanning, standing like a couple in their wedding photo. I spot myself hanging on the edge of the frame and remember that I'd had to be cajoled into posing for make-believe happy families. I hated photos being taken of me and only the veiled threat from my dad that I'd miss the present opening got me there. I should've run upstairs. The presents hadn't been worth waiting for because Keira had picked mine. I'd asked for a bike but instead I got a set of wildly inappropriate designer clothes that made me look like a child prostitute. She said they were the fashion in New York, which I can believe, and insisted on photographing me in them. I'd got some enjoyment from the gift though as I'd dressed the gardener's dog in them and roped the Labrador in as my wicked stepmother in my latest game. The sparkly outfit hadn't survived our romp through the woods. Keira had not been pleased, though I recall that hadn't stopped her moving on to photograph the dog with the shreds of sequins hanging off her. She won an award for that photo.

I hated her far more than I hated Sylvester. She never gave up pursuing me.

I close down the tab, shutting the images back in digital limbo. There's no internet service, otherwise I'd be googling how to do a factory reset on the machine and scrub all the pictures for ever. That is probably illegal. I imagine that in some way everything on here belongs to the estate. I'd be depriving his children, against whom I bear no grudge, of possible income from image rights. OK, no googling.

Click on the documents and I go to most recent. There's no dramatic secret revealed as far as I can see, no last words, or final manuscript. Unless this folder called 'The Children' is in fact the name of a play and not his long-distance correspondence with his family.

Only one way to find out.

18

The more you give your trust,
The more you're bound to lose
Noel Coward, 'If Love Were All'

There are three subfolders named after each of his children: Lucinda, Ralph and Johnny. OK, so no last play. That's actually a relief as I won't have the dilemma of what to do with it.

Out of interest I click on 'Lucinda'. There's a series of what looks like annual reports as each is dated by year. Opening the one entitled 2000, I find a document from a firm called Broad and Partners. I scroll through it. It's a detailed description of what Lucinda was getting up to when on her maternity leave with her second child, a list of the places she went, childcare arrangements, how her husband was doing in his job as a doctor in a large hospital in Chicago, all the minutiae of their life. I've not had any experience of an ordinary family but this feels very weird.

There's another subfolder containing photos but these aren't posed like the ones in the image cache: these are shots through restaurant windows, on the street, long-distance in parks.

Light dawns: they're surveillance photos.

I read the small print on the firm's letterhead and find, as I now expect, that they are private investigators, specialising in fraud.

Curiosity piqued, I open the folders on the sons. Different firms have been employed but essentially the same material is contained within each collection: information on family, photos, news on jobs or social achievements, such as Johnny having a golf handicap of nineteen, which apparently is pretty good, and Ralph's kids adopting a stray cat.

Why did Sylvester gather the information in this way? Was he particularly obsessive about his children and grandchildren's welfare and not believe what they told him? I can't reconcile that with what I remember about him.

Or was this something my father arranged? That would fit like a glove. My father would want to know what his opposition—and that's how he'd see the children—was up to in case they staged an intervention. He could've been using Sylvester's name and money to dig the dirt.

Not that he'd turned any up. From my quick scan of highlighted passages, Lucinda was in counselling back in the 2000s, but it might've been more shocking to find a middle-class American not seeing a shrink. It seems from the file that she had an abusive first marriage; but the second husband sounds a nice guy, nothing to alarm a father or give my dad fuel for his blackmail.

Yet if it were gathered with the intention of finding something to open the way for blackmail, why did the files start before my father worked for Sylvester? Or maybe he took over the practice of collecting the information? He had to know it existed as it isn't hidden, sitting right there on the desktop.

I'm coming back round to Sylvester being responsible. It's his computer after all.

Whatever the reason and whoever commissioned it, this material is definitely not normal and some of it highly sensitive. I wouldn't want anyone else to know about my hospitalisation for mistreatment at the hands of an ex, such as is detailed in a mid-nineties instalment in Lucinda's folder. Even the innocuous stray cat seems too private to be flashed up on some social media site. But it's all sitting here on a machine that's ridiculously easy to break into.

But that's just it, I realise: the decision what to do with it isn't mine. Even if technically the contents of the house do belong to me, I'm not custodian of the Sligo family secrets. I'll have to contact his heirs.

I open the most recent file from the year Sylvester died, and take down Lucinda's details, hoping something will still be current. As I feel I know her through her bookshelf, I'll ask her directly what she wants done. I don't have a current email address myself, so I have to wait until I can use the computer at the shop and piggyback on theirs, but I'm pleased to have a plan of action. I can move on.

The computer has told me all I want to know for now. I shut it down and switch off the power at the wall. And I've learned what I need to know about the house too: it's in a good state of repair; I don't want it myself; it'll probably be relatively easy to sell as it's in a desirable part of the world with the cachet of literary celebrity to add a shine. Those three realisations are worth the price of the train ticket.

I lock the pantry door from the inside, pocket the key,

and climb out the broken window. Sylvester's magical kingdom can go back to sleep until the estate agents arrive.

Anticipating a long walk, I head down the drive, tote settled comfortably on my shoulder. The shadows are deep in the woods but I have no desire to turn off the path and revisit them. I used to love the copse when the trees were in full leaf like this; there were so many hiding places for an adventurous child. At least, that was how I saw it at first, before the magic turned to something darker.

My problem had been that I wasn't the only one hiding in there.

I DON'T HAVE an opportunity to send the email the next day because the shop is caught up in preparations for a book launch that evening. An artistic director of one of the major theatres, and once a Hollywood darling, has picked Last Chance to celebrate the publishing of his memoire. I'd like to say this is because we are an attractive venue, but it probably has more to do with Larry being his editor and the fact that the shop is within in reach of all the West End theatres so guests can still make their 'beginners, please' call. Looking down the guest list, it is a who's who of the stage and I can't help but be a little excited even if my duties are confined to manning a cloakroom for bags and coats (a.k.a. racks in the stockroom). Viv has warned me that Charles Collins, the director, is a fading star in the profession so we might not get everyone we hoped for, but I'm banking on actors all wanting the chance to gossip while being served free drinks.

Prior to everyone's arrival, I flick through one of the books from the stack on the signing table. Habit has me looking for entries about Sligo. I discover that Sylvester and

Charles started out in the sixties together, rubbing shoulders with Michael Caine, Maggie Smith and Vidal Sassoon. I like his description of life then before you made it—the flat shares with people who are now big names; the counting out of rent in pounds, shillings and pence into the palm of your censorious landlady; the jobs you could do to earn a living while you tried to make it—postman, milkman, typist. I can imagine Sylvester enjoying driving a milk float, waking suburbia with his tuneless whistling. There isn't much about Sligo after the sixties as the two men went their separate ways. I feel happier for it.

The crowd begins to arrive at five-thirty. The author, a genial man with a monk's tonsure of white hair and alert blue eyes, surprises me by making sure he says hello to all of us before we start. I'd not expected this because Viv had told me she found him difficult. But then many people find her difficult so it is probably just the sparks that two strong characters are apt to strike from each other. He hugs Bette and whispers something to her, provoking a laugh and an 'Oh you!' from her. Viv and Charles nod coolly at each other.

Larry breezes in with his husband in tow. He kisses his sisters, hugs Rupert, greets June, and sprinkles the room with adrenaline fuelled energy. Taking in the fact that what he thought was an unchanging place has in fact changed, he praises the new decor and, when told I had a hand in it, congratulates me on achieving the impossible. He is introduced to Brutus who is sitting as if he is the guest of honour in his favourite lounging spot in the children's corner. The introduction goes well and we are all relieved that there is no sign Larry is going to object to this new canine addition to the PiP payroll (Viv has enrolled him as watch dog for tax purposes so we can claim for his food and vet bills). Greg, Larry's partner, comes over to introduce himself. He's a big, quiet man, a restful foil to Larry's dynamism. I learn that he's a lighting director at the National which explains how two such different people met and why I hadn't encountered him on our night out—he was lighting a show. He looks enviously at my position half in the stockroom where I don't have to make conversation.

'Do you need a hand?' he asks as the guests arrive in force. There's been a brief rain shower so there are more coats and umbrellas to manage than expected. I've commandeered extra coat hangers from June for the former and two more buckets for the latter.

'I'm fine. But if you need a bolt hole...?'

He sighs. 'Tempting but I'd better go and show willing. Larry's put a lot into this book.'

He slopes off, martyr on the way to the scaffold.

George sneaks up on me and kisses me from behind. 'Hi.'

'George! You almost gave me a heart attack!'

He grins and tosses his bag into the stockroom. 'This will be me soon.'

'Manning the coat station?'

'No! Launching a book!'

I chuckle. 'Fetch me a drink, will you?'

He taps his forehead and heads off into the crowd to find Lillian at the drinks table near the door.

I try not to show how star-struck I am when some of my favourite great actors turn up. Sipping on the juice George brought me in-between customers, I imagine how these events are rather like going on Safari: lots of zebra and antelope, then suddenly you glimpse one of the big five, a McKellen in the bush, a Dench behind a tree, a Gambon nose up in a mud pool, very little chance of a Maggie because she's nocturnal and hates crowded spaces...

Rather wonderfully, I see Robert, the man from the Bagwell players, has scored an invitation. Wise, because he will reliably buy the book. He's cornered Kenneth Branagh against the Restoration Comedies. The actor-director's eyes are sliding away in hope of rescue and, yes, Bette has spotted the disturbance and sent her ranger in the form of Rupert to save him, swapping a Kenneth for June. 'June, do tell Robert about the latest production you dressed—the Birmingham one—I'm sure he'll be fascinated. Ken, let me introduce you to...' And the pair head off for safer pastures. Robert is not offended; he will be dining out on that brief encounter for the rest of his life—and his loyalty to the shop is ensured.

Then Larry taps his glass and makes a little speech about Charles Collin's contribution to the modern stage. He glides over Charles's brief and spectacularly unsuccessful time in Hollywood, before returning to his triumphant occupation of one of the top jobs in theatre. The man himself then steps forward to our applause and reads one of the more amusing sections from the book, the staging of *The Importance of Being Earnest* in a prison in the 1970s. In an unmatched piece of fortuitous casting, the Lady Bracknell actor had been put inside for, among other things, counterfeiting designer handbags.

'So when he said "A handbag?", some wit in the audience asked if it was one of his. I tell you, that old lag who played Lady Bracknall out-acted any other one I've seen in my entire career, including Edith Evans!' concluded Charles, to laughter and applause.

I'd forgotten I liked this—the warmth of theatre people, their ability to turn a tale about themselves, the old chestnut stories handed down generation to generation of actors. As a child I'd often listened in to dinner parties or drinks on the terrace, wondering who all these people were that were mentioned like royalty—Edmund Kean, Ellen Terry, the Redgraves, the Cusacks... If I could have had a choice, that was the kind of family I would've liked to have belonged to, one who knew where they fitted and passed down the acting genes.

'Merle.' My father arrives late and passes me his damp umbrella.

'Mr Carlisle.' I give him a ticket for it, hoping that will be the end of our conversation for the evening.

He doesn't move. 'I've been thinking...' The audience has now broken up into a dutiful line of book-buyers and a scraggly crowd of those downing a quick drink before their performance.

I resist the usual comebacks for that, like 'wonders will never cease'. I just think it.

'Would you like to come to dinner one night at my place? I think we need to talk and we can't here for obvious reasons,' Dad continues.

'I've nothing to talk about.'

'I have. There are things I've put off telling you. Things about your mother.'

It's not the first time he's used my curiosity about her to lure me into his orbit when really I wanted to escape his gravity.

'And I've mementos of hers I want to give you.'

'I'm surprised you kept anything.' But that reminds me. 'Do you have my birth certificate?' I won't tell him but I've been thinking that I'll need a way of proving I am who I say I am when I go to the lawyers about the house.

'Why do you want it?'

I realise my tactical error. I should never've mentioned it

when he wants something from me. I should've made it seem no big deal. If he knows what I'm thinking of doing, he'll start to be difficult—correction, *more* difficult than he already is. I know already he'll see anything I get from the house as half his—or more. *You were only ever there because I got us there! You owe me!* Yes, that's exactly what he'll say.

'I just want it. It's past time I looked after my own paperwork.'

He folds his arms, pretending to be watching the room. 'But you're homeless.'

'I'm renting. And I have a job. That's pretty stable. Do you?'

'Do I what?'

'Have a job?' Or are you living off the proceeds of the paintings you stole?

'Of course I do. I'm a writer.'

So that was the persona he's currently inhabiting. No wonder he's hanging around the bookshop so much: he's probably cultivating Larry. George is lucky he got the biography commission before my dad came on the scene.

'Good for you.'

'Dinner then? I mean, if you want me to dig out your birth certificate.'

That's his price. 'I can't come to Bath for an evening. It's too far.'

'I don't live in Bath.'

'But...' I close my mouth. Of course he doesn't.

He takes the ticket I gave him and writes down an address in East London. 'Seven-thirty tomorrow night?'

I nod and tuck the scrap of paper away. Part of me is angry he's manoeuvred me into this, but the other part is resigned. I never won a battle with my father, not till I walked out and made sure he didn't know where I was. Maybe that was more a judicious retreat than a victory?

'I'd better go and mingle,' he says with a social smile as George approaches. 'George! How's the great work?'

George diverts from me on to the more alluring track of someone as interested in Sligo as he. I try not to feel offended. At least they take the discussion away from where I can hear them.

The crowd thins out and I'm too busy handing over coats, bags and umbrellas to notice that my father has left. His umbrella remains, slouching in its bucket—probably purloined from a cafe so never really his. I decide not to hate it on principle.

Charles has had a good evening and is very kind when he comes to say goodbye and thank me for doing the unglamorous task I'd been allotted. He already knows George, who is standing with me, due to an interview George did with him early on in his research.

'I hear from Larry you've finished?' he asks.

'Yes, finally.' George puts an arm round me. 'Just as well because after living and breathing the man for eighteen months, I'm afraid I was becoming a bit of a Sligo bore.'

'Only a bit?' I murmur.

Charles smiles. 'Yes, too much Sylvester was never good for anyone. Small doses.'

'Did you meet his old secretary, Evan Carlisle? He was here earlier,' says George, using his height to see if my father is left among the stragglers.

'That man? No, and I can't say I'm sad to have missed him.' There's a bite in Charles's tone. Despite Viv's dislike, I find I'm warming to him.

'Oh? Why?' asks George. 'He's perfectly charming.'

Charles picks up his coat which I'm holding out to him. 'That is exactly the problem. Goodnight.'

And he goes.

George rubs his chin then looks down at me. 'Do you know what he meant?'

I do. 'Maybe he thinks he's smug or something?' I say airily. 'You said yourself you thought he was a bullshitter. Do you want to go out for a pizza?'

'Sorry, I'm going to Larry and Greg's. There's a dinner thing for Charles. How about tomorrow?'

I remember my engagement with a sinking heart. 'Sorry, I'm busy.'

'You? Busy?' He actually laughs a little.

'Why's that funny?'

'Just that, unless June or I coax you out, you stay inside like a...like a cloistered nun.'

'Well, for your information, I have plans.'

'Who with?'

'None of your business.'

'Now I'm intrigued. Has Lillian thawed enough to ask her to meet some of her college crowd?'

As if. 'I'm just busy. Can we leave it at that?'

He shrugs but the agreement is no longer good humoured. We're both a little irritated with the other. 'Fine. See you maybe then later in the week? If you don't have plans.'

'OK.' It's hardly the parting words of the world's greatest lovers, so I'm left wondering if our fledgling relationship has just fallen from the nest to be left spluttering and dying on the pavement beneath.

Damn, my father is good at what he does.

19

It's boring living in the past; you always know what's going to happen.

David Hare, 'The Breath of Life'

My father's flat is in Mile End, an area estate agents describe as 'up-and-coming' which actually means a grungy area with some recent, cheaply built apartments with the requisite balcony for the storage of the bikes to speed young bankers into the city. Not for them the purgatory of the Underground. There's a few coffee shops to show the gentrification but ethnic grocers, community centres and burger bars predominate. The block is opposite a large secondary school and mosque, which I imagine annoys him. He'd prefer a loft in the childless Canary Wharf rather than this proof of life and new generations who don't care about him and his ways on his doorstep. He's the foreigner here.

Steeling myself, I press the buzzer. He doesn't check,

just triggers the door release. I take the stairs up to the third floor, struck by the lingering new smell of the building. It hasn't lived long enough to take on the personality of its occupants. Unless that *is* the personality of the tenants?

My father is waiting in the open door to his flat.

'I wasn't sure you'd come,' he says, playing genial host. 'Shoes off, please.' He points to mat where his brogues are lined up. He's wearing a pair of slip-ons and offers me a set, still in their hotel plastic bag. I decline. I look around and see signs of someone else sharing the apartment with him—a woman's coat and shoes, closed bedroom door, faint scent of perfume. I can now understand how he can afford the place. More evidence is presented by the framed photo of him with an attractive woman in her thirties on the sideboard in the kitchen-living space.

'Who is she?' I ask bluntly.

'Rima? Oh, she's my wife.'

That's a step further than I had imagined. 'Congratulations.'

'I would've asked you to the wedding, of course, but you were sulking.' He gets out a bottle of wine from the fridge and unscrews the cap.

'Not for me, thanks. I don't drink now.' Funny how he dismisses my breakdown as 'sulking'. No story really exists for him but his own. I think he's the dictionary definition of a narcissistic disorder.

With a snort of disdain, he pours himself a wine, then gets out mineral water for me and waves it before me. 'Yes?'

I'm not going to get away without some kind of drink. 'Fine.'

He pours it with a waiter's flourish and hands me the glass. 'You might meet Rima later. She's working.'

'What does she do?' Look at me, with the small talk! I'm almost grown up with him. That's a first.

'She's in finance—pensions advice—that kind of thing.' He goes to the window and looks out. There's a gap in the buildings that gives a canyon view to the horizon where the tops of the city towers can be seen.

So vague as to tell me nothing except that she probably has money of her own. I hope she has it tied up so he can't get to it.

'Does she know about me?'

'Of course. I said you were travelling—finding yourself. She's eager to meet you as we're having a baby in three months.'

That pulls the rug from under me like nothing else. 'A baby?'

'A half-brother, or sister, for you. I hope you're pleased? So you can see why having an asset like the house doing nothing seems particularly foolish.'

How to explain to a narcissist that his decision to start a second family has absolutely nothing to do with what I decide about my inheritance? It's not worth the bother.

'Congratulations—I think. You're happy?' Poor kid.

'Of course I am. Rima wanted a child before she turned forty so we're delighted.'

I read the subtext. His current cash cow (sorry, Rima, but that's what you are to him) is primarily in the relationship due to ticking biological clock. How many of us settle with the good-enough partner just so we can have the children before the chance passes us by? He eventually had to fulfil his part of that bargain. At least it sounds as if she's got power in this relationship, not like the other ones I've seen him in with my mother and Sylvester. And me, I suppose.

'Do you have my birth certificate?' I ask, hoping I can

slip away before meeting Rima. The lies I'd have to tell the pregnant mother are too many for me tonight.

'Later. Let's eat. I'll just get it out of the oven.' Donning oven mitts like a knight his gauntlets, he pulls out a lasagna. Bubbling and browned, it looks perfect. 'Rima made this for us, knowing it was a special reunion supper.' He opens the fridge and gazes inside for inspiration. He then takes out a bag of salad and upends it into a bowl. 'She'd be cross seeing me doing the final preparations with you here. She likes to have everything set out ready when we have dinner parties. But you're family, aren't you? No need to impress.'

I sip my water, trying to pick my way through what he's telling me. You see, you might be hearing a slightly henpecked, older husband charmingly getting to grips with cooking solo, but I know it's a pose. He's playing 'reformed man' for me—the one who in the Hollywood movies goes from career-driven tyrant to family-orientated guy—the modern Scrooge story retold millions of times. And the goal? Watch the hands and work out what he wants. His hands are already reaching for the wine bottle to refill his glass, not offering any to me. And he wants, what else? Money.

'That looks good,' I say neutrally when he serves me a slice of lasagna.

'I helped cook.' He's proud of the fact, like a six-year-old baking cookies. 'Made the sauce.'

'Good for you.' I'm being ironic and he knows it. We do understand each other far too well to get away with anything.

Here comes the sly counter-punch. 'When's the last time you cooked?'

I shrug. 'I can't—nothing more than cheese on toast.'

'I thought Mrs Brampton taught you?'

'She showed me how to make cakes—kid's stuff. Can't live on cake.'

He passes the salad bowl to me and I spoon a mound onto the plate. 'How's it going with George? Is it serious?'

'Not really.' I'm not sure that's true but never let him know you care for anything because it becomes a weapon in his hands.

'He talks about you a lot. I think the so-called coincidence of you sharing the name with my daughter makes him think I like to hear about you. You're obviously very intelligent.'

I say nothing because that is the intelligent thing to do.

'You always were. Your vocabulary when you were at primary school outstripped those leaving secondary, did you know that? Your teachers used to show me your stories with awe at your imagination. I told George about that. I had to tell him something about my daughter, after all. Do you still write?'

'No.'

'You should. Then we'd be a family of professional writers.'

That's a good way of killing off that ambition in me. I turn him to his favourite topic: himself. 'What are you writing, Dad?'

He dissects his lasagna, eating each layer separately. 'A play. I've been talking to Larry about it. He sounds interested.'

I wonder how many pitches Larry has had to smile his way through. 'What's it about?'

'Loss. Very much the hot topic at the moment and what with your mother...' He leaves that trailing. He's cannibalising our family pain for his own advancement. He doesn't feel it—something at some point cauterised his soul against real emotion—so is happy to play with the pose of bereft widower using his private agony as a place of authority from which to write.

'You said you had something to give me of hers—and something to tell me?' I prompt.

'That's right. Now I've got my new life with Rima, it no longer feels right to have your mother's things here. We're clearing out space for the baby's stuff too, as you can imagine.'

Pack up one life to make room for another. He is good at that. 'What've you got?'

'Just a minute.' He gets up and goes into one of the bedrooms. I let my eye wander and see in an alcove the John Piper, gleaming in its golds and dark blue against magnolia walls. The bare-faced cheek of it! Does he think I won't mind? He probably doesn't consider my point of view at all.

He returns and puts a plastic storage box in front of me. It's the kind that has clips to keep the lid on so I flick them open and look inside.

'Those are CDs of her singing with her group. They made three recordings.'

Surprised that there really is something he wants to give me, I pick one up. The jewel case has a sleeve showing my mother in a white dress, looking younger than I am now, sitting on a hay bale. She's surrounded by moody denim-clad guys with a banjo, accordion and violin. They called themselves The Green Willows and their repertoire was folk songs, some I already know, some that I've never heard of, like 'The Golden Vanity', a song for my father if ever there was one.

'Thanks,' I choke out.

'I knew you'd like them. She had a glorious voice. Do you sing?'

'Only in the shower.' I actually have quite a nice one but I don't display it in public unless drunk.

'Like me then. Tone deaf. And there went my plans to be a rock star.' He smiles with automatic self-deprecation but I'm not in the game of smoothing his ego.

'The world breathes a sigh of relief,' I say instead. His voice is actually OK, and he knows that I know it. I remember him singing to me as a child, Rolling Stones' songs mainly. I think Mick Jagger is one of his idols. He admires his marriage technique: six-hour Hindu ceremony on a beach at Bali? Come the divorce: of course it wasn't legally binding, Jerry.

'There are some photos in there too. I thought you'd like them.'

I fish out a familiar pouch of Boots snaps. I'd already filched one years ago and he never noticed. 'Thanks. I'll look after them.'

'And then there's this.' He dangles a silver cross from a chain. Mum is wearing it in all her photos—or one very much like it. I reach out my hand. 'The hospital gave it to me after she died.'

I pull back. 'She was wearing it?' I don't want to carry with me a memory of that last night on the railway tracks where the car she was travelling in was hit by a train. Terrible accident. The driver, her brother, was badly injured and the train derailed but Mum was the only fatality. Not wearing a seatbelt, they wrote, so she went through the windscreen.

My dad shakes his head. 'Obviously not. It was in her things.'

I take it. 'Thanks.' I can't be certain it is actually the necklace she had or if Dad had got hold of one like it as part of his emotional manipulation. But then, does it matter? I can decide it is real and stick with that. I slip it in my pocket and return to eating. 'What happened to her brother?'

He pulls a face. 'He was what they call now bipolar—high as a kite one day, chased by the black dog of depression another. It made him more alive than anyone I ever met, and Mandi felt responsible for him. But she paid such a huge price for it. He should never've been driving. Sacrificed to sisterly love.' He's just given me a précis of his play, I realise, inflating what he felt for her into the grand passion of his life, operatic in its tragedy.

'Is he still alive?'

Evan shrugs. 'Doubt it. Last I heard he was in a depressive spiral. Guilt. Served a few months for dangerous driving.'

Such a tragic figure would not appeal to him. He might find himself having to take care of someone for once in his life, without any prospect of reward.

I finish my portion and refuse seconds. 'I'm full but tell Rima it was great and I say thanks.'

'You can tell her yourself.' Dad clears the plates and puts them in the dishwasher.

'I'd better get back. I don't like travelling on my own after dark.'

I hand him the excuse he can use with his wife and he seems pleased. He isn't that eager to get us together: I'm not reliable as a witness; his old and new lives might clash. A reconciled but distant daughter who he can tap for cash is what he'd prefer.

'Dessert?'

'No thanks. I'll just take the birth certificate and head home.'

He pats his own tummy, weighing up gluttony and the

desire to be appealing to his younger wife. 'Right then. I'll dig it out.'

Astonished he's actually going to give it to me without more bargaining, I sit for a moment as he goes into the bedroom again. Then inspiration strikes. I climb on the sofa, unhook the John Piper from the alcove and slide it into my tote, back of the painting against the box he gave me so I don't damage the surface. Going into the hall, I put my shoes on, ready to make a fast getaway.

He comes back with a manila envelope, which I take without checking.

'Thanks, Dad.' I open the door.

He reaches for me for a fatherly hug, but I'm not playing that game. He picks up the signals and instead pats my arm.

'I'm pleased we did this. Let me know if you need any advice on the house, won't you? You really should think of selling while the market is high.'

'Sure. By the way, did the will include contents?' I back away, keeping the tote behind me, then turn at the last moment to go down the stairs.

'Yes, it did.' He's gratified I'm showing an interest.

'I thought so. Thanks for supper.'

The door closes. I'll give him five minutes before he realises the picture is gone. That means I should run.

20

Gus is the Cat at the Theatre Door.
His name, as I ought to have told you before,
Is really Asparagus.
T. S. Eliot, 'Gus: The Theatre Cat'

I sit the picture on a box by my bed and gaze at it happily. A dark flag waves over the fallen walls of the ruin and storm clouds rage across painted sky but yet it feels strangely cheerful, like someone facing inevitable defeat with defiance.

June snips a thread. 'That's a lovely picture. Where did you get it?'

I hug my knees. 'At a flea market in Camden Lock.'

She selects another button. 'You might've found a bargain then. Who's it by?'

'The signature says John Piper so it's probably a fake.'

'How much did you pay?'

'Twenty pounds—mainly for the frame.' How easy it is to lie. I am my father's daughter in this.

'Then you've either come across the most inept market stall owner in London or you're right. But even as a fake it might be worth more than twenty quid. You should get it valued.'

'Maybe I will.'

June assumes that is assent. 'Right: let's try this on you.'

Knowing my role by now, I stand on the stool and let her drop the latest creation over my shoulders. It's a tabard for Joan of Arc in a revival of the Bernard Shaw play about the French martyr.

'Don't you look the part!' she exclaims. I suppose my short hair is fitting for the heroine who led the French armies.

'June?'

'Hmm?' She's fussing with the hem.

'What were your parents like? Did you get on with your father?'

She snorts. '*Do* get on, darling: they're both still alive and kicking and in their eighties. I did get on with him, until I announced in my teens that I was gay. Funnily enough, my father found it easier when I transitioned. I was now playing on the right team as he understood things.'

'Is he religious?'

'Oh no. Complete pagan, just slow to adapt. My mother is an Anglican like me and she took it all in her stride, bless her.' June an Anglican? She is full of surprises! 'When I visit home, she introduces me to all her friends at church with great pride.' June tweaks the *Fleur de Lis* straight over my breasts. 'I think she finds it rather flatteringly worldly to have a trans daughter. She's caught up on all the jargon and has even got herself on a panel in her local diocese to deal with LGBTQI issues.' June sits back on her heels, letting us both appreciate the image of a little white haired lady among the activists. I'm sure already that they must all love her mother. 'Last time I visited during Open Gardens week, she'd persuaded my father to plant the back garden in rainbow colours. I'm not sure he quite grasped the message of the flags she sprinkled about the place. You should've seen his face when the local newspaper covered it.'

'They sound adorable.'

She pauses. 'Aren't they? I should go and visit them soon. It's been weeks since I last called in—work being so busy. And they're not getting any younger. How about you, hon?'

This is why I don't usually ask people about themselves. 'My mum died when I was little. Car accident.'

Crouched beside me, June briefly touches my knee. 'I'm sorry.'

'And Dad? Well, Dad is a law unto himself. Toxic. I keep clear.'

'Any brothers or sisters?'

Not yet but on the way. 'No. Just an uncle in New Zealand.' And possibly another who killed my mum.

'No wonder.' She pulls the tabard over my head.

'No wonder what?'

'That you ended up on Viv and Bette's doorstep. You've got nothing to fall back on.'

'I'm kind of aiming to stand on my own two feet.'

'Good for you. But you've got us now, haven't you?' I can hear that she's worried for me and I wonder why.

'Is there something I should know?' I ask.

'Oh, nothing.' But she says it in the exact tone that I would use to hide an unpleasant truth from another person.

'June, what is it?'

'It's just...oh I might as well tell you. It's just that I'm worried you're falling too much for George.'

'Don't you like George?'

'I love George, but he's...' She twirls her wrist.

'He's what?'

'He likes people who are useful to him, haven't you noticed? His sudden friendship with Rupert and you, how he hangs around Larry. It's not malicious, I'm sure. He's just focused on his project, in love with that, and likes people connected with that by extension; so I'm worried when he moves on to some new area of research, he'll swap all his current friends for ones that can help him with the next.'

I've been so used to everyone agreeing how splendid George is that it comes as a shock to find June is a sceptic. 'But I think he likes me.'

'Of course he likes you. I'm not saying that he doesn't. I'm just saying he isn't serious about his relationships, not yet at least. Maybe you'll be the one to change his mind, fix him with this set of friends so he doesn't move on to pastures new.' She doesn't sound convinced.

'How do you know all this about him?' I step down off the stool.

June spreads the tabard out by the sewing machine. 'Hon, I see a lot of me in him. I've just used you as a clothes horse, haven't I? I use everyone that way because I'm obsessive about my craft. I hang clothes, he hangs ideas off people. It's what we do.'

SOBERED by this assessment of George, I play it cool next time I see him. I had been going to apologise after our spiky last parting, but I decide he should be the first to make the effort to repair things. Either he puts the metaphorical dab of clear nail varnish on the ladder in our relationship, or lets it run all the way so it is fit for nothing but the bin.

He comes in just as I'm composing the email to Lucinda to ask what she wants to do with the files. I don't spell out what I've found, just explain that I lived with her father in the last decade or so of his life and that I need to talk to her about something arising from that. I press send quickly before he sees to whom I'm writing.

'Did you have a nice evening?' he asks. He's looking huggable in a lightweight blue jersey and black jeans. It's annoying to find out that my attraction to him hasn't fizzled out.

'Yes, thanks.' I don't elaborate. One surprise I haven't quite yet absorbed is the fact that according to my birth certificate I'm a year younger than I thought. I wonder what scam had made it necessary for Dad to inflate my age? I expect he'd forgotten he'd done it. He had so many fake IDs for me that I'd never thought to question my date of birth.

'Are you free tonight?'

'I can be. What do you want to do?'

'There's a promenade performance on the South Bank—free to all. I thought you'd like to see it, then maybe come back to mine?'

'Sounds good.' That's a step forward. I've not been to his flat yet.

George brushes a finger over the back of my hand. 'Merle, are you OK?'

'I'm fine, thanks. You?'

'Yes, good. It's just that you seem a little...distant.'

'I'm fine, really.'

He shakes his head as if to force himself into more positive thoughts. 'I've made a start on Coward. Do you want to have a look?'

'Sure. Show me after work when we get to yours. I've got a lot on here.' I point to the books I'm cataloguing.

He picks one up and grimaces. 'Olivier. Never felt much interest in him.'

'He's been well covered by biographies already.'

Brutus pads over and snuffles George's hems. He scratches the dog's head absent-mindedly. 'Right then, I'll leave you to it. I'll pick you up about six?'

'Sounds good.'

'From here or June's?'

'Here. I don't need to wear anything special, do I?'

'No, come as you are.' He grins as if recalling his lines after floundering in the text a little. 'You always look perfect to me.'

'You really go for the serious bookseller look?'

'My private fantasy.' He kisses me on the cheek and heads out.

Lillian has been discreetly watching us from the other side of the shop. She comes over.

'Everything OK between you two?'

I shrug. 'You know...' I always have found a hanging sentence like that useful as people fill in what they really think.

'If you need to talk...?'

'Thanks, but basically we're fine.'

'Just the shine is wearing off?' She nods. 'That's what I find after a few weeks. There's this gorgeous guy in my improv class—even better looking than Rupert, if you can imagine that? I dated him for a month and now I can't bear to be in the same room as him.'

Lillian is actually confiding in me. This is bizarre. Maybe she feels she has the edge in relationship knowledge whereas I'm always embarrassing her about playwrights and theatre lore. I resolve to be less of a know-it-all.

'What did he do?' I ask.

Her eyes widen as she shares what she's convinced I will agree is a shocking fact. 'I think the passion killer was when he hummed along to *Les Mis*, including in all the tense bits. And he was out of tune! Everyone looked at me as if I were doing it. So embarrassing.'

'Definitely not a keeper.' I'm on the same page as her about that.

'Looks can only get you so far.' She's rather wistful now, perhaps having a moment of self-revelation that I really shouldn't interrupt. I slip away into the stockroom and play ball with Brutus until the impulse to share has passed and we can go back to our usual 'two houses both alike in dignity' stand-off.

I AM EXPECTING the visit but it still catches me out when my father—Evan, I must get used to calling him Evan—corners me during Lillian's lunch hour. I'm covering the shop alone which is what he's been waiting for.

'Give it back!' he growls, seizing me by the elbow. It's an odd tone for someone still trying to look like they are smiling in polite enquiry for any onlookers.

'I don't have anything of yours to give you back,' I say, pulling my arm free and continuing with the shelving I'm doing in the children's corner.

'Don't play cute with me. I know you stole it!'

'Stole what, Mr Carlisle?'

He looks around him, checking no one can overhear us. It's hard for him to appear impressive when we are kneeling on unicorn cushions and surrounded by fairy lights.

'My painting!'

'*Your* painting?'

'I had to tell Rima I'd sent to have it cleaned! She was furious. She loves that painting. I gave it to her when we got married.'

'Did you now?' I squeeze *Angelina Ballerina* in beside *Backstage Cat*.

'Give it back right this moment!'

It's odd to see him so genuinely feeling something. I've found the one true emotion he has left: rage.

'I had a little look on the internet today. Did you know that an Alfred Wallis seascape was sold a year ago at auction for a tidy sum? I recognised it.'

He stands up and squeezes a Winnie the Pooh Bear neck in lieu of mine. 'Sylvester gifted it to me before he died.'

'Really? So if I ask the very efficient lawyers for an inventory of the house contents after death, it won't appear?'

'He gave it to me but I left it hanging in the dining room because I was still living there.'

I wrinkle my brow. 'And you have a record of the gift, I suppose?'

'It was a promise, not a contract.'

'So we only have your word on it?'

'And that should be good enough for you, my daughter.'

I shove T.S. Eliot's *Old Possum's Book of Practical Cats* in the wrong slot, retrieve it and place it more gently in the right place.

'Merle! Are you listening?'

'To every word that falls from your lips, Father dear.'

'I have to have that picture back! At once!'

'You can't have back something you never owned in the first place. Or are you claiming the Piper was a gift too?'

'I earned it!'

'How exactly?' I get up, pins and needles in my calves from kneeling.

'I was a loyal servant for sixteen years.'

'Total crap, Dad.'

'Vulgarities are for dolts!'

'Congratulations, you raised a dolt. But not a fool.' I retreat behind the counter and click my fingers so Brutus comes to heel, adding an extra barrier. 'It's my painting and you're not getting it back. You can put that in your Piper and smoke it.'

As I WAS on the early shift, Bette agrees that it is fine for me to leave a little early to get to the South Bank. Just as I'm closing down the computer for the day, a reply from Lucinda pops into the shop's inbox. I'm relieved I am here to intercept it.

Let's talk. Call me any time. Her mobile number follows with an invitation to communicate by Skype.

Short and to the point. I jot down the number and delete the message. Only I don't have a mobile. I wonder if I can risk borrowing someone else's. George's? But he would be the one person who could quickly work out who Lucinda is. Lillian? She's been almost friendly today and would probably not care as long as no charges appeared on her bill.

'Lillian, have you got Skype?' I ask.

'Of course.'

'May I borrow your phone?' I see George approaching the shop. 'Tomorrow? I need to call the US.'

'Fine.' And she returns to the sandwich she's eating for dinner.

'Thanks.' I grab my bag.

21

The play was, at least, a full hour too long; and had Job *himself sat to hear it, he must have lost his patience.*

George Colman the Younger, Preface to 'The Iron Chest'

Remind me not to voluntarily watch a promenade performance of anything in Central London. Nice idea to stage *Twelfth Night* by the Thames, what with the shipwreck and characters staggering ashore, but not so clever in reality as traffic and the Heathrow flight path make it almost impossible to hear what is said. Shakespeare works in many forms, but not as a mime. The play floundered along the bank like patient losing blood fast. We flowed away after about an hour to leave it sprawled before the last few die-hards—probably family and friends who promised to stick it out to the end.

'Did you know anyone in it?' I ask George as we head off across Waterloo Bridge.

'The guy playing Sir Toby, but not well.' He takes my

hand, which feels nice. Look at me: I'm in a couple! My previous boyfriends had never allowed that. But they hadn't really been boyfriends, had they? Just relationships.

'Just steer clear of him for a few weeks.' I bump shoulders consolingly but I don't offer to go back. I'm not that nice.

'I'll try catch it again. They're performing in Battersea Park next week. That should work much better than this. It's such a shame, though, that they built this one up to be their big moment.'

'You never wanted to go on stage?'

'Of course I did.'

'What stopped you?'

'A little thing called lack of talent.'

I'm laughing as we enter the Underground. I'm not sure what's going on between us but I'm thinking this might be a decisive night. Thanks to the public nature of June's workroom, we've not yet spent a night together. In fact, we've not gone beyond some heated kisses and touching in dark corners like a couple of teenagers who can't get enough of each other. Now our road is clear to take things to the next level. But do I want to? He is making the running as I'd resolved to play it cool after June's warning. I glance up at my companion. He looks determined to get me home with him so no need for a degree in psychology to know he thinks it's time. And me? Maybe I'll know afterwards where we stand? It might be a stupid way to test out my feelings, but it could make the relationship clear: a brief fling or something deeper? I have to know.

George has a room in a flat in Little Venice so we get on the service to Paddington and walk the final stretch along the canal. I'm surprised by this sudden serving of boating culture right in the heart of the city, quirky canal boats moored alongside shopping precincts and flashy new office buildings. The Elizabeth Line rumbles somewhere beneath, a new monster in the tunnels that lie under this city. We arrive outside a portico'ed white building that looks like a set for a Richard Curtis film about dating Londoners, the kind of place real people only occupy in their dreams.

'How on earth can you afford this?' I marvel. 'The rent must be astronomical.'

George gives me one of his trademark warm smiles. 'I think you're getting the wrong idea. This is my mum and dad's place.'

'You mum and dad can afford this?'

'You're joking? No, they're caretakers. It's owned by a businessman from Dubai. They live in a flat at the top. I've a cottage near Hastings for writing but they're letting me stay while I'm researching.'

'So I'm about to meet your parents?' Whoa, this is going way too fast and not towards sex. I don't think I'm ready.

'Don't panic. They're in Paris for a few days for their anniversary. We're got the place to ourselves.'

Now I get both why he's asked me over and why he hasn't asked me before: major buzzkill to have the parents popping their heads around the door to ask if we could keep the noise down. With our chaperones, no wonder we've both been hanging back.

The door opens with that smooth heavy swing of a place that's had serious amount of money spent on it when recently renovated. Millions probably. A white stone tile entryway gives a chilly welcome but George doesn't seem to notice. He's heading straight upstairs. I linger a little to peek at a life I'll never know, a life where you have a grand piano by a window overlooking a shared garden square, paintings by what are probably notable modern artists, a collection of antique weapons over the fireplace and in display cases, a kitchen that looks like the bridge of the Starship Enterprise, and white sofas. Who in their right minds has white sofas?

'Merle?'

'Yes?'

'Are you casing the joint or something?'

'Coming!'

I hurry up the stairs. Right at the top there's another door and it is in this one that George is standing to greet me. I have a sudden flashback to my father the day before, but shake it off. Thoughts of Evan are definitely not wanted here.

'Welcome to the maid's quarters,' he says, waving me in like a *maître d'* showing me to my table.

Some maid. The family lives in a two bedroom flat with a very decent sized kitchen and living room. There are no windows in the bathroom but it is kitted out with a power shower and one of those toilets that jut from the wall rather than squat humbly on the floor.

'What's the owner's line of work?' I ask suspiciously.

'No idea. I always thought it best not to enquire. He sponsored me through private education so I'd be a hypocrite to bite the hand that fed me.' Another child educated on the spoils of possibly illicit or climate-destroying earnings. The private school sector must've grown fat with it. 'What can I get you to drink?'

'You know, what I'd really like is a cup of tea.'

He pulls a face.

'What?'

'I just think it might be hard to seduce someone over a mug of PG Tips.'

I tug at the neck of his t-shirt. 'Give it your best shot, Romeo.'

And so he does. Rising to the challenge, he lowers the lights, puts on some soft music, and gradually undresses me in the kitchen, kissing each new patch of skin that he bares. Then I return the compliment. We discover that a slow disrobing is the perfect amount of time to let tea brew. We laugh at this revelation and then resume in the lounge, putting the sofa to good use. Part of me wonders why we've not taken it into the bedroom but I guess he's making the most of having the place to ourselves. He is tender, making me feel worthy after so many years of self-disgust. My slim curves he tells me are perfect, and he proves it by running lips and oh-so-clever fingers over every part. He doesn't just pay attention to the more obvious areas, but lingers on the dip in my throat, the lob of my left ear, the tip of the fingers of my right hand.

'What are you doing?' I ask. It feels like a pleasurable kind of torment as his lips cruise.

'Researching you,' he says. 'What you like, and what you don't.' He nuzzles my belly button.

'I...I think I like everything.'

'That's good, because so do I.'

AFTERWARDS, we lie together, his hand stroking my arm, hip and thigh over and over, like he's testing to see if it's still as smooth each time. It feels even more intimate that what we've just done. His chin rests lightly on my head.

'How did you get into writing about the theatre?' I ask, in a very mellow mood.

'Mum used to take me. And there was a kids drama club on Saturdays at the Young Vic. I got interested in the writers and writing when I realised I was ever going to be one of the actors.'

I kiss his collar bone in thanks for the answer.

'I've never asked you, how did you end up dropping out?'

I nestle against his chest, listening to the words rumble. 'Bad choices.'

He doesn't say anything. I know that's not really an explanation. But if this thing between us is going to end soon, then why share?

But if it isn't? What if June is wrong about him? I take a chance.

'It was part way through my second year.' And the last time I saw Sylvester alive—one very unhappy Christmas that was, sending me spiralling down as the full horror of what had been done became clear.

'What caused it? You said health problems?'

'I had a breakdown. Stress.' That covers a multitude of sins and is also the truth. 'I walked out on my life.'

'So you've still got family to walk back to?'

'Not really. I don't count a blood tie as family. They have to act like a parent to earn the title.'

His reply is to keep on stroking.

'I hid for a few years. I had a couple of dead-end jobs to start with, then gave up on those—or my employers gave up on me. I got ill for a bit and end up in hospital with pneumonia. Came out, then kind of sofa-surfed. I have no favours left with any of my old friends. They were giving up on me until Bette and Viv offered me the job.'

He sits up behind me so I'm between his spread legs. 'I'm sorry. I've spoiled the mood, waking bad memories.' I shrug, but he's right. I'm back to remembering just where I came from. 'Come here. Let me help you forget.' He laced his fingers with mine and raises my arms above my head. 'We'll do yoga together.'

That's so unexpected, I laugh. 'Yoga?'

'Us geeky types have to get some exercise if we don't like team sports.'

'You, George Appiah, do yoga?'

'Oh yeah. Have you seen some of the poses? Don't tell me it's not really about sex.'

He's now kissing his way down my arm and neck. 'OK.' I shiver. 'Then I won't.'

THERE'S no talk of me going home. After his own brand of very interesting yoga, we take a shower together, fool around some more, have a late night snack, then go to bed on the pull-out sofa. When I ask about his room, he explains he's only got a single and that it's his childhood bedroom. I can get why he might find that a turn off. I never took anyone into Lucinda's bedroom either. He fetches me a t-shirt of his own and a duvet for us to share and we settle down, his arm thrown over my waist in a possessive fashion. The light on the TV box glows a pinprick of red in the darkened room. There's very little sound even outside thanks to the double glazing. It's like we've been set apart from ordinary life, here at the top of this rich man's mansion.

I wake in the early hours with the need for the loo. Padding out, I quickly see to that, wash my face and clean up a little. The mirror shows me an electrocuted elf so I try to smooth down my startled hair. Yawning, I head back to bed but by now my feet are freezing. Experience tells me they will take an age to warm up unless I inflict them against a warm part of George's body and even I'm not that cruel. Maybe I can find a pair of clean socks in his room? The first door I try is his parent's. I close it again. The next is the utility room but there's no clean washing folded up on the counter for me to steal. The last door nearest the entrance proves to be his as it does indeed have just a single bed. I flick on the light. Then I'm distracted from my sock quest by the large desk under the window—the centre of his research operation. To the left there's a cork board, a blizzard of information. In the middle, he's pinned a picture of Dogberry Cottage and then photos of the people who inhabited it at one time or another. It's weirdly reminiscent of the crime scene boards you see on TV cop shows. At the top is Sylvester, of course. His three children are either side of him: the two boys on one, his daughter on the other, school photos from their primary years. His ex-wife is next: Caroline Sligo, now Barrett as she's married again. I estimate she must be in her seventies by now so the photo is also from the era when she was with Sylvester. Multiple strings then point to the rest of us: Mrs Brampton, the gardeners (though he only has faces with question marks for those), previous secretaries, editors, directors, friends, Keira Fanning, my father, and lastly, me. I'm right down in the corner, one of Keira's images photocopied from the book. But there's another string that leads on from my photo. I follow it to find, under a sheet of A4 with a family tree, a picture George took of me a week ago.

No. I must be interpreting this wrong.

I sit down on the bed and stare at the string. From Dogberry to my father to younger me to my face now.

George knows.

He knows but hasn't asked, hasn't said anything.

How long has he known?

Then I can feel him behind me, standing in the door. 'Merle?'

'I was looking for socks. My feet are cold,' I say quietly.

'Right.' He opens a drawer. 'I don't keep them over there.

Here's a pair.' He lobs them in my direction. They fall by my hand where it rests nerveless on the mattress. He must be hoping I never lifted the white sheet of paper. Do I un-see this? Pretend?

I clutch the black socks and squeeze. I've got to get out. Pulling them on, I go back to the kitchen to collect my clothes. That striptease that had seemed so fun and sexy, now seems stupid. He's been studying Sylvester's muse. June had warned me. I'm attractive to George because I represent the world with which he became obsessed. No need to call in Dr Freud to see how having sex with me allowed him to penetrate that world. He can't shag a dead writer so he settles for the inspiration.

I've been so blind. Remember what I looked like when I was first taken in off the doorstep? Yet even before I'd had a few weeks of rest and decent meals, he was sniffing around me.

George is following me with his lost puppy look. 'Merle, what are you doing?'

'I'm going home.'

'But it's three in the morning. Come back to bed.'

I feel stronger now I'm dressed. 'You're a bastard, do you know that?'

'What? I mean, I think my parents would beg to differ.'

'Don't play cute with me. I saw.' What have I done with my tote? I think I'd dropped it in the living room on arrival. I push past him.

He swallows and doesn't try to defend himself. 'I'll put some clothes on. Walk you to the bus stop. There's a night bus.' He's hopping into trackies even as I find my bag.

'I don't need an escort—don't want one.' Oh, this hurts. I feel like he's stabbed a bluebell wood fencepost in my back and twisted.

'Would it help to say I'm sorry that I didn't tell you I knew?' He's standing there, big palms open in appeal.

I lean against the front door and close my eyes. 'How long have you known?'

'A day or so after I saw the book of photographs. The penny dropped. You haven't changed so much that the face, your name... And the accounts show payments for fees at UCL. It was too much of a coincidence.'

Since the beginning then. 'And you still arranged to meet my father at the shop?'

He puts on a shirt. 'I hoped you'd tell me then yourself.'

'You were thinking there'd be some big Oprah style reconciliation and you'd get the credit for reconnecting father and daughter?'

He rubs the back of his neck. 'Maybe. I don't know. Evan's a nice guy. I thought, maybe, you could work it out?'

I hold up my hand to get him to stop talking. I need to see the last few weeks with the benefit of the full information. 'The house? You knew it belongs to me?'

'Well, yeah.'

'Why? Why play me like this? You didn't have to make me care for you. And don't you think having sex with me was way over the line?'

'It wasn't like that!'

'Wasn't it?' The pain—red, raw, excruciating—is ripping through me.

'I really do care for you—I might even love you.'

'No! No, you don't get to say that!' I'm sobbing now when really I want to beat him into a pulp. 'You lied to me. George!'

'And so did you. You lie to everyone!'

'So that made it OK, to manipulate me like this? Oh God, I can see it all now. You wanted this as your big scoop, the publicity would be amazing when you dig up the lost heir to Sligo's house. You could unveil me at the book launch, get booked on the news programmes as well as the arts ones. I was just a project to you!'

I open the door and head down the stairs.

'Merle, wait, there's an alarm!' He hurries after me, hitting the timer switches on every landing.

Keeping my distance I let him beat me to the door to the street. He pauses just before punching in the number.

'What's between us, it isn't about Sligo, or who you really are, not for a while now. Please, believe me.'

I say nothing, just wrap my arms around myself.

'I know you're upset—I can get why—but let's talk tomorrow, OK? I'll apologise again and again until you believe me. I really only wanted what was best for you.'

I refuse to look at him. 'Open. The. Door.'

Finally, he does so. 'Do you know where you're going?'

I'm too exhausted either to swear or wave two fingers, which are the only replies I can think of making. I stumble over the first step, then fast walk away from him, careless of my direction.

Of course I don't bloody well know where I'm going. But I do know that I can't be where he is.

ACT 2

22

We want more order than we ever meet
And art keeps driving us most hopefully on.
Elizabeth Jennings, 'Works of Art'

There is no comfort to be found running away.

I don't go to the shop or to June's. George can walk into the shop at any time and June would let him in; I just can't live with that possibility. I need to hide. I check into a cheap hotel and brood, smoke and drink until my head spins and nausea rises. I'm repeating all the self-destructive habits I formed when I dropped out but I can't seem to stop myself. I know it is foolish – reckless – self-defeating, but there's so much pain I can only do things that dull the edges.

My thoughts go in fruitless circles.

I'd taken a chance on him and, like so many others in my life, he exploited my trust. I'd built a little fantasy romance and he'd bleached it barren with his scheming.

It is my father all over again.

I'm never going to escape this story of betrayal.

It's a dark time. All lights are out in my theatre.

FINALLY I SURFACE when my money runs out. I still have my key to June's. The best I can come up with is to go back and collect my stuff, then escape the Sligo web I keep getting caught in. I should've done that weeks ago.

Checking out, I take some deep breaths. I should've paid attention to my early misgivings. I'd asked myself what I was doing involving myself with George and the shop, but it's like the Narnian Turkish Delight the White Witch hands out—you can never get enough once you start eating. My real addiction—the thing I keep falling into—is the playwright's world. And I don't leave because maybe deep down I don't want to? The girl never really returned from her walk in bluebell woods.

That is the most depressing thought of all.

Crossing my fingers that there's no one at home, I let myself into the flat and climb the stairs. Silence greets me: no sound of voices or drill of the sewing machine. Pushing the door open, I enter the attic room. June is sitting in the window tacking a hem.

'I wondered if I'd see you again,' she says with only the briefest look up.

'Sorry. I'll just fetch my stuff. It won't take long.'

'You'll do no such thing. You'll have a cup of tea and we'll talk.'

'Really, June, I can't stay. Would you look after my painting for me?' I can hardly bear to think what might happen to John Piper if I drag him round with me.

'Go put the kettle on.' June puts her sewing aside, tugs

the bag off my shoulder, and prods me with one fastidious fingertip in the direction of the kitchen.

I owe her at least a conversation before I leave. I come back with two mugs of tea. I hand her one and sit on the bed.

'So,' she says.

'So,' I echo.

'George told us everything.'

I almost spit out my mouthful. I swallow, but it is the painful kind where it's already half gone down the wrong way. 'He did?'

'He said he upset you really badly and that he feared he'd sent you away in a terrible state. He's been looking for you.'

'Did he say anything else?' Like who I am?

'Please, dear, give us credit for more manners than that. Lovers' quarrels only ever make sense to those involved.'

Not this one.

She looks over the top of the little glasses she wears for close work like this. 'I have my theories, of course. I was right about him, wasn't I?'

I nod.

'It's foolish of you to take on so. That's the kind of man he is. It's the deal you get if you go to bed with him. You shouldn't expect more.'

'I don't.'

She gives me that pained look, calling out my lie. 'Apparently your heart and your head are at odds then, because he's hurt you.'

I rub my forehead. She's right.

'Bette said to ring as soon as you turned up. She was upset you didn't go to her.'

'It's not her problem to solve.'

'We know that, but Bette doesn't. You must've seen that she has this compulsion to save the world? She even took on that ridiculous dog no one else wanted. I rang her while you were in the kitchen so she'll be here shortly.'

'June, I don't think I can do this.'

'Do what? Apologise to Bette for leaving them without an assistant for two days?'

'I was thinking more that I can't do this.' I gesture to the room. 'Live, work, do normal things.' Live in Sligo's world.

'Listen to her: the drama queen!' tuts June. 'Darling girl, none of us really feel as though we can bear normal life, but we do because there isn't an alternative. You just put one foot in front of the other and get on with it.'

I put the mug on the little bedside table and stretch out. I don't mind a lecture. It's oddly comforting. I wish she'd adopt me. Perhaps she already has?

'Throwing yourself off battlements is for opera divas only. You aren't the star of a grand tragedy but a young woman trying to live her life to the best of her ability.' June puts her mug aside and smooths the scarlet dress she is hemming. 'Don't mistake the stage for real life. Plays make patterns that give the illusion it all makes sense, or at least has some form or purpose. I'm sorry to be the bearer of bad tidings: life doesn't.'

I'd never quite got over her revelation that she was a churchgoer. It didn't fit with my stereotypes. 'But you're C of E – don't you believe in something?'

'I'm C of E *because* life is senseless.'

'But all that stuff promises just what plays do—that there's a reason for it all?'

'Good lord, you've obviously not read *Job*.' She snips off the last thread and hangs up the scarlet dress, red as any blood on a Catholic crucifix. 'I'm travelling in hope. Anyway, we aren't discussing my beliefs or lack of them here but your situation. You've a problem with heartache, Merle, not metaphysics. Take the support of your friends when it is being offered to you.'

Right now I'll agree to anything to be allowed to stay here and sleep. 'OK.'

And I fall into unconsciousness.

BETTE IS SITTING in June's chair when I wake up. She doesn't say anything, just looks at me and smiles sadly.

I start to sob.

A glass of water is put in my hand and my shoulder patted. She waits patiently for me to cry myself out.

'I'm sorry,' I manage.

'We know. It wasn't about us though, was it? That silly young man!'

I drained the glass and lie back. 'I broke the rules. I let you down. I'm as bad as Cristofor.'

'You lasted far longer than he did. I know what you're thinking.'

'You do?'

'You're thinking you can't serve in the shop again in case you see George.'

I wish I could deny it but she's right. I'm scare of the confrontation.

'Let me tell you, young lady, you can't go through life avoiding awkward moments. You've got to get back out there.'

I'm not sure betrayal is best described as awkwardness but I get where she is coming from. She doesn't know the secret George could expose at any moment. 'I don't want to.'

'Of course you don't, but you will, because otherwise

you'll always cower and run. This is your time to make a stand.'

I get shakily to my feet, feeling like a newborn foal. 'Do I have to?'

'Oh yes, you definitely do.'

'I don't think I can.'

'You can and you must.' She rubbed her heart. 'I learned that the hard way when I left my marriage. I'm not giving up on you so you mustn't give up on yourself!'

I realise that is exactly what I've been doing the last two days and feel a swell of annoyance. I hate to be pathetic. And they are all thinking it's over a young man like some pining heroine, like Marianne in *Sense and Sensibility*. She's infuriating to read and I certainly don't want to be her in real life. My particular downfall isn't a man though, or not the one they think.

'Are you feeling better now you know we want you back?' says Bette as she gets up to leave.

'Yes, thank you.'

'Then we'll expect you at the shop tomorrow at your usual time.'

'Bette, I don't—'

She holds up a hand to stop whatever I'm going to say. 'I suggest you go back to your usual routine as soon as possible. Doing nothing is the biggest temptation for us—because that's when we're most likely to pull the blanket over our heads. The shop isn't your destiny, my dear, not like it is ours. You can look for work from the stronger position of already being in employment. And if he comes in, you have my permission to retreat to upstairs.'

Of course she's correct. 'Viv will let me back?'

Bette pats my arm. 'Viv is rooting for you, just like me. She just has a different way of showing it.'

And so I resume my life in the shop. One strange result of my meltdown is Lillian's new interest in me. She senses drama, I think, and wants to know what that's like as her own life has been so crisis-free. Maybe I'm being cynical? She might just care. What there is no doubt about is her new role as my defender from George. Every time he approaches, she ushers me upstairs or into the stockroom like we're in some carry-on farce. Her excuses for my absence are getting increasingly creative. When I hear her say that I'm auditioning for a TV commercial for dog food and have taken Brutus (I suppose in her world that is entirely plausible) I decide that I have to stage an intervention. I'm feeling strong enough now with a week of normality under my belt. Better to face him. He's the one who should be scared.

I step out of the stockroom. 'Hey, George.' Brutus follows me, perhaps hoping the dog food will materialise.

'Merle! Oh, thank God. I'm so sorry.' He's holding a bouquet of flowers this time. Previous attempts have included chocolate and a novel. I wish he didn't look so desirable, all shamefaced and ready to fight dragons for me.

Lillian decides this would be a good moment to check that the second-hand section is tidy.

'I liked the book.'

'Good, you got that?'

'Evelyn Waugh's a favourite.'

I see him consider and reject various rejoinders. He settles for. 'I'm pleased. Peace-offering, you know?' He's shifting from foot to foot, suffering with the suspense I'm putting him through.

'I did read it that way.'

'I know I've let you down. Badly.'

That's just what the men in my life do, so I shrug.

'But I would like a chance to prove to you that it wasn't about...isn't about who you are.'

I take the flowers from him. 'That ship has sailed, George. I'm not sure I'm even interested.' It feels good to be strong and resist the temptation to fold. I need to put a higher value on my trust.

'Then I'm getting in a rowing boat and coming after you.'

A smile escapes at the image. 'It's not going to work.'

'But I'm still going to try.'

'And will you promise never to tell about...about me?'

'Of course! Please, Merle, can we at least go for a drink together.' He realises how crass that sounds. 'Have coffee? I need to know at least what you want me to do with what I know.'

I suppose I do have to get that folded neatly away and decide what I do with my identity now it's partially out there. 'Coffee then. Sunday's my day off. Meet me at June's at eleven—if you're free.'

'I'll be there.' He enters it in his phone diary.

'Oh, and if Mr Carlisle gets in touch, don't tell him you know where I live.'

He nods with determination. 'Absolutely. You have my word.'

Deciding to meet with George actually makes me feel a lot better. I'm no longer looking at the door with anxiety in case the next customer is him. Life can return to its old pattern, serving the students, tourists, drama enthusiasts that make up our clientele. I even find myself volunteering to serve Robert of the Bagwell Players when he arrives. His brand of bumptious enthusiasm endears rather than infuriates. He's self-deluded rather than out to fool anyone else. What harm is there in that?

'How are rehearsals going?' I ask him.

'Not bad, always a problem finding enough young men to fill the parts,' he confides. 'Do you know the play?'

'*She Stoops to Conquer*? Yes, quite well.'

'I've decided to cast it gender blind. That's quite the thing these days and solves my problem of not having enough of the right sort.'

'I imagine it does.'

'I'm hoping people won't find it too much like a pantomime.'

'I'm sure your audience will adapt.'

He smiles at me, grateful for reassurance. 'They will, won't they? And I've found a very talented coloured girl to play Kate Hardcastle. We're moving on in Bagwell, oh yes, we're moving on.'

He's trying to move with the times but he's reached about 1970. 'I'm sure it'll be a triumph. Anything else I can get you?' He's purchasing a glossy guide to eighteenth-century style and has already told me that he has ambitious plans for the scenery and costumes.

'No, no, this is what I came for. Thank you, my dear!' He waves a jaunty salute with his rolled umbrella and struts out. If ever there is a modern man who fits a character from eighteenth-century comedy then it is him, a kind of Squire Bob Acres from Sheridan's *The Rivals*, the well-meaning but foolish country suitor. I start a little sketch of him in a notebook, thinking of him as the pompous but yet somehow the moral centre of a play, the fool character like Bottom the Weaver.

'What's that?' asks Lillian, an hour later.

I look down and realise I've written a whole scene of an imagined rehearsal at Bagwell. 'Nothing.'

'Screenplay or play play?' she asks, taking no notice of my lie.

'Good question.' I frown and chew the end of my pen. 'Play play.'

'Most of my friends are writing screenplays now. For Netflix and so on.'

It's depressing to think of joining all those aspiring writers, so many words, so many wasted hours. I don't want to be like my father. I put the notebook away.

'I didn't say that to put you off. I think it's great that you're having a go. We need more women writers and, working here, Larry will at least read it. Just make sure it has some good female roles.'

'You mean for aspiring young actresses of about your age?' I smile.

'Yes, exactly.'

I get the notebook out again. She's right. I've defaulted to think about men because they are the ones who have dominated both my life and literature. I put a line through what I've written and start again.

23

So it's not what you're given, it's how you take it.
Carrie Fisher, 'Wishful Drinking'

Caught up in my personal drama, I have totally forgotten the promised phone call to Lucinda. I'm reminded when she emails me with a query as to whether I received her last message.

I check the international clock online. It's late afternoon here and morning in Chicago. I could ring her right now. I could speak to her this moment.

But I'm terrified. I'm not sure why but some part of me wants to run screaming from the room.

I'm a coward.

I think of June's disappointment if she knew. Viv would say I am only living up to her low expectations. Bette would shake her head and forgive me. My fairy godmothers.

'Lillian, can I borrow your phone. I need to Skype someone.'

Lillian tosses it to me without further ado. She's serving a customer so I take it into the stockroom and open the app. It takes a moment to work out how to use it, send an email to Lucinda warning her what number I'm on, then I put in her mobile.

'Merle? Is that you?' Video is enabled so I see a glamorous woman in her late forties, bobbed blonde hair and kind blue eyes.

'Yes, er, hi. Sorry it took me a while to ring.'

'Not to worry. How can I help?'

'We've never met but I lived at Dogberry Cottage. I read your books.'

'Oh my word, they're still there!' She laughs and I know that I like her. 'What's your favourite?'

'It's cruel of you to make me choose, but I took *The Children of Green Knowe* when I last called in. I hope you don't mind?'

She shakes her head. 'I haven't thought about that story for years. I never read it to my own children and now it's too late. They've grown up.'

'I...er...inherited the house.'

Her expression turns sober. 'Yes, I know.'

'I wanted to talk to you...about something your father did.'

She holds up a hand to stop me in my tracks. 'I knew that was why you were getting in touch. I'm so sorry. It was irresponsible of me to shake the dust from my feet and not check on what he was doing. I just couldn't cope any other way. He said he'd changed. Please, forgive me. But that's so not enough! How can you forgive me? I mean that I am very, very sorry.'

'Um...' This isn't going quite how I expect.

'My best advice is get yourself some good counselling. It

saved my life. I'd say torch the house—you must hate that as much as I do—but it would buy a lifetime's supply of therapy so I suggest you sell it. Get rid of it. You have to move on.'

I take a breath. I want to ask 'Did your father abuse you?' but she's telling me, isn't she? Instead I say, 'You don't need to worry about me.'

'Don't I? I heard from the lawyers that you'd disappeared. It often really hits hard in your early twenties, when you start your own first serious relationships. I know I found that. You must be so angry with your own father for not protecting you, but I get how he might not have known.' She looks away, pressing her heart as if it troubles her. 'It's like a terrible secret that gnaws away at you, isn't it? Shame, disbelief—oh the emotions are so, so complicated. You think it was your fault but let me be the first to tell you, it was *not* your fault.'

We're not thinking about the same thing—our experiences are worlds apart—but her words do help with my own private pain. 'That's kind of you to say that. I knew I liked you because of your books. You had to be a nice person.'

She laughs a little tearfully. 'You'll be OK, Merle. I can see that in you—a survivor like me.'

I wish. 'I didn't actually contact you about that.' I can't explain how my situation is very different from hers. I'll leave her thinking she understands my story—it's part-way to the truth after all, just got the victim and victimiser swapped. 'There's something else. Your dad kept files on you all—you, Johnny and Ralph. He paid private investigators to keep tabs. There are photos and updates.'

'He did *what*?' She gets up from her desk, making the screen lurch and I'm looking at her midriff. 'That bastard!'

She whirls around and sits back down. 'Did he take photos of my kids? Oh my God, I want to kill him!'

'Just long distance. Nothing, you know, close up so you can distinguish features?'

She collapses back in the chair, hands pressed to her forehead. 'He was such a nightmare.'

'I can make it go away—destroy the files—the computer hard drive if you want me to, get rid of everything on there.'

She drops her hands. 'Would you? Make a bonfire of it and livestream it to me so I can toast my marshmallows my end over its demise? We should've had it put in his coffin with him—didn't even occur to me.'

'If it'd make you feel better, I can do that now.'

'Oh yes, it absolutely would.' She's fierce in her affirmation.

'You don't need to check with your brothers?' I'm thinking of all the other things that might be on there, the photos collection, the manuscripts.

'I will, of course, but take it from me, they'll dance their own jig around the flames if they know you're doing that for us. They have no illusions about what he was.'

'OK. I'll do that next time I go.'

'When will that be?' She's worried now she knows the files exist. I don't blame her.

'Sunday? I can go on Sunday.'

She nods. 'Good enough. And Merle, thank you. I wish I...'

'You were the best part of my childhood, you know? My imaginary friend whose books I borrowed.'

She laughs tearfully. 'Oh, that makes it worse. I'm sorry.'

'I'll let you know when I'm lighting the match. I'll have to get myself a phone but this seems a good enough excuse.'

'You don't have a phone?' She's scandalised by the idea, like I've announced I don't wear shoes.

'Yeah, I know. Dogberry Cottage produces some weirdos, doesn't it?'

She laughs at that. 'Like you and me? Thank you for calling, Merle. Speak soon?'

'Yes. Get yourself some marshmallows.'

I THINK LONG and hard over this but I make up my mind that this is the very best way to settle things. When George calls for me at eleven on Sunday, I come down the stairs, jacket hooked over my shoulder, and announce:

'Change of plan. No coffee.'

'Oh.' He looks crestfallen. 'Right.' Poor sad hot scholar.

'We're going to Dogberry Cottage. Do you have a car?'

'Yes, back at my house.'

'Will you drive me? It'll save hours.'

'Yes, sure, of course I will.' His face brightens. 'You're letting me go there, after everything I've done?'

'No reason why not.' And it's going to be an interesting test of what he puts first: me or his project.

I feel no need to prepare him. If I give him too long to think about it, then he might find a way of thwarting me. Instead, when we've collected the car and are heading out on the A40, I talk about my father.

'You've got the wrong idea about Evan Carlisle, you know?'

'Uh-huh?' He is concentrating on overtaking a minibus, but I can tell he's listening.

I hug a knee as we sail across the Hammersmith flyover. It gives the illusion you are escaping the city, rising above the traffic snarls beneath. 'My dad is a con artist—and a very good one because sometimes he cons even himself. He probably told you what a close relationship he had with Sylvester, but that's not what it was like. Sligo was scared of him.'

George darts me a look. 'Scared? How and why?'

I roll my shoulders. I'm not going to tell him what Lucinda has told me in confidence. If she'd wanted to expose her father, she would've done so long ago. She must've realised, after she'd broken off all contact, that he'd sent his letter of apology through the medium of his last play. It was almost a cry for her to come back and shoot him, put him out of his misery. The man I knew allowed Evan to abuse him almost as some kind of expiation of his sins, I now realise. He wasn't guilty of the wrong my father accused him of, but he knew he was guilty of much else. 'Sylvester was old and vulnerable; my father is ruthless in exploiting the weakness of others. I'd suggest you steer clear now you've finished your book.'

'But if what you say is correct, then I need to change what I've written!'

'On the basis of what evidence? I don't want you to quote me. I'd just cut it down, keep it to the barest of facts: my dad was his secretary for well over a decade. He dealt with emails, arranged appearances and sorted out the house. That's all true. Sylvester was fading, heading into his second childhood if you want to give it a Shakespearian ring.'

I shift so my back is again the door and I've a good view of George's face. 'Have you told Evan you know who I am?'

'No! I wouldn't do that!' His tone seems convincingly offended that I even ask. Do I give him the benefit of the doubt?

'I don't mind if you do. It'll mean he has one less weapon to use against me.'

'I don't understand.'

'Oh, he'll threaten to tell you or spill the beans accidentally on purpose because I've got something he wants very badly—other than the house, that is.'

George is silent for a moment. 'Is it a picture by any chance?'

'I knew it! He's so predictable! What did he say?'

'That he'd lent it to you but hadn't had a chance to get it back because he heard you'd been ill.' That was the story Bette and Viv had told Larry and any customer who asked after me when I was missing. 'He came over all embarrassed with a story about how it really belonged to his wife and he was in trouble for letting it out of the house.' He goes quiet again.

'And?'

'He wondered if I could fetch it for him. He was going to give me some of Sylvester's letters as a "thank you".'

I make a mental note to report to the lawyers that Evan is bartering Sylvester's archive. 'What did you say?'

'This was while you were missing so I wasn't in the right place to think about anything but finding you. I told him I'd get back to him.'

'And did you?'

'No.'

'OK. Yeah, that's best. Leave him hanging so he doesn't come up with another fiendish plan. What he's not telling you is how he nicked the three best pictures that were left to me and flogged at least one of them to enrich himself. The one he wants back is mine but he gave it to his wife.'

'Wow. You're serious about him being a nasty piece of work?'

'The nastiest. And I should know because he's gifted me with many of his least pleasant personality traits.'

'Like what?'

'That's for you to find out. A woman is allowed her mysteries.'

He bites on his bottom lip and I have a sudden urge to kiss him—awkward when travelling on the M40. 'How am I supposed to trust you then?'

'I never said you should.'

I turn the conversation to other matters. We discuss Noel Coward anecdotes, which ones are real and which ones are probably only attributed to him as a way of hanging wit off a likely person. Coward suffers from the same malady as Churchill, Mark Twain and Oscar Wilde: half the things the internet claims they said are quotes that have floated about for a bit before snagging on their reputation, like seaweed attaching itself to rocks.

I don't need to tell George the way as he's been here already. He mutters an apology for that as we turn into the drive. I hop out to open the gate, the close it again behind the car in case any nosey neighbours come to see who's visiting the empty house. George parks by the front door, gets out and waits by the entrance.

'Where are you going?' he asks as I head off down the side.

'I don't have a key.'

'What?' He jogs to catch up. 'So what are we doing here?'

'Breaking in.' I stop by the pantry window. Still broken as I've forgotten to send a message to the lawyers. I got distracted by the whole life meltdown thing.

'We can't do that!' Rule-abiding George sounds scandalised.

I just look at him.

'Oh. Your house. I get it.'

I tap his chest consolingly. 'Don't worry, babe, I've got

this. You won't fit through the window. Give me a boost up and I'll let you in one of the French windows on the terrace.'

'What does it say about me that I like it when you call me babe?' He makes a stirrup of his hands and helps me up. It's much easier this way so I get in without any more blood sacrifice to the household gods. I don't stop to revisit the ghost either. I walk right through to the study and open the window. George is waiting by the dining room ones which makes me laugh. My life keeps dipping into farce.

'Hey, handsome, over here!'

He grins. My good humour is encouraging him to think I've forgiven him, like bringing me here is the labour of Hercules he has successfully passed. But that's not the test; that's still to come.

He pauses in the doorway. 'The study.' His tone is reverential. I can see how he might genuinely be having a moment here but I'm on a mission.

'George, do you know anything about computers?'

'Yes, a little.'

I pull out the tower from under the desk. 'Can you work out which one is the hard drive?'

'You want to take the hard drive? From Sylvester's computer?'

I fold my arms. 'Yes.'

He actually looks delighted, poor lamb. 'Oh wow—think of what might be on there!'

'I think you should know before we go any further I'm doing this with the permission of Sylvester's children.'

He's battling his research excitement and trying to play it cool. 'In that case, I'll get it out for you. Is there a little set of screwdrivers?' He's pulling it out and disconnecting the cables.

'Yes. Won't be a moment.' I fetch what he needs from the

drawer in the kitchen where we kept miscellaneous stuff like that.

'This model actually has two,' he says. He's got out a little pen light from his pocket which he clamps between his teeth. I slap the screwdriver in his hand like a nurse assisting during surgery. He eases the two disks out and puts them on the desk.

'Am I right in thinking that this means there's nothing left on the machine?'

'Yeah, essentially that's its brain.'

'Great.'

'Unless someone else has a back-up of it, or he used cloud storage, everything is on there.'

Possible, but I can't kill off every copy—the firms involved would have their records too and there's probably some email somewhere if he didn't delete everything—but I can deal with the most vulnerable ones. If my father had had anything to do with it, I can't see that he'd get any mileage about dragging it all out into the light because there's nothing in the files that anyone need be ashamed of, nothing worthy of blackmail. It was just the project of a sad old man to monitor the family from which he'd been cut off. They kept their silence if Sylvester kept his distance—that must have been the bargain.

'OK, next stop the kitchen.'

George trails after me. I can tell he's desperate to look around. I pause for the moment and consider letting him do just that while I burn these outside, but I really want to know how he'll react. It's too good an opportunity to miss.

I grab matches and head out for the bonfire patch behind the old greenhouse. A vine has run wild in there, tendrils forcing themselves out of the window like a bottled octopus.

'This garden is unbelievable. Can I take a photo?' George asks tentatively.

'Knock yourself out,' I say blithely.

I find the old drum incinerator in its usual place. It's got a few holes in the side thanks to rust but it look serviceable. I pile twigs and a few dry leaves in the bottom and light the tinder. Once the flame takes, I feed in a couple of larger branches, then a log or two.

'OK, George, I'm ready.'

George emerges from the glasshouse, leaves in his hair and dirt on his shoulders. 'What an amazing place!'

'Yeah, it is. None of this is the house's fault.' I get out my new phone and check I've got enough signal to use Skype. I call Lucinda. 'Ready with the marshmallows?'

'I am.'

'George, this is Lucinda, Sylvester's daughter. Can you tell George, Lucinda, that you're fine for me to do this?'

'Ecstatic,' she says, deadpan. I do like her.

'You heard that, George?'

'I did. And, er, hi, Lucinda. Nice to talk to you at last.' He looks at the hard disks in my hand and the fire I've made. 'What are you going to do, Merle?'

'I'm destroying these hard drives. I can't tell you why, but I need you to stand by my decision, and by Lucinda's wishes, without trying to stop me.'

He opens his mouth but pauses. He shakes his head. 'Of course you've thought it through.' He swallows. 'You'll have your reasons. Neither of you is insane.'

'Thanks, er, George,' says Lucinda. 'Kind of you to allow us not to be mad women.'

He digs his hands in his pockets as if to stop his body reacting against the wishes of his brain. 'OK.'

I grin at him. 'Oh, George, *now* you are forgiven!' I drop

the hard disks into the fire. Tilting the phone I try to get an angle so Lucinda can see them blacking and melting. 'Have you got those marshmallows, Lucinda?'

'You bet!'

I turn the screen and she has one of a skewer which she's toasting over a candle.

'It's summer. Far too hot here for a bonfire,' she says with a smile.

I look back into incinerator. Those hard drives are rendered beyond retrieval. 'Job done.'

'Thank you, Merle. And if ever you're in Chicago, come look up your imaginary friend, won't you?'

'Yeah, I'll do that.' In the life where I do things like fly to America. I end the call.

George is wiping sweat from his brow, far more stressed than either Lucinda or me.

'Not going to ask me what that was about?' I ask as we head back to the house.

'No, even though it's killing me not to.'

I stop on the weedy terrace near the struggling geranium. 'Thank you, George.'

He looks at me hopefully. 'Are we OK now?'

'We are.' I go up on tiptoe and kiss his chin. 'But I'm not sleeping with you again.'

His face falls but he rallies. 'Good to know. I'm going to have to find something better than chocolate, novels, flowers and breaking and entering to change your mind about that.'

'That wasn't a challenge.'

'Still, challenge accepted, my liege.' He bows me into the house.

. . .

I SIT on the front step by the car while George wanders around the house. It would've been cruel to bring him all this way and not let him look his fill. I don't need to see it again. When he comes out, he gazes over my head to the trees.

'Can I go into the wood?'

I wave permission.

'Do you want to come?'

'No, I don't want to come.'

He doesn't press me but heads off into the copse. What few paths there were must now be lost so it will be heavy going. Sure enough, he comes back a quarter of an hour later nursing numerous scratches. He goes inside to wash hands, then returns.

'All done?' I ask.

He sits beside me. 'It's just a wood. No bluebells.'

'You've missed them, city boy.'

'You played there?'

'Yes. It was my kingdom.'

He pauses, puzzling this out. He knows the play. 'Merle, did...?'

I get up. 'Let's go back home.'

'I'm not stupid, you know?'

'I never said you were.'

'Lucinda—you—there are things you're not telling me.'

'There are lots of things I'm not telling you.'

'You're leaving me to think the worst?'

'What you do with your thoughts is your own business. What I can tell you is that a wood is just a wood, a house, a house. They aren't guilty of anything.'

'So why didn't you want to go into your wood.'

'Because, Mastermind, I'm wearing sandals.'

He seizes on this explanation with relief. 'Oh, right,

voice of experience. I get it now. My ankles are shredded. Thanks for the warning. Could've done with that half an hour ago. There are some vicious brambles in there.'

'And now you know. Shall we head back?'

He nods.

'I'll lock up then.'

I pass through the house, securing the French windows, returning matches and screwdriver to their original spots. Yes, a house is just a house. It's a pathetic fallacy to project fear and misery onto a place. My memories are the things haunting it—the rats in the attic—and these have nothing to do with the bricks and mortar. Another family can buy it, build dens in the wood, slide down the bannister; there's absolutely no reason why they can't be happy here. I'll take the memories away with me and leave it free and clear.

24

That bill is forged, 'tis sign'd by forgery.
Thomas Dekker, 'The Shoemakers' Holiday'

I make an appointment to meet with the lawyers. Fortunately for me, it's a firm based in the West End so I can do this in a lunch hour. Simmons and Cox specialise in theatrical contracts and have an office just off Cambridge Circus, tucked in a building behind a big signboard for *Harry Potter and the Cursed Child.* I hope the play's title isn't prophetic: Simmons and Cox and the Cursed Child...

Mr Cox himself has made space in his diary to see me. I've borrowed a suit from June so I hope I'm looking formidable. Short blonde hair can be read that way, aggressive if ruthlessly styled back with gel, which is how I've combed it. Lillian did my eyes for me so they have a heavy wing of eyeliner that makes me look sphinx rather than elf

—or that's the intention. It's rather fascinating the big change a small flick of a pencil can achieve.

June thinks I'm going for a job interview and gives me a double thumbs-up as I leave.

'Miss Carlisle.' Mr Cox, a short, light-on-his-feet fifty something, offers me his hand. He moves like a retired dancer, which is entirely possible in his business. 'I'm sorry to start off on this note but do you have some ID to prove who you are?'

I hand over the birth certificate. He checks it against the top sheet of the fat file he has in front of him.

'Oh, I think we've got your date of birth incorrectly recorded. Do you mind if I photocopy this?'

I let him assume the mistake is his. 'No problem.'

He hands the certificate to the intern who has just delivered coffee to us, instructing him to copy the document.

'Excellent. Your father has been in touch of course but this is the first time we've met, isn't it? Apart from my visits to Sylvester when you were a child, of course. A great man.'

I let this all wash over me as social chat to which I need not respond as I accept coffee with a splash of milk.

'You were travelling when he died?'

So my father has supplied a cover story. To lie or not to lie? That is the question.

Sitting here in this office with the Cursed Child logo on the wall of the building opposite, I've unexpectedly reached a crossroads. What would happened if I just start telling the truth? It's a strange thought—one that feels like parachuting in the dark with no notion of the landing zone. Years of training say to hide, but whose training it that? My nightmare of a father. Do I still want to live the life he mapped out for me—the life of the long con?

No.

But can I change habits of a lifetime?

My fingernails are digging into my palms, leaving little half moon marks. I have to or I'll be condemned to repeating my failures.

'Miss Carlisle?'

Here goes. 'Actually, I dropped out because I had a breakdown.'

'Oh.' This jolts him from the smooth path he'd been anticipating, remarks about the Outback, or the beaches in India, or some other fleeting experience of the Gap Year student. 'Well then, I'm very glad you now feel able to contact us. There's a lot that needs deciding.'

'I've visited the house. I understand I got the contents as part of the settlement of the estate?'

'Yes. I thought you knew?'

'It's best you assume I don't know any of the details, Mr Cox. I noticed that several paintings are missing from the dining room.'

He flicks through his inventory. 'These three?'

'Yes. I recovered the John Piper myself but I think the other two have been sold without my permission. I'd like you to get them back.'

He turns the file to a letter that's treasury tagged to some email printouts. 'But your father gave me a letter from you authorising the removal—though I must admit I didn't know about the subsequent sale.'

I don't make the mistake of touching the letter. 'That's not my handwriting or signature.'

He looks at me with kindly patience. 'It's the one we have on file for you. It would've been checked against that.'

'Ah, here's the thing: I've never given you a sample so you can't possibly have one. If you want to check, I can ask my bank to show you what they have on their files for me since I was sixteen. My signature hasn't changed. If you test that letter and any other documents purporting to be from me for fingerprints, you won't find mine on them.'

'But your father...' He trails off. I let him work it out for himself. 'But we have procedures! This shouldn't have happened!'

'Let me guess: he said I was travelling so he brought you a letter from me saying whatever—"here's my signature, see you after Sri Lanka"?'

Mr Cox frowns. 'It was China. You were on the Great Wall.'

'Nice. I imagine time passed and you forgot you'd ever been waiting for confirmation? Why worry? He was just looking after the pictures for his daughter.'

Mr Cox pulls on his tie. I am definitely not good for his blood pressure. 'Oh my word, this is serious—this is fraud.'

'You'll have to take that up with my father.'

'And the money, for studies?'

Interesting. 'What studies?' I lean back in my chair and cross my ankles.

'The postgraduate course in Montreal?'

So that's how my father has been living. 'Would it shock you to find I've never been to Canada, Mr Cox?'

He looks defeated. 'No.'

'How much has he skimmed from my share of the estate?'

Mr Cox looks down at his figures. 'About a hundred thousand.'

And I'd been sleeping on sofas. It's almost funny. 'Then I instruct you to get it back. If you don't, I suppose I'll have to see what can be done about making a case about the mishandling money left in your care. I expect there's somewhere I can complain?'

'There is, but we have insurance and... oh I hope it won't come to that. I'll contact your father.'

'Good luck with that. I'd go straight to court order if I were you. He'll do a runner otherwise.'

'I'll have to...I'll speak to my criminal colleagues.'

I think he means experts in criminal law, but the image of him setting some East End tough guys on my father is rather beguiling. 'That's probably best. But what can you do for me?'

Recalled to his primary purpose, he straightens. 'We'll pursue the issue of the paintings. If an auction house went ahead without proof of ownership, they'll be in hot water too. We'll attempt to get them back.'

My money is on my father having forged documents to prove he owned them. 'And my missing money?'

'I...er...I'll get back to you on that. We took it from the royalties on *A Walk in Bluebell Woods*.'

'I'd like to go to college, you see, so my need is urgent.'

'Oh, there's enough left to cover university fees and living costs, don't worry about that.'

I recalibrate my expectations. 'How much exactly?'

'About five hundred thousand. We sold the film rights a year ago.'

Oh hell. I can't bear the idea of a film being made. All the wounds would reopen in multiplex cinemas across the world. 'Under who's authority?'

'Well, we just assumed you'd want to maximise your income. Your father said...' He falters.

'Exactly. Mr Cox, how much did we get from the film company?'

'What are you thinking of doing, Miss Carlisle?' He sounds frightened now. 'The film is in pre-production. I was actually going to mention to you today that they've asked about using the house. They're offering a very impressive sum.'

And if I put the house on the market right now, what was the odds they'd try to buy it? I shelve that plan for the moment; there is too much else here to sort out.

'Can we stop them?'

'We'd be sued for damages—for the costs they've incurred.' He swallows. 'It'd wipe us out.'

I pinch the bridge of my nose. I'd been hoping to come in here, announce the intention to sell Dogberry Cottage and put the boot into my conniving father; now I'm wrestling with Hollywood. 'Who has the power to agree an adaptation under the terms of the will?'

He shuffles papers again and reaches a copy of the will. 'The majority of the literary estate has gone to his children; that play alone came to you, though many would say it was the jewel in the crown. You or your appointed representative have the final say. Your father...' He is finding sentences beginning with those two words impossible to finish, so I give him the correct ending.

'My father lied. I wouldn't appoint him to feed my cat while I was on holiday, let alone to manage my money.'

Mr Cox pours himself a glass of water. 'You said you had a problems – a breakdown. Were you by any chance sectioned—or did someone else have power of attorney while you were ill?'

'No. I've been legally competent despite my problems, Mr Cox. I've not been locked up in the asylum; I just dropped out for a while.'

'I apologise. I was just looking for an explanation.'

'The explanation is that my father is a liar. I'm sorry you've fallen foul of him but I've had to live with him since I was born so perhaps you can guess what it's like to be me?' I mustn't get angry but this is pressing on some painful scars. I seek a silver lining. 'Perhaps the film is going to come and go without much attention. Who's in it?'

He names two of the world's most bankable stars.

I swear.

'You really don't want it made?' His hands are shaking now.

'Mr Cox, if I could sink every copy of the play at the bottom of the Mariana Trench that's what I would do.'

'Oh dear. I…I think you might have to get yourself other representation because your case would be against us.'

'The film company would come after you?'

'Well, inadvertently we've given permission and taken the money on your behalf. The fact that we believed your father was acting in your stead is clearly a defence but…' He looks quite distressed. He's telling me that I might bring about the end of his firm. This responsibility is getting too much for me.

'Can you give me a minute? I just need to take a quick walk—get some air. This is all a bit much to absorb.'

He stands up, ever the gentleman. 'Take all the time you need.'

I pass the intern on my way out.

'Shall I send in your next client?' he asks Mr Cox.

'No, Luke. Please transfer all my meetings and call Mrs Simmons.'

'She's in a meeting with Warner Brothers.'

'Believe me, she won't mind me interrupting.'

I leave Mr Cox to sort out his existential crisis and return to the street. The afternoon audience for the Harry Potter play is queuing up for their bag search, excitement bubbling from everyone lucky enough to have got hold of tickets. This same scene is repeated elsewhere across the West End for whatever is the hot property at the moment, the rap musical or the star-powered Shakespeare. Sylvester's play will attract a different crowd, as will the film, but it might end up being the kind of piece that appeals to the awards season judges if the two actors they've cast are playing at the top of their game.

I lean against the wall of the theatre feeling as if my bones are crumbling. I'm like some fragile fossil that turns to dust on exposure to air.

If I try and pull the plug, I'll cost a lot of people their jobs, not just the lawyers who have been decent to me even if they've been woefully misguided about the nature of my father. There are the camera people, the script writers, actors, directors, producers, scenery, props, costumes, sound, outside catering—I can't even begin to imagine everyone involved in the making of a film. They probably will even use special effects as no movie seems to be without that these days. Computer generated bluebells because they've missed the season, maybe?

A homeless woman ambles past, clutching fistfuls of plastic bags. She doesn't see me hunched in my misery, but I see her.

And why do I want to stop it? Because it hurts me—that old wound of having my story stolen. I expect it'll hurt Lucinda too.

Does she even know?

That I can find out. I text her.

Hi. Merle here. Just come from lawyers. Did you know about the movie of A Walk in Bluebell Woods?

Her reply is immediate. *Yes. I thought you approved it?*

No.

Then who did?

My bastard father without my permission. Do you want me to cancel it?

Can you do that?

I don't know. I can try.

There's a longer pause. The three dots show she's typing, or at least hovering over a message.

The play is out there already, she types at last.

Meaning...?

Genie is out of the bottle. No one has ever connected it to me so they are not likely to now. I know you are in more danger of being identified as Anna as you were living there when he wrote it. You do what you feel is best for your recovery.

But you're fine either way?

Yes. My brothers will feel the same. It didn't touch them quite as much as me—our father trying to apologise like that. In public. He always was devious. He found a way none of us could ignore.

OK. Thanks.

Take care.

I close the message chain. My issue isn't the same as hers. Mine is complicated by the theft of my fantasy and winding it into his own imagination, violating its innocence. There's no apology to me in it, unless my father was for once telling the truth and that it was Sylvester's deathbed wish that I hear that he was sorry. Leaving me the play might bear that out. Who knows with my father as the message bearer?

I start walking slowly back to Simmons and Cox. And there's something else I need to consider: do work of arts rise above their maker? Do they become universal stories, rather than specific to the mind that created them? Testimony exists against some popular singers, impossible now to prove either way, but does that make their music off-limits? Or going back in history, would we ban the plays of Ben Johnson because he killed a fellow actor? Or Byron because he committed incest? What about the paintings of Caravaggio who murdered someone? Maybe, just maybe, these people who know the dark side of the soul have something worth saying about humanity? I might not like it, but wouldn't I be acting like some kind of Big Brother censor if I tried to stop Sylvester's play? It explores the repercussions of child abuse from a position of hidden but real experience. I have to remind myself that the balance of the play, though seeking to understand the drive to this kind of appalling behaviour, powerfully condemns the man for his sin against Anna. He eventually begs to be killed but she seizes back her agency by not shooting him, leaving him to suffer his guilt with no quick end in sight. Letting the film and new productions of the play go ahead—is that not my Anna-moment? I have the power here and I can choose not to use it.

I return to the office. Mr Cox has been joined by Mrs Simmons. I imagine all other clients have been unceremoniously redirected to understudies. How theatrical of them. Mr Cox makes the introductions. They remain on their feet while I sit down, like defendants waiting to hear the judge's sentence. I've no desire to make them sweat.

'I've decided to let the film go ahead,' I say.

'Oh, thank God,' says Mr Cox, sinking into his chair. Mrs Simmons presses his shoulder in solidarity.

'You're probably wondering why I might even consider the question at all. It's complicated—and personal.'

The two lawyers are no fools. They know what the play is about, but they don't know what it means to me; they just think they can guess. They reach the right conclusion for the wrong reasons.

'I see,' says Mrs Simmons. She takes a chair at the end of the table so we are in a triangle formation rather than across-the-table confrontation.

'There are aspects of my life which I wish to keep private.'

'Completely understandable.'

'It seems to me that the publicity surrounding me demanding the film be stopped would achieve the exact opposite—and it might go ahead in any case if a court case doesn't decide in my favour.'

'There is definitely a risk, seeing how everyone entered into the agreement in what they thought was good faith.'

Mr Cox clears his throat. 'Mr Sligo's standing instructions were to take as many offers that came to us, exploit his properties to their full income potential for the benefit of his heirs. You hadn't told us otherwise and were out of contact.'

'OK then. It's a good job I've decided not to try to stop the juggernaut. However, I would like my paintings back, and the money, if you can squeeze that out of my...Evan Carlisle.'

'Absolutely. We'll get a team on it right away,' says Mr Cox.

'You're our number one priority, Miss Carlisle.' Mrs Simmons rises when I do. 'We'll get justice for you one way or another. Would you like us to hand the evidence of fraud over to the police? It's the Metropolitan Police that would take it forward as a criminal matter.'

'Why not? It's about time some of Evan's chickens came home to roost.'

'We'll prepare the files immediately. And thank you.'

I shake her hand. 'For what?'

'For not destroying the firm we built up over twenty-five

years of hard graft,' says Mr Cox. 'I can assure you that Mrs Simmons and I will not forget for one moment what we owe you.'

'Oh.' I actually blush. 'I didn't...you know...actually want to make anyone suffer for an honest mistake?'

'That's very decent of you,' says Mrs Simmons. 'Let's see if we can start getting those chickens back in their coop.'

25

Sir Anthony Absolute: Come here, sirrah, who the devil are you?

Captain Absolute: Faith, sir, I am not quite clear myself; but I'll endeavour to recollect.

R B Sheridan, 'The Rivals'

George is still attempting to win me over so I allow him to take me out for dinner—nothing over-the-top, just a pizza and salad. An expensive restaurant would feel too much like a date with expectations. I'm trying to squash those. It doesn't stop my own expectations blooming. He is just so attractive, sitting there, trying to make amends. He used me, yes, but maybe, just maybe, he meant what he said that I became more to him than a research project? Dare I hope?

Once the waiter has brought our food, I tell George about my visit to the solicitors. It is liberating to have someone who knows me in whom I can confide. I can't remember ever having that before.

'You've sent them after your father—the police—gone the whole nine yards?' asks George in an awed tone. 'I might have to write an addendum to my biography.' He sees my expression. 'Kidding!'

'Why is it nine yards?' I sprinkle parmesan cheese on my salad. I trust him not to betray me. About seventy-five percent of me does, anyway. 'Not three or five?'

'No idea. Google it later. But are you sure you want the police involved?'

'Why not? I don't think I've done anything that's officially criminal?' I wrinkle my nose, thinking. 'At least, nothing that's relevant to this case.'

'You're working under an assumed name.'

'The lack of paperwork is fairly stunning considering how Last Chance belongs to Past is Prologue, a publisher, and books are their thing. I've been taking cash in hand.'

'Bette and Viv can get into trouble for that.' He shakes his head and folds over a piece of pizza to trap a mushroom inside.

'Are you going to report them?'

'No!'

'Then why would the police even be interested?'

'I hope you're right. It just feels like...a vulnerability. One your father might exploit if only half what you tell me about him is true.'

George might be correct about that. Evan has a way of identifying my weakness and aiming for that spot. 'I'll tell them soon. I'm not sure my father will be able to use it against me though, as he started it. I'm only using one of the many names I was given as a child.' I flash him a grin. 'I can be forgiven for being confused, m'lord. I had one messed up childhood.'

George's fork stops half way on the journey to his mouth. He's staring at me.

'What?' I playfully complete the trip for him, nudging the tines up to his lips. He eats, then swallows.

'You sound different. Confident. You're talking more than you used to. Smiling.'

'I think I am different.'

'How?'

'I decided that I'm done with pretending. OK, I'm not going to run down the street shouting who I am to everyone, not that they'd care, but I'm now officially me and I don't intend to change.'

'And who is that?'

'According to my birth certificate, I'm Merle Amanda Carlisle, daughter of con artist Evan Carlisle, and folk singer, Mandi Carlisle. I'm a year younger than I thought, so I'm in fact twenty-six, which means I did a whole load of things underage without knowing it. I'd've probably done them anyway but it would've been nice to know I was a rebel.'

George holds out his hand. 'Nice to meet you, rebel.'

I shake. 'Nice to meet you too.'

'Folk singer, huh?'

'Yep.'

'That's cool.'

'I have some of her music. I'll play it to you one day. But don't expect me to crack out the flower garlands and cheese-cloth dresses.'

When I get home that night, I kiss George's cheek and leave him standing on the pavement. He accepts this with a rueful shrug.

'I'm serious about not getting back together,' I tell him. I'm probably lying to us both but making him wait is his penance – and mine for being so naïve. 'This is just friends. I'm not playing a game with you, George.' But I probably am.

'Aren't you? I was rather hoping you were.'

I laugh softly and close the door on him. I have to admit, though, it took every ounce of will power not to grab him by the front of his shirt and tow him upstairs. My mind plays out the little fantasy, but haven't I run this circuit and know what's at the finishing line?

Being in two minds: look it up in a dictionary and you'll see a picture of my face at this moment.

It's just as well I restrained myself as June is working late in the attic. She is at the sewing machine so I have a trilled warning that's she's in occupation. She lifts her foot from the pedal and the machine subsides as I enter. From what I can see, she's sewing together something that looks like a skeleton suit. And isn't it wonderful that that's not weird?

'No George?' she asks, adjusting the rib cage.

'You know we're not, like, together?' I say, putting my bag down on the bed. I sit down to take off my shoes.

'You're not?'

'We're never, ever, ever, getting back together,' I murmur but I think my Taylor Swift echo goes over June's head.

'Never say never. Look at Sean Connery.'

'Sorry?'

'Did a late Bond after having sworn off.'

'Was it any good?'

'Now you mention it, he was a bit creaky and the plot was a letdown.'

'I don't think that's a good advertisement.' I flop back on the bed.

'My point isn't about the film; it's that you shouldn't rule things out, especially not at your age.'

I tucked my hands behind my head, elbows like batwings. 'You were the one who warned me off.'

'I'm giving him points for persistence. I thought he'd move on, but he hasn't. So I'm allowed to change my mind. As are you.' She cuts the thread and shakes out the skeleton suit. 'Three down, only another twenty-nine to go.'

I prop myself up on my elbows. 'Can I help?'

'No, hon. I'll do the rest tomorrow. The cutting out is complete; I just need to sew them together.'

Relieved, I collapse back down. '*Knee bone connected to the...thigh bone*,' I sing.

'Don't. Not funny.' But she's smiling.

'What are they for? Bit early for Halloween.'

'The Opera House. The director wants to do a Day of the Dead scene.'

I close my eyes, imagining thirty-two skeleton-suited chorus dancing and singing. Awesome. 'I love it here.'

'I love having you here.' She switches off the light on the machine.

'June? Do you want me to tell you who I really am?'

'Do *you* want to tell me?'

'I don't know.'

'Then don't. I believe in the power of reinvention. You can be who you want to be now with me.'

'OK.' I role on my side, hands tucked under my cheek. 'Thanks. I'm just Merle then.'

'Goodnight, Merle.' She brushes a fingertip over my nose. I'm reminded of my mother. She always like a last touch before turning off the light. I'd forgotten that but June has just gifted me the memory.

'Goodnight, June.'

. . .

Of course, the feeling of triumph, of finally overcoming my past, doesn't last long. My father hasn't been surviving on his wits for so many years without a few tricks of his own. Mr Cox is the bearer of the first bad news.

'Your father–'

'Please, call him Evan,' I say as I sit in the same chair in his office that I occupied ten days ago. Luke brings the coffee and this time stays to make notes. He's about my age and, out of the corner of my eye, I notice that he is looking at me with interest. I can't tell if this is because of the notoriety of who I am or just because he likes what he sees.

'Mr Carlisle has told the police that he definitely had your permission to sell the paintings,' says Mr Cox, handing me my cup. He's remembered I take it with milk. 'He claims you were desperate for money so he'd reluctantly sold them to get you some emergency cash as you'd got into trouble with your dealer.'

'So I'm a drug addict now? Lovely. And he has a record of all this?'

'Yes—except for the handover of money as he accepted it in notes from the auction house.'

'That would appeal to him, walking round with a briefcase of money.'

'He says you have a vendetta against him and you've only now changed your tune. Apparently you're jealous that you're being usurped in his affections by a new arrival.'

I snort and coffee sloshes into the saucer. 'I'm a bit old to play jealous older sister.' I imagine he's telling his new wife this version too. It would explain my 'spiteful' removal of the John Piper. You have to admire his ingenuity if nothing else.

'Quite. He stands by the letter being from you.'

'He would; he doesn't have any choice.'

'Unfortunately for the prosecution's case, the fingerprint analysis wasn't conclusive. Paper isn't a very good surface for making prints visible. The police didn't find yours but neither did they find clear prints belonging to anyone other than me and the secretary who added it to the file.'

'Where does that leave me?'

'You still have a good case—the signature is nothing like any your bank has on record, just as you said. The handwriting is more like yours but from when you were younger.'

'He has my old school books, or some of them. He would've copied.'

'Our handwriting expert says that she can show many points that suggest exactly that, but it is a conceivable another expert will explain it away as lapses due to your poor state of health at the time.'

'I was out of my head when I wrote it?'

'Something like that.'

I wish now I had recorded my first meeting with my father outside the shop where he admitted not to knowing where I was for years. Clearly, I'm not as well trained in the art of being devious despite my upbringing.

'And the postgraduate course?'

'Apparently that was a euphemism for rehab. He was trying to spare your feelings.'

'And where was I supposedly in rehab?'

'In a Swiss clinic that has since gone out of business, money wired via a Swiss bank.'

'Handy that.'

'Yes, I think the judge might see it that way too if the Crown Prosecution decide to go ahead to trial. His story is a tissue of lies but a criminal case has to be proved beyond reasonable doubt and it is very expensive to prove all this wrong. You might be better off suing him in a civil court where the burden of proof is on the balance of probabilities.'

'Is there anything to stop me pursuing the criminal case first and going to the civil court for a do-over if we don't win?'

'Absolutely not. It just all costs money.'

'But I have that—and he can't raid my piggy bank any longer so it'll hurt him more than it does me.'

'Well, there is that silver lining I suppose.' Mr Cox smiles. 'If that's what you want to spend your money on?'

'I can't think of a worthier cause.'

Mr Cox looks down at his coffee and stirs it thoughtfully. 'Oh, and he's seeking an injunction against you. Apparently he's scared of you. He wants the courts to rule that you won't go near him or his pregnant wife.'

'What?'

'You invaded his home, flung insults around, and argued.'

'I was invited to dinner, his absent wife had cooked us lasagna, and he gave me my birth certificate and some memorabilia belonging to my mother.'

'You have proof of this?'

'Well, I have the certificate and some CDs that he gave me that night.'

'Good. Perhaps you can send an image to Luke for your file. I'll pass that on to the police.'

Luke hands me his card. 'My email, Miss Carlisle.'

I rub my forehead. Dealing with my father always brings a headache. 'He's playing victim—his favourite role.'

'That was my surmise,' says Mr Cox. 'Don't worry, Miss Carlisle, he won't get very far with his injunction seeing how he's the one being investigated. He's just blowing smoke.'

'Can I get an injunction the other way round?'

Mr Cox frowns. 'Do you have cause to be scared of him?'

I'm not frightened of Evan, I realise. He's never run to being a physical threat; I'm just so tired of him. 'No.'

'Then I suggest you leave the histrionics to him. The police won't look favourably on his fuss as they've not had any complaints filed against you before you started this action. It's not hard to join the dots. We'll keep it under review, naturally. Let us know immediately if he contacts you. Don't see him on your own.'

'OK, I'll sit tight. He might come into the shop though. I can't stop that.'

'That would be very foolish of him but if he does, phone us. During office hours, one of us can be with you in five minutes. Outside of those hours, we'll at least have a record on the phone of what's said and one of us will come.'

They really are giving me the royal treatment. 'The shop closes at seven thirty.'

'Mrs Simmons and I are often here until that late. Hazard of the job.'

'I can cover times when you or Mrs Simmons have to be elsewhere,' offers Luke.

'Thank you, Luke,' says Mr Cox. 'Yes, we can make sure we have coverage for the next few weeks with Luke and some of the others involved in the team we've put on your case. I don't imagine it will be for long, just while feelings are going to be at their height.'

'When will this go to trial—if it goes to trial?' I ask.

'Maybe by the end of the year, or sometime next? The courts are backed up. There should be a preliminary hearing by then if the police feel they've gathered sufficient evidence and have passed the file to the CPS and they in turn decide to charge him.'

What a chain of 'ifs'. 'But you're saying that I might not get my triumphant day in court?'

'There's no such thing, Miss Carlisle. Don't believe the TV. Nothing happens half as fast as they suggest and never as satisfactorily.'

'Got it: no air punching as he gets sent down for ten years.'

'I'm afraid not. But we can still hope that we might get your paintings back and some of the money.'

'But I shouldn't hold my breath?' I stand up.

He shows me to the door. 'Exactly.'

26

Fortune has thrust me forth to prowl, like the wolf; but the wolf is anxious for its young.

George Colman the Younger, 'The Iron Chest'

The fraud case goes silent over the summer. Mr Cox assures me that this is completely normal; such things take months to investigate and the police do not communicate what they're doing to witnesses so I'm to remain in the dark.

I can live with that. Evan hasn't come by the shop so I can enjoy the thought of him wallowing in the same uncertainty. His wife will've had her baby by now so that will be another distraction for him. If he feels it plays well, he'll be acting the model father, showing his prowess at juggling baby and nappy on the changing table, little smile for his wife as he asks for her admiration that the old dog can learn new tricks. Or at least remember them from when he had me. There was some tenderness, if I remember it correctly, but it is hard to work out what's true and what's a false memory when it comes to my father. He has probably persuaded himself, and attempted to persuade me, that he was the best single dad in existence. That was one of the reasons I came to Last Chance, hoping I'd meet someone who knew us then. I haven't yet had the courage to out myself and begin the list of things I don't know or half remember.

The baby isn't quite real to me—brother or sister, alien words in my mouth. I look Rima up, of course, to find out if she's a safe harbour for my half-sibling. The baby will need someone stable in their life. From her profile on her firm's website, Rima does sound refreshingly normal. If not in jail, perhaps my father will end up being the stay-at-home dad while playing at being the writer waiting to be discovered. That's one of the most exhausting things about the world of theatre: all these people with ambitions and only a fraction who will make it through the gate. Myself included, I suppose, as I've carried on with my own writing. I've abandoned the Bagwell theme for a piece about female homelessness. It might be quite good—I'm not sure. I've only shown fragments of it to George and he's encouraging. Not a crowd pleaser though, so I'm not optimistic about its future.

The end of August brings a renewed focus on Sylvester Sligo. I grit my teeth because I can see that it is all going to come together in one plastic strewn tidal wave. I'll have to get out my metaphorical rake and clear the beach once it's passed. First concession I make is that I allow the film company to use the house. The benefit to me is that they'll tidy it up and decorate so it will be easier to sell, not knowing that it looked a bit of a dump when we lived there. The photos don't show that side of the dogeared Dogberry life. They've invited me down but so far I'm keeping aloof.

I've sent George instead as he actually laps up all this stuff and is able to report back. He does get me autographs of the lead actors. I had a girl crush on the actress playing Anna when she had the part of an elf in my favourite fantasy series so that dedication is added to my growing collection of memorabilia. The actor playing Julius, the role Rupert has in the stage production, is a current heartthrob from a spy franchise so that goes down well too. I let George keep the signature belonging to the actor playing Edmund—not because I have anything against him (he's a fine RSC stalwart) but because I don't want a connection to Sylvester in my box, even at this remove.

It makes me feel better about myself that I'm enjoying vicariously the fact that George is having the time of his life. Even if I do continue to frustrate his plans to get us back together, he is riding high. The film company are using him as their expert on life at Dogberry Cottage. Sylvester always said in interviews that he used his home as his inspiration (neglecting to add that he used himself too) so they want it to be authentic. I'm happy for George to play this role, else they'd be going to my father, wouldn't they? At least I've managed to cut off that idea by telling George I have no problem with him making himself available. He is also now in possession of an advance copy of his biography. Being brave, I decide to read it and find it an easier experience than I imagined. He focuses on the early years, the unsullied Sylvester as he comes to fame, one that sets off few alarms bells for me as his work was so different in that first phase. The later years are dealt with briskly, my father's role minimised, my presence only mentioned in passing. It's a long life so there's nothing odd about this. I skip the chapter on *A Walk in Bluebell Woods*, apart from checking what was said about Keira's photos. Not much. I'm 'child of one of

Sylvester's employees', treated on a par with the fixtures and fitting of the house. He makes the muse the cottage rather than me.

I hand it back to him. 'Thank you, George.'

He looks up from his notes on the Noel Coward project he has started, having persuade Larry that it's time for a reassessment. 'For what?'

'For handling it like that.'

'You're OK with it? I found it a difficult balance when I came to correcting the second draft, knowing what I know now. I don't want to print a lie.'

'It's not the full truth but nothing is a lie.'

He bites the end of his pen. 'Ri—ight.'

'I know the researcher in you wants to do more but you just can't. Those involved will deny anything.'

'You mean you and your father?'

I was actually thinking of Sylvester's children but if his mind hasn't gone there then I won't encourage him to do so. So I shrug. I'm trying to be truthful with him. It's like my Mid Year resolution.

George sighs. 'All right then. It's a relief to know we're still OK.'

I sit down beside him and curl up my legs on the bed. He spends more time here than at his cottage near Hastings or at his parents. My attic is emptier than usual as the skeleton suits have all marched off to the Opera House and June is giving herself a Mediterranean holiday now the world is travelling again.

'We're OK. Now show me where you've got with Noel Coward.'

Viv and Bette attend Rupert's preview and come back reporting that it's a good production. The film won't be released till next year at the earliest so there's no danger of that stealing the thunder of the staged version. I'm a little surprised to see Viv has her arm threaded through her escort for the evening: Charles Collins, the artistic director whose book we launched a couple of months ago. They are having an earnest discussion about the director's decisions on various cuts and additions to *A Walk*.

'What's that about?' I whisper to Bette. 'Don't they dislike each other intensely?'

'Charles? He's an old flame. They really should just move in together and stop this shilly-shallying,' says Bette. 'It's been going on for thirty years.'

'So when we had the launch here, that was what, in a shally? Now we are in a shilly?'

Bette laughs. 'Exactly. Couldn't put it better myself.'

'I didn't know shilly-shallying could last so long.'

'Neither did I.'

Lillian, who also went to a preview, spends more time telling me about Rupert's six pack than his acting, but I don't blame her. I've seen the photos in the programme Bette insists on leaving on the counter of the shop. We try not to drool over it when she's around. The show officially opens on 28th September, the same day George's biography comes out and I've been invited to the launches for both. I brace myself for the curling wave. Excuses for not attending the first night and the launch party are getting more and more difficult to come up with; perhaps a strategic cold might do, but I feel bad about leaving my kind employers a woman down on the most important night for Last Chance that season.

George is the only one to understand my dilemma. The night before, when he comes to inspect the special exhibition of his books I've set up on the display table by the entrance, he kisses the top of my head and hugs me.

'Do what you need to do,' he tells me. 'None of us will hold it against you.'

'Viv will. She hasn't had a cold since 1982—she told me when I sneezed in front of her.'

'Apart from Viv.' I can feel his cheeks crinkling with a smile.

I hug him back. 'I hope it goes well tomorrow. I really do.'

'Enjoy your duvet day. How are you going to spend it?'

'Watching TV and reading.'

'Sounds perfect.' He gives me a final hug then heads out. He may have been a bad boyfriend but he is making an ideal best mate. Maybe we could try again?

When I wake up the next morning, I allow myself to feel a little real scratchiness in my throat. It's enough to give me cover for my conscience as I'm no longer a fan of falsehoods. I ring in and am relieved when I get Bette on the other end. She doesn't question my symptoms for a second and is full of good wishes and advice.

I end the call promising I'll make myself some lemon and honey. I actually do so, taking my duvet downstairs to set up camp on the sofa in June's living room. Wrapped in goose down, cradling a steaming mug, novel on my knee, I feel foolishly happy and about eight years old. A few hours pass in contentment, then I decide to catch the lunchtime news, and after that watch a drama serial I've been meaning to start. If I begin now, I can watch a whole season. Waving my controller like a wand, I say 'Alohomora!' as I did as a kid—I'm showing symptoms of a Potterhead, so sue me.

The news is already on. State visit. Political squabbles. Cuts in spending. War somewhere with appalling civilian consequences—all depressingly familiar scenes. Then the announcer says they are returning as promised to one of the stories in the headlines: the shocking revelation that world-renown playwright, Sylvester Sligo, stole the plot of his most famous play from a child who lived in his household.

I sit bolt upright.

The news item cuts to an interview with my father. He's holding my exercise book containing 'The Queen of Berry-doggia'—you can see the title quite clearly.

'Mr Carlisle, when did you realise that Sligo had done this?' asks the interviewer with that gentle tone they reserve for victims. Sylvester's name has been cropped to his surname with sinister emphasis on the first syllable.

'You may have heard that there's a new biography on the writer? I was interviewed by the author, naturally enough, as I was the one who knew Sylvester best in his last years. That prompted me to go back and look at the belongings I removed from the house—and I found this in my daughter's things.' He tilts the book so all can see my childish hand-writing.

'And how did that make you feel?'

Evan swallows bravely but the camera picks up on the tears in his eyes. 'I was devastated. It's all here—the fantasy that is the backbone to the play, *A Walk In Bluebells Woods*. And it made me wonder.'

'Made you wonder what?'

'What else he might've stolen from my daughter. I never understood why she blamed me for so much, and now I begin to see.'

'Are you saying...?'

'That Anna might be based on her? Yes, I am. I was so blind.' He allows a little hitch in his breathing like a man battling strong emotions.

'And your daughter? What does she think about this?'

'She's angry with me—I suppose because the guilty

party is dead. Who else can she blame? Sylvester left her the house and proceeds from the play so I believe he was trying to make amends, but that won't repair my relationship with her. She, poor girl, is quite viciously set against me—pursuing me in the courts over some small financial matters. I think her real problem is with what I allowed to happen through ignorance, nothing I actually did myself.'

My vision turns red with black edges—blood pounds in my ears. I can't breathe.

'And where is she now, your daughter? Is she all right? Is she getting help?'

'She's working here in London but I'm afraid she's not in a good place. I'd appreciate it if you spared her feelings and don't try and contact Merle at Last Chance.'

Oh my God, the man is a monster! He just gave everyone watching a hotline to me. He's stripped away my anonymity and hung me out to dry.

The reporter winds up with a short sentence or two about the new production and biography beginning the Sligo season, the question that raises about how we deal with allegations of abuse against people who are dead. She says that Evan has made extracts from the notebook available and these are on the website so readers can compare them to the passages in the play to see that he is telling the truth. Then back to the studio for the sports news.

I can't move. A howl gathers in my chest and erupts. I scrunch up the pages of my novel, rip them out, though Neil Gaiman never did anything to me. I can't...I don't know what to do with this agony.

My phone start pinging with texts. At a glance, I see it's Mr Cox but it's beyond me to reply. This is so like my father—think of the worst thing he might do, then double it. I want to murder him. Take that gun from the play and shoot him!

There's a banging on the door downstairs. My phone chimes. *It's me.* George.

Forcing my feet out from the duvet nest, I go to answer.

He looks at me. 'You know?'

I take some breaths, struggling to string coherent sentences together. 'I was watching the news. You'd better come in.'

'I'm so sorry. So sorry. I want to kill him!'

'That makes two of us.'

I go upstairs but the steps feel like the slow climb to the gallows.

'What can I do to help?' ask George desperately. He glances at the confetti I've made of *American Gods*.

'Take out a hit on him? I've got the money.'

There's a brief pause while he struggles with the fact that I might not be lying. 'OK. Anything else?'

I sit back on the sofa. He looks about at the evidence of my duvet day. 'At least you were here. Rupert tells me that the shop is besieged.'

'Good publicity for the launch, hey?' I can't help my bitter tone.

'I'll cancel it.'

I rest my head on my hands. 'No, no, don't do that. Don't let my father steal the limelight. That's what he wants.'

My phone rattles again. This time I do look down.

I've taken out an injunction against the news programme. That material he gave them is yours. They have no right to show it and will have to take it down immediately and issue an apology. Nor should your name have been mentioned even by your father. You have a right to privacy.

Not taken down before thousands of people have screen-shot-ed it. Not beeped out in time to prevent me being identified. With a sigh, I pick up the phone and reply. *Thanks. Will call shortly.*

'Oh bugger this.' George, who has been pacing, sits beside me and pulls me into a hug. 'Just tell me what I can do!'

'I don't know, George. This is what life with my father is like: one losing battle after another. I was an idiot to think I might win. I should've left as soon as he turned up.'

'We need to do something. We need to fight!'

I spread my hands. 'How? With what?'

'How about the truth?'

'The truth isn't what you think it is.' I close my eyes and allow myself to rest against his chest. His arm tightens, trying to infuse me with some of his strength.

'So tell me then: what is the truth?'

27

Sooner or later we all have to pay for what we do.
Oscar Wilde, 'An Ideal Husband'

Six years ago

I was in digs in Brixton with uni friends in my second year. Not a bad place by student standards: the usual thistle crop front garden crammed with council bins, paint peeling on the front door and windowsills, but inside it was clean—before we moved in at least—and we each had our own room. Jodie kept us all on the chores rota so it didn't descend into squalor. My friends had already gone home for Christmas when our landlord announced he was getting the boiler replaced over the holidays. Apparently the current one had been inspected and declared unsafe. That left me with little choice: I had to go home.

I'd been avoiding the place, naturally enough, now that I could. As I'd grown older, I'd come to understand just how unhealthy the relationships were under that roof and I hated to be a witness and participant in the mind games. I wished Sylvester would chuck out my father but he never did. He must've realised he was being dominated and exploited, surely? The invitations he accepted for lectures or premiers were only the ones my father wanted to go to, usually somewhere sunny or exclusive; no draughty festival tents for him. Evan awarded himself frequent bonuses as Sylvester's outstanding employee and ensured all my bills were paid too. We were throttling the man, squeezing out every last spark of life in him. He was a wreck—and I hated to see it. The anger over the theft of my story had long since faded and I'd begun to strategically forget whole swathes of my childhood—it was far easier that way. The problem I had at Dogberry these days was seeing my father slice and dice Sylvester's soul without any sign he had the least inkling what he was doing.

But of course my father knew. He had to!

Unless he believe his own fantasy of loyal servanthood? I never actually worked out if my father ever surfaced from his subterfuge to find reality.

I returned that Christmas determined that, now I was an adult, I would confront my father and see what could be done to rescue Sylvester from us. I hated being complicit in this slow strangulation.

Dad picked me up from Oxford station in Sylvester's Jaguar. He had parked in the disabled spot and got one of the special badges on the dashboard. Was Sylvester that infirm now or another scam?

'Merle, haven't seen you for ages!' my dad exclaimed for the benefit of our audience at the station. 'How've you been?'

'Fine.' I slung my bag in the back of the car. 'Still driving Sylvester's jag?'

'He doesn't drive anymore. He gave it to me.'

'Oh yeah?'

'Yes. You'll notice a big difference. Age is catching up with him.'

'What will you do when he, you know, actually dies?' Rather than stagger on in this half-life we've condemned Sylvester to, I meant.

'Oh, he's got many more years ahead, I'm sure. He'll see you through uni.'

'That was obviously my first consideration,' I drawled.

'You're worried about me?' My dad sounded surprised.

'Not in the least. You'll survive whatever happens. I was just wondering.'

My dad gripped the wheel a little tighter. He preferred it when I pretended to love him. 'He's in his twilight but that can last a very long time.'

I wouldn't put it past my father, when the day came, to keep Sylvester's dead body on ice somewhere and carry on with the pretence that he was still alive. 'Yeah, I'm sure it can.'

We pulled up to Dogberry Cottage, which was unchanged since I left for college sixteen months ago. I'd made sure I'd not been back, finding jobs during the holidays that gave me excuses. Dad would've preferred me to come home to top up the torture sessions with Sylvester but I found ways around that. This meant I lied, claiming my course required the work experience. He never bothered to check, or even ask himself, why an English degree asked students to work in retail. It was surprisingly easy to fool a professional liar.

'Sylvester, look who I have here!' My dad called out as we neared the open study door.

Sylvester was sitting gazing out at a geranium struggling on the wintry terrace.

'You should probably put that in the greenhouse,' I offered. 'The gardener once told me that they aren't very hardy.'

He looked round and smiled at me. 'That one is. Comes back every spring despite the frosts. Some things are like that. Can't kill them.' The lion of my childhood has turned into Saruman: hair longer than it should be, fingernails unclipped, eyebrows bristling dark over sharp eyes. 'You look well. How are your studies going, Merle?'

'Good, thanks.'

'You must tell me all about them. I'm getting very behind with what's what in literature these days.' He gestured to pile of books with review slips sticking out of them. 'At least they still think of me.'

'Sure. You can help me with my holiday assignment. Twentieth century playwrights. You probably knew most of them. I have to pick one and turn in a paper in the New Year.'

'I expect Merle will pick you, sir,' said my father, playing the obsequious servant.

'I doubt that very much,' replied Sylvester, gaze flicking back to the geranium. 'And who could blame her?'

This was why I hated coming home—so much history between us. Neither of us could breathe freely in the other's presence.

'I'll just go upstairs and unpack,' I said, eager to escape.

'Mrs Brampton's put clean sheets on your bed. She's looking froward to seeing you tomorrow,' my father announced to my retreating back, still playing this like it was an entirely normal holiday visit.

I waved that I had heard and took the stairs two at a time.

The next morning, I had coffee with Mrs Brampton. She

never liked to speak ill of my father in my presence but I could tell she was struggling with his way of handling Sylvester.

'We hardly see any of his old friends now,' she said regretfully. 'I'm left cooking for two. They barely need me.'

'Of course Sylvester needs you!' I exclaimed. She'd baked biscuits for me, thankful, I think, finally to have someone in the house to mother.

'Your father has a knack of putting people off, if you know what I mean? Very brusque on the telephone, he is. He says they're a bad influence on Sylvester—make him sad—but I don't know. I would think sitting staring out the window with nothing to do all day would make Mr Sligo feel sadder—and that's all he does.' She got up and poured a cup of coffee on a little tray. 'Take this to him, will you? A change of face will do him good. He must be tired of seeing my ugly old mug day in, day out.'

'None of that!' I warned her. 'He's lucky to have you.' She actually had a lovely smiley face that only got better with age in my estimation. She was an odd note in this house, living life far from the level of drama the rest of us managed. If we all wove ours into a dark theme for a thriller, she was *The Archers*' jaunty theme tune breaking through to remind us that a batch of scones had just come out of the oven.

To oblige her, I sought out Sylvester in his study. I knew my father was away for the morning, playing squash at his sport's club, membership fee part of his employment package. Maybe Sylvester didn't begrudge the cost as it got him some peace. Placing the cup on the table beside him, I took a seat in the chair opposite.

'How've you been keeping?' I could do politeness when pushed, even with him.

'Not so good, Merle, not so good.' His hands were fretting in his lap.

'I'm sorry to hear that.'

'I've been a bad man.'

There was not much I could say in response. Yes? No? Don't be silly? Instead I let my silence speak for me.

'You know what I think as I sit here?'

Really not. I shake my head.

'My artistic achievements? Negligible when it comes down to it.' He spread his gnarled fingers in a symbol of life slipping through them. 'I wanted to rival Shakespeare, did you know that?'

'Bit of a tall order, isn't it? Hubristic.'

'Hah! Yes, I'd say so. But I think everyone, if they're honest with themselves, start out wanting to do that—thinking surely someone must come along to be his equal? There've been many false dawns.'

'There have?'

'You're doing the Twentieth century. Just look at the towering ego of George Bernard Shaw! They heaped praise on him before the war but I doubt his plays will still be performed in a hundred years' time.'

'They're not performed much now.'

'Ah, then I suppose he'll be remembered as the inspiration for *My Fair Lady*. He'd hate that.'

I hooked my ankle under me, hands around my bent knee. 'I wrote about Shakespeare last term, trying to work out what made him still relevant.'

He turned to look at me. 'Oh? And did you? Did the second-year UCL undergraduate solve the mystery?'

'What do you think?'

He chuckled. Were we making a new kind of relationship between us? I wondered. We'd gone from mentor and acolyte, to betrayed and betrayer; torturer and victim; maybe now we could be, on an intellectual level, friends? It was an intriguing thought, finding that we could talk as almost equals. I remembered now with some compassion that he had been very gentle with me that day when I found out the truth about my mother, carrying me inside, drying me off with a warm towel, then reading stories to me to drive away the nightmares. There was kindness between us, as well as so much else.

'And did you reach any conclusions, Merle?' he prompted when it was clear I'd lost my place in our little scene.

What was my line now? Oh yes. 'Only that Shakespeare deserves his reputation for being for all time, whereas many others don't. Bit like you said about Shaw.'

Sylvester picked up his cup. It wavered in his hand so he used his other to brace it. He sipped, grimaced, and put it down. 'They'll forget me—and I deserve to be forgotten. Can you imagine someone raking over all this stuff up to reassess me? My future judges.' He gestured to his shelves and desk. 'No one will be interested. Best to burn the lot.'

'I used to think I was writing for posterity when I wrote in my diary.'

He tapped the rim of his cup absent-mindedly. 'Do you still keep one?'

'No. Do you?'

'Notebooks. Everything interesting about my writing is in there. I think I'll donate them.'

So he wasn't really planning to burn his legacy. There was some ego left. 'Where?'

'Would UCL like them?'

'I can't see why not.'

'They can put me in a case alongside Bentham.'

'You want to be preserved? That's gross.' I'd never liked the spooky presence of the utilitarian philosopher sitting on display in the college. His philosophy had been to be useful but what earthly use was a stuffed Victorian gentleman except as a *memento mori*?

'Lord, no. No one wants this clapped-out old body. I meant the notebooks. They are me. My writing is more real than I am.' He put the cup down aslant on the saucer. I resisted the temptation to correct it. 'It's better than me, that's for certain. A finer version, one who can control themselves.'

We sat in silence for a while as Mrs Brampton switched on the vacuum cleaner upstairs. A crow landed on the planter and wagged it tail at us like an admonition.

'You should get rid of my father, you know. He's not good for you. Sack him. Retire somewhere sunny.'

He didn't reply.

'Sylvester?'

'I heard you. And don't think I haven't thought of it.' He didn't continue but I could hear the 'but I don't deserve that' in his tone.

'So why not?'

He shook his head. 'I don't think I really understand people, for all that I made them my study.'

'My father?'

'No, I understand him. Unfortunately.'

'Then how do you mean?'

Another long silence followed. Then he spoke.

'I don't understand myself. I had a problem once. My... affections were wrongly directed. I hated myself for it. I swore I'd never do anything like that again so I cut it off—the feeling anything for anyone. Of course you can't completely get rid of passion—we're all human. So I sublimated it, you might say, by putting it all into what I wrote. I felt safer for it. But lonely—so terribly lonely.'

I had no idea what he was saying but I could tell he believed it intensely.

The crow flew off, brushing petals from the geranium. I was only surprised it hadn't carried the whole thing away in its beak. That single flower was the only thing of colour left on the terrace among the dull bricks.

'And were you—safer?'

He darted a look at me. 'Yes. I didn't put a foot wrong for years. But then, when the internet started, I lost my way again. Images—tasteful ones. There are communities who like the same thing—easy to get in touch with them. So easy. And people who produce the images—some are true artists, exploring old styles of photography. I invited one over to capture my household. I wanted that whimsy—that golden glow here. Pretty girls and boys, sunshine, eternal spring. I didn't think about you being here too.'

I hugged my knee closer to my chest. I'm no longer feeling safe in this conversation: I'm feeling trapped—powerless—how I'd felt so many times before.

'I want to say that I didn't know what she was doing, but I encouraged a small part of it, didn't I?'

That order among the bluebells to take my picture—that had been the start. I could only hiss an affirmative.

'She didn't stop there, did she?'

'I don't want to talk about this.'

'I'm sorry, Merle. I left you with her. Told myself because she was a woman, nothing would happen.'

I stood up. 'Nothing did happen. Everything was completely...nor...normal.' But it hadn't been. It really hadn't been.

Tears were trickling down his cheeks now and not the

crocodile ones my father sometimes shed. 'I've got so much to answer for.'

'There's nothing...you haven't...'

'I know what happened, Merle.'

I put my hands over my ears. 'Shut up! Nothing happened—nothing!' Because if I did not let myself remember, then that was the case.

'I'm sorry.'

I couldn't stay here. I ran from the study, past the limp decorations in the hallway, prickly holly and anaemic paper chains strangling the bannisters. At the bottom of the stairs, I could hear the hoover still running. I couldn't face Mrs Brampton—not lovely sane Mrs Brampton. This...this pollution couldn't touch her. I grabbed my coat and handbag off the coat rail and headed for the door.

Sylvester appeared in the corridor, having made the crossing from his chair to the door in the time it had taken for me to make my decision. 'I can make it right if you ask it of me, Merle. I have that much power left.'

I didn't turn to face him—couldn't. 'Why don't you just die, Sylvester? Free us all from this hell!'

With that, I walked out. The door slammed like a gunshot.

28

A youth, who yet has lived enough to know
That life has thorns, and taste the cup of woe.
M G Lewis, 'The Castle Spectre'

George is very patient as I tell him these things that I've never told anyone else. He's breathing unevenly, trying not to explode with fury on my behalf, but that makes me feel safer. At least he's feeling something normal, whereas I've spent years trying to be abnormally numb.

'What happened after that?' he asks when I fall silent.

'Oh I kept my promise. Sylvester did his best to fulfil my last command. He took to his bed and died sometime after he'd given up living. Two—three years ago, wasn't it, when he physically died?' George nods. 'I never returned while Sylvester was alive, believing I'd put it all behind me.'

'Had you?'

'What do you think? I'd been all right until I knew

someone else had seen what she did. I went immediately from there, without passing Go, without collecting two hundred pounds, to dropping out. University abandoned. Living abandoned. I existed, but barely. Both Sylvester and I were effectively dead. So no. I'd say I just dragged all the crappiness out with me, my ball and chain.' I lift my foot from the floor. 'If you squint you can see it's still there.'

He runs his hand down to my ankle and squeezes. 'Look, I've taken it off.'

'It's not as easy as that.'

'No, but we've got to keep doing that until you believe it.'

'Fine, fine. It's off.'

'Therapy would help.'

'That's what Lucinda said.'

'She knows?'

I wince. I hadn't meant to bring her into this discussion. 'Not the details—just that bad stuff went down in that house.'

'And her own father involved? That must've been a shock. Did she know or suspect what he allowed?'

Difficult territory. 'About me? No. She doesn't know me really. We've never met.'

Leaving aside the question of Fanning, am I right in thinking that you're saying Sylvester didn't...?'

'No, he didn't abuse me. He just stole my story.'

'How did he even know it existed?'

'Because when I first lived there, that first summer, we used to share what we were writing.'

'You did?' He's excited by this new snippet about Sligo. 'Down, boy!' I want to say to the researcher.

'He talked about famous writers sharing their work. Flattered me.'

'He...he groomed you?' Having just been given an excuse

to think his hero was not as twisted as my father claimed, George really doesn't want him to turn out to be a villain after all. I can understand that, but I can only help him so far.

'In a way. I think now he was encouraging me because he wanted to use me for inspiration. He saw me playing in the woods and wanted to understand what was going on inside my head.' And I think now the so-called collaboration was all a pathetic attempt to possess the innocent imagination he'd killed off inside himself; he wanted to go back to a time before he'd put a foot wrong. But I don't offer that reading to George.

'So your father's insinuations are only half right—about stealing the story but nothing else?'

'I suppose so.' He's reminded me of the impossible situation I now find myself in with the news bomb my father's detonated. 'But Sylvester isn't here to defend himself.'

George sits up a little straighter. 'But you are! That's exactly how to take over the narrative. You come forward and tell the world your own tale: you and Sylvester had a lovely creative relationship. He didn't steal from you...'

'He did!'

'I'm telling a story to help you regain the power from your father, not the truth. In this story, you edit it to say that you were delighted to collaborate with Sligo. You didn't understand the adult themes in the play at your age, but you did know he was riffing off your imagination to produce a great piece of art. That's why he gave you the rights to the play—that had been the plan all along. In short, he was a wonderful writing mentor for you. Your father, late to the party, totally misconstrued the relationship, confusing fact with fiction.'

I lay with my head on his chest for a moment, thinking it through. 'You mean beat the storyteller with another story?'

'Hell yeah.'

'I'll have to do this myself, won't I? You can't do it for me?'

He pulls a face. 'I could try, seeing how you have a cold and everything.'

I take his hands in mine, repeating the yoga move he'd once tried on me to calm me down.

'What does this mean?' he whispers, voice gone hoarse.

'Not that, pal. Not sleeping with you. I'm just trying to screw my courage to sticking place.'

'You're channelling Lady Macbeth now?'

'OK, not the best female role model. But I am going to stab my father's story with a proverbial dagger, so maybe not entirely wrong.'

'How would you like to do this?' He folds our arms so we are now both hugging me.

I twist to look up at him. 'Fancy an extra bit of publicity for your book launch?'

Shortly afterwards, June rings from Minorca.

'Is that you?' she asks urgently as I'm getting ready to take my bow before the world.

'Hello, June. How's the holiday?'

'Fabulous, until I checked the news websites. I should be there with you!'

'I'm OK. George is here.'

'Put him on the line!'

I hand over the phone and continue with my quest to find the perfect outfit. For once my resemblance to a startled pixie might play in my favour as I do still look a little like the photos the press have been using in those slideshow montages to illustrate the story. I hope they're not paying Keira Fanning for the privilege. That would be an irony too far.

'Ask June if I can raid her wardrobe!' I call over to George.

He lifts the handset away from his ear. 'She says take whatever you need.'

'Thanks, June!'

I select a green minidress. A little bit Peter Pan but maybe that's a good association? I've just flown in from extended absence in Neverland. I go behind the rack to slip it on. When I come out I hold out my arms.

'Ask her if this works.'

George takes a photo and sends it to her. 'She says it's perfect. There are green pumps in her shoe store and apparently you already know where that is.'

'It's where Cinderella left her slippers.' I go to the storage box and root through until I find the shoes she means.

George hands me back the phone.

'I told him to look after you,' says June.

'He will.'

'Wear the green Alice band and spike up your hair some more. A little bit of makeup but not Lady Netta levels.'

'Yes, Mum.'

'I should be there!' she wails. I can hear Lady Netta and Regan adding their own commentary at her end. They must be having a riot in Mahon. I hope the town will survive their invasion.

'Don't you dare cut your holiday short! We've got this,' I assure her.

'Go knock 'em dead, Merle,' shouts Lady Netta.

'That's the plan,' I reply.

I end the call and hug the phone a second. 'She didn't even ask if any of it was true.'

George hands me my coat. 'She doesn't need to. She just needs you to know she's on your side. Team Merle.'

I slip my arms into the light raincoat. 'And who's on Team Evan? Absolutely no one.' That made me feel better.

We slip into the shop through the back entrance. Viv, Bette, Lillian, and Brutus are all waiting for me in the stockroom.

'Who's minding the shop?' I ask. I can hear that the room beyond is heaving with people, come early for the launch.

'Larry's sent some people to help out,' says Viv, arms crossed. 'You look well. Cold gone?'

I'm sure I'm looking sheepish. 'I'm sorry I didn't tell you.'

'Don't be a goose. Of course you couldn't. With a father like that, I'd've shot him long before now and fled to a country without an extradition agreement. I'm surprised you're still in the same country as him.'

'So am I surprised. Every day.'

'I realise I remember him from Sylvester's house,' muses Viv. 'He always steered clear of me.'

And he had each time he came into the shop, heading out as soon as he saw her coming, I realise. But she had also answered my first question: she is the one I vaguely recall. 'You do?'

'I hung around in those circles when I dated Charles. We found the gilded youth a bit hard to take, used to laugh about it as we motored away. We had no idea what was really going on, did we?'

I shrugged. 'I'm not even sure myself. Memory is a strange thing.'

'And you were the little girl who darted around the place

like some fey creature.' She cradles my face gently. 'I didn't know.'

'Can we...talk? Later?'

She nods.

'There's so much I don't understand. Was Sylvester a monster or was he kind?'

'I'd say he was that most dangerous creature: a writer who is ruthless about his art. So a little of both. I liked him, despite the flummery of his court, if that helps?'

She doesn't know everything but neither had I. It helps to know his charm was real and not just something I made up to excuse my feelings for him.

Bette touches my arm tentatively. 'What do you want us to say, dear, about all this?'

'Oh, you won't need to say anything. I'm going to say it.'

'Good for you!'

I look around for their brother. 'Is Larry here?'

'Out there.' Viv nods to the crowd. 'He's quite good when he gets angry.'

'I'm sorry about the bad publicity.'

'It's not the publicity, Merle, it's you he's angry for.'

'Rupert's there too. He can only stay another thirty minutes before he has to get to the theatre. They're having cancellations. People don't like the...well...you know... rumours,' says Bette delicately.

'I can help with that, I think.' It is ironic, being put in the situation of denying a slur on Sylvester's reputation that I, in fact, know has a basis in truth. But that's not my battle or even my truth to tell. 'Are there press out there?'

'We can't get rid of them,' says Viv nodding. 'They claim to be staying for the book launch.'

'Can you get them to stand back a bit. I've got a statement I want to make.'

'Good girl,' says Viv. 'I'll bring them to heel, don't you worry about that.'

While she does so, I hug Brutus. 'Wish me luck.'

He licks me, but that's nothing special. He does that to everyone who puts their face close enough to him. He's not a dog with a sense of occasion.

'We're ready,' Viv calls, poking her head around the door.

Lillian gives me a hug. 'Good luck.'

'Thanks.' I look across the room at George.

'It's OK. I'll stand with you,' he says. I don't even have to ask.

'Team Merle,' I say under my breath. And I'm becoming a bit Team George now too.

I head out into the shop. It is packed. In fact, there are people on the pavement outside who can't even get in. I see Ayesha looking annoyed she can't get to be with her friends. Real guests for the book launch are squeezed out by journalists. I have to get rid of them or George won't get his due. I look for somewhere to stand but George solves that by boosting me onto the counter. It's a bit high but at least now I'm dominating the room. He gets up beside me so I no longer feel so exposed.

'You start,' I hiss, as words once again fly out of my brain with terror. The camera clicks are what do it for me. I hate them.

'Ladies and gentleman,' George begins. The hubbub dies down. He's missed his vocation as Radio Four announcer: he has a lovely speaking voice. 'It's flattering to see so many of you have come for my book launch. We'll be starting that in a few minutes time.' There are a few awkward coughs. 'But first, my friend, Merle Carlisle, would like to say a word or two to correct the record. Merle?'

'Um…thanks, George.' Heavens, I sound like a complete idiot. Dig deeper. 'I saw the news this lunchtime—the same news you all did. I'd completely forgotten that a copy existed of that little story of mine—the one that my father was so kind as to share with you without my permission. Nice of him to…er…show how bad my spelling was when I was nine.'

There's embarrassed laughter.

'Anyway, what he doesn't know is that he's got it all completely wrong. Mr Sligo, Uncle Sylvester…' the word is ashy in my mouth but it has to go this way, '…he and I shared our stories together when I was little. He was a very generous man; he encouraged my writing and read me his play as a work in progress. Not the adult stuff, but the scenes he thought I'd like.'

'He read you a play about a child abuser?' calls one rude woman from the rear.

George puts his hand on my back but I'm OK. 'Aren't you listening over there? I said he read the bits suitable to my age.' I leave it all vague. Looking back, it had been unsuitable, of course, but that doesn't fit today's story. 'My estranged father misunderstood the relevance of the fantasy I wrote. It was something I was pleased to share with Sylvester and he always promised to acknowledge his debt to me. I preferred not to be named—thanks for that, Dad—but Sylvester fulfilled his pledge by leaving the play to me.'

'He left you the house too!'

Someone has been doing her homework. 'As I said, he felt a debt to me. There's the proof.'

'Your father claims Sligo left it to you out of guilt,' shouts another reporter.

I put my hands on my hips. 'When I was at school, I remember being told to raise my hand if I wanted to ask something. I now know why teacher said it. That's what we'll do here.' A forest of hands shoots up. 'I've not finished. I want to state once and for all: I am not Anna. Nothing like that ever happened between Sylvester and myself. He created fiction. I am fact. Separate the two from now on. OK, I'll take...' I glance up at George, '...three questions before we start the book launch. If you want more answers then you'll find what you need to know in my friend's excellent book, which I've read by the way, and can endorse. Yes?' I point to a man by the door.

'Your father claims you blame him for not protecting you from Sylvester. Is this true?'

'No. Next question?'

The reporters are not dumb. They know where the bad blood lies.

'Why have you fallen out with your father then?'

'That's a matter for the courts so I can't say any more on that subject. One more question.'

'How do you think we should remember Sylvester Sligo?' This question is for someone who looks like an arts correspondent rather than a news journalist.

'You should remember him as an extraordinary talent. Those who knew him personally will remember him as their friend. I will remember him as...as the most important person in my life between the ages of nine and twenty-six.' Damned if I'll let my father claim that position. 'Now that's all the time I have for questions.' They groan and mutter. 'Look, guys, I'm basically telling you there's no news story—sorry, everyone. But stay and have a drink. Buy lots of books.'

As I turn to get down, the persistent woman at the back calls out. 'So if there's no news story, why did you disappear and only just come forward now?'

I turn back. 'Were you the least bit interested in my

whereabouts until one o'clock today? No? Well then, maybe you've got that wrong too. Avoiding my father is not the same as disappearing.' I point at her. 'I expect you to buy at least two copies of the book as you got an extra question.'

There's good natured laughter at that and I'm finally back on the floor.

'How did I do?' I whisper in George's ear.

'You've got the job—as my salesperson.' He kisses me. 'Well done.'

29

His faults can never hurt another's ease,
His crime, at worst, a bad attempt to please.
R. B. Sheridan, 'The Rivals'

There is some satisfaction in seeing my father's insinuations cut off before they have time to seed themselves into the productive acre that is Sylvester's posthumous reputation. The biography, play and film are safe. I decide not to push my resilience by attending the first night of the play after the book launch. I let George go with my blessing and I take Brutus, on Bette's suggestion, back to my room for company. We sit together, me using him as a useful backrest. I flip through the channels, stopping at the nature programmes as these are the only ones Brutus pays any attention to, ears twitching at every bark and howl. Curiosity has me checking the reception of my counter story on my phone every few minutes until I get annoyed at myself. The item has sunk from headline to footnote and disappears from view after a new round of political squabbles takes over. That's what I wanted, wasn't it? The 'nothing to see here, move along' approach.

I do get a text from Lucinda. It's short and says simply: *Good call.*

We can both live in this version of the story, the one where Sylvester retains his status and not too many questions are asked. To do otherwise would only hurt those who were hurt in the first place. Neither of us want to punch ourselves in the face.

Letting the images on the screen blur, I lay back on my doggy cushion and try to understand Sylvester, but it's an ugly place to force my imagination and I find I don't want to go there. What's that French phrase: *tout comprendre c'est tout pardonner*? If you understand everything, you forgive all. Maybe that was what Sylvester was telling me: it was impossible to understand everything in this case, so he never forgave himself. He spent the rest of his life crying out for the mercy of others, and when that was withheld, made himself vulnerable to punishment. My father was his sick accomplice in this.

But what about me? Had I forgiven myself for my part in the punishment? I'd eventually broken-down under the strain. The causes had been many: my father's heartless manipulation of me; the guilt that it had been my ignorant claim of abuse when I meant theft that opened the door to Evan's years of blackmail; Sylvester challenging me at the end to drop the veil I'd placed between me and memories of what had really happened... No, I think the straw that broke the camel's back was finding on that last visit that I felt something for Sylvester—some childish love and gratitude still. It had killed me to know that he was aware of what I couldn't bring myself to acknowledge...

I go cold even now at that thought.

Therapy. I definitely need therapy.

Brutus grunts his agreement, dislodges me, turns in a circle, and lies down again.

'Like that is it?' I grumble.

Switching off the TV, I take myself off the bed, leaving him in occupation of the rug.

A WEEK LATER, I'm organising a new delivery of books when a woman enters the shop with a baby in a sling. It's a bit young for our children's corner but she takes a seat there anyway and shifts him. Ah, she's looking for somewhere quiet to feed him. I turn away to give her privacy.

Five minutes later I hear a soft voice behind me.

'Merle?'

I look round. The woman is holding out to me a saggy baby in a blue babygro like the cub in Lion King.

'Yes?'

'I'm Rima. Would you like to meet your brother?'

Of course she is. In that no-makeup-because-I've-been-woken-six-times-last-night-thank-you-very-much look of the new parent, I'd not recognised her. I now can see the pretty, groomed brunette from the photo under the tired eyes and scrappy ponytail.

'Oh. Er...'

'Please. He's your family.'

It would be rude to refuse so I take him and settle him in my arms. The kid is very chill because he doesn't even wake up to fuss. 'You've made him drunk on milk. He's out of it.'

'Little fiend. He sleeps now when I can't!' She's trying to make a link with me, baby as ice breaker. Not a bad strategy.

I grin and put a finger in his little palm. He's perfect. Unspoiled. 'What's his name?'

'Orson.'

'Really?' Poor kid. 'So Evan hasn't moved on from film stars then?'

'We like it. It's unusual.' Her tone is defensive, as well it might be.

'He's cute.'

'All babies are cute.'

'No, I think this one is really special. Take it from me: I'm not a baby person normally but he rocks. Oh, and he blows milk bubbles.'

She whips out a muslin cloth and dabs his lips. 'He has his moments. Like his father.' She flashes me a smile as if she thinks I'll understand.

Right. I hand Orson back. 'Thank you for bringing him to meet me. I appreciate it.'

She takes him and slots him into the pouch on her front. 'Can we have a word—just the two of us? In private?'

There's nowhere nice to take a baby in the shop itself. I cross to Bette and ask if I can borrow her kitchen.

'Of course, sweetie. Does the lady need someone to cuddle the baby?' She looking hopeful. Rupert better hurry up and give her grandchildren.

'I don't think so. Actually, he's my brother.'

'Really?' She sounds thrilled for me, but then remembers. 'Oh.'

'Yes. Awkward.'

'Use the kitchen. I'll keep Viv away.'

I go back to Rima. 'Follow me. The owner is letting us use her flat.'

Rima looks across and smiles at Bette. 'Thank you.'

We go upstairs. The kitchen is tidy, all evidence of their

usual breakfast cleared away. Now that I'm at June's, Ayesha no longer brings me a croissant, more's the pity, and I can't get used to the idea that I could actually afford one if I wanted. That level of luxury is hard to command no matter what my bank account is now telling me.

'Tea?' I ask. 'Coffee?'

'Tea, please.' She undoes some buttons on the sling so she can lay the sleeping baby on her knee. 'There you go, Sunny.'

I smile into the cupboard. She's not admitting it but she's already backed off from my father's pretentious choice of name. I wish my own was as easy to adapt. Filling the tea pot, I put it down between us and get out two cups.

'Milk?'

'Please. No sugar.'

So now we really have exhausted all tea-related small talk, she's going to have to tell me what she wants.

'Merle, I wanted to talk to you about your dispute with Evan.'

And there it is. I add milk to my tea and stir. 'OK. Fire away.'

'He explained what happened—how he took control of your inheritance when you were in difficulties.' She's not meeting my eyes, apart from darting glances to read my reactions.

I say nothing, just watch her through the fragrant steam of my chai.

'He really was trying to do the best for you, even if you don't agree with how he handled it.'

'I see.' I'm feeling bad for her. I don't think she knows this is a con.

'And now that Orson's here, and you're back in touch,

we've a chance to make a new start as a family. I'd very much like you to be part of your brother's life.'

She's found my one weakness—my desire for my own people. Evan probably sniffed that out himself then sent her as his emissary. How did I not anticipate this?

'I'd love to get to know Sunny—and be there for him as he grows up.' He'll probably need me one day.

'I know, wouldn't that be great?' Rima leans forward, thinking she's persuaded me. 'He'll have an amazing older sister to come and take him out for kids' films and ice-cream.'

The picture she paints fills me with longing. But there's always a 'but' with my father. 'I'd like that too, but not at any price.'

'This isn't about money!'

'Isn't it? Pleased to hear that. Rima, I don't want to get between you and my father but there's more to this situation than you understand.'

'Can't we just talk it over as a family? Did you have to go to the police?'

'Of course I didn't have to; I wanted to.'

That floors her. 'Why?'

'If you don't know, then I'm really the worst person to tell you. I think we should talk about other things, don't you? How's Sunny sleeping?'

'Please, don't change the subject.' I can now see the financial adviser Rima rather than the new mum version who had introduced herself. 'If it's about the painting...?'

She wants to go there, does she? 'And what do you think happened over the painting?'

'That Sylvester gave it to him—and he gave it to me—but the arrangement was never official.'

'And I being the vindictive daughter swooped back in and took it out of spite? Really?'

She says nothing, just sips her tea with a righteous expression. That's exactly what she thinks. Evan has got her well and truly bedazzled. Is it better to leave her like this? At least she's happy.

But the wheels will come off the wagon eventually. They always do with Evan.

'How can I put this? The picture was part of the inventory of the house, as were two others that Evan sold without permission. He forged a letter from me.'

'He said you'd say that. I get it: you're angry with him.'

This is going to be futile so I decide not to embark down that path. I stand up and put my empty cup in the dishwasher. 'I'd better get back to work. Have you finished?'

She looks down in her cup which is still half full. I keep my hand outstretched. 'I guess I am then.' The cup goes in alongside mine.

'Thanks for coming. It was lovely to meet Sunny. I'd appreciate it if you could keep the disagreement between my dad and me out of what relationship you allow me to have with my brother but I'll understand if you want to keep your distance—at least till the case is settled.' And maybe afterwards if my father ends up in jail where he belongs.

She buttons the little boy back against her chest. 'I'll...I'll be in touch. Christening party will be in a few weeks.'

Imagine that: a family party one day, battle in court the next, just like a TV soap.

'Thanks. I'll show you out.'

As she turns to go, I find myself adding despite myself.

'Just do one thing for me, Rima, please?'

She looks at me a little haughtily. 'What?'

'Protect yourself—and Sunny. Do what you would advise a client to do to make sure their assets are safe.'

'Safe from whom?' She raises a brow.

'You don't need me to tell you really, do you?' And I show her out.

30

Indeed, as a rule, everybody turns out to be somebody else.
Oscar Wilde, 'An Ideal Husband'

There's one big cloud on my horizon that I've tried to ignore. It's been the only way I know how to deal with what I've parcelled up as my own walk in bluebell woods. I'd shut that play script and left it on a shelf gathering dust. George knows it's going to come down one day soon and is worried.

'What do you want me to do?' he asks as he gets an email from Larry asking for his copy for the exhibition brochure for Keira Fanning's show.

'How do you mean?'

'Do you want me to put in there that she's a lying twisted bitch? Do you want me to report her to the police?'

I've made polite George turn vindictive. I don't think that's a win. 'I can't talk about this, George.' I curl up on the sofa, clear of costumes for once.

'When are you going to talk about it to someone? It doesn't have to be me.'

'I'm a more stiff-upper-lip than spill-your-guts-to-a-shrink type.'

'Don't believe you. I think you're a scared-out-of-your-mind type—as you have every right to be.' He opens his reply. 'I'll tell Larry I'm not doing it.'

I press my face into a cushion. 'Don't. Take the money, write the damn piece and move on. She'll come, she'll go, a couple of obscure arts reviewers will cover the show, life will carry on.'

He types in a search to Google. I don't want to know what he's researching. 'What if she's still doing it?'

'Doing what?'

'Whatever the hell she did to you.'

I threw the cushion at him, knocking his laptop askew.

'Hey, watch it!' He clutches it to his chest.

'I've gotta go to bed.'

He checks his watch. 'It's early yet. And you're not working tomorrow.'

'Yeah. But I need sleep.' I've fire ants crawling under my skin and I'm planning on a long shower.

He puts the computer down. 'I'm sorry. It's just that I want to make things right.'

'I know what you're saying comes from a good place.' I'm looking at my toes, not at him.

'Can I at least look up some numbers for you—people who might be a good fit as a counsellor?'

'Sure.' Easy to promise that. Doesn't mean I have to contact anyone.

He looks relieved to have something positive he can do. 'I don't think I can bring myself to meet the bitch.'

'Let's drop the subject, OK?' I pick up his jacket. It was

raining when we arrived and the sky still looks gloomy as the sun slips away.

'See you tomorrow?'

'I'll ring you.' I escort him downstairs. At the bottom he leans down to take his normal goodbye kiss but I step back. 'Not today, OK?'

He digs his hands in his pockets. 'OK.'

'Nothing personal.' But how can he take it otherwise?

I want to kill the photographer—or at least strangle the one in my memories. Kick her out of my subconscious so she can't invade again.

Once he's gone I grab my keys and phone. I won't get rid of this feeling until I confront it. I jump on the Bakerloo service and go northbound to Paddington. Forcing myself not to think about what I'm doing, I head for the overground trains and get on the first service to Oxford, summoning an Uber ride to meet me at the other end. Having money is something I'm still not used to.

The driver is waiting outside the station.

'You know where you're going?' I ask as I slip in the back.

'Had to look it up, but I think so.' He indicates that he's pulling out. 'It'll take about forty-five minutes.'

'I can help if you get lost near the end. I know the lanes.' I then lean against the window and pretend to sleep. Conversation is beyond me.

It's night when we pull up outside the gates.

The driver looks down the dark drive, then back at me. 'Do you want me to wait?'

'No, it's fine. It's my place.'

'Oh, OK. Goodnight.' Thankfully a driver from Oxford has no idea what lies at the other end. It could be a caravan in the woods for all he knows. I certainly don't look like I own a house.

I wait until the taillights disappear around the bend before going to the gate.

Damn, it's got a new padlock. The film company's been taking liberties. I hook my thumbs in my belt loops and laugh at myself. Shut out of my own mansion. I'm not a con man's daughter for nothing though. I can climb a gate if needs be. With a groan, I boost myself up on an iron curlicue, lucky that my foot fits between the bars. At the top there's some arrow points to negotiate. I get one poke in the inner thigh which makes me curse but as my jeans don't rip I'm not badly hurt, just bruised. I grip the bottom of the arrows to swing down, hang for a second, then drop to the ground.

As I walk down the drive I'm composing pissed off emails to the producers. I feel a little less angry when I notice that they've weeded the approach and laid new gravel. Nice. I walk around the house, though that's not why I'm here. New pots have appeared on the steps with fancy bay trees that have twisted stems. Sylvester would never've let anything like that by his front door. He'd've found it very pretentious. I peer in at the windows. The curtains are now drawn back but with no lights on it's hard to make out how much they've done inside. I can see big coils of cable snaking across carpets to lighting rigs and the furniture has been shifted about. I'd stipulated that they put any personal items in my bedroom and made that a no-go zone, so I wonder which room they've chosen as Anna's. I lean back and look up. My money is on Evan's old one. I should've asked George but until coming here I hadn't been much interested in the details.

I go round the side. The pantry window has been mended so there's no easy entry even if I did want to go in. The terrace has been weeded too with lush planters now replacing the tired ones that had struggled here. I wonder what they've done with the brave geranium. Maybe it will be back once they leave? I should've stipulated that in the contract. The furniture too is new—white wrought iron rather than Sylvester's worm-ridden wooden set. Maybe health and safety meant they couldn't risk their actors' expensive bottoms on those chairs.

I sit down on one and look out across the lawn to the wood. It almost surrounds the house, apart from one boundary on the north side that gives onto a pasture. Sylvester had once described it like a cupped hand cradling Dogberry Cottage; I think of it more like a fist squeezing.

But I shouldn't bear a grudge against a bunch of trees. That's just childish. I have to see past my own experiences and recognise that they're just trees and, in fact, I own a bloody good nature sanctuary. It's a safe place for many species now even if it hadn't been for me as a child.

'Get over yourself, Merle,' I whisper.

A light floods the terrace, startling me. It doesn't have lights like that. Not normally. One of the French windows opens and a security guard steps out, walkie-talkie to his ear.

'Yeah, found the intruder. Sitting on the terrace, cool as a cucumber. OK. Yeah. Tell them I'll keep her here.'

Now my racing heart has subsided a little, I don't turn to look at him but keep my eyes fixed facing forwards. 'If that's you telling your buddy to call the police, I really wouldn't do that.'

He laughs. 'Miss, you're trespassing. I'm just doing my job.'

'Put here by the film company?'

'Yes. Sunshine and Showers Productions.'

'And did they provide you with any information about the owner of the property?'

He lays a hand on my upper arm. 'Come along. You can tell your story to the police.'

'Take your hand off of me.'

He grips tighter. 'Don't make this any more difficult than it should be.'

I pull back a finger—that usually works. He curses. 'I said: don't touch! I own this house so you get the hell away!'

He starts to sneer but something in my expression must've warned him that would be a bad move. Lifting the walkie-talkie, he speaks to his partner. 'Stu, the intruder says she's the householder. Is there any way in which that might be the case? Doesn't look like one—not much more than a kid. Do her parents own it?'

I don't catch much of the answer that comes back among the crackles and pops but I do hear his 'oh shit'.

'Yeah, yeah, she has got short blonde hair. No, I don't watch the news. Bloody depressing. Right. Will do.'

He takes several steps back and clears his throat. I preempt the apology.

'It's OK, I get it, just doing your job. Now piss off—and turn that light off. Go back to watching sport or whatever the hell it is you do.'

'Yes, Miss Carlisle.' He retreats back inside and the floodlight clunk off.

I wait for my night vision to return. The interruption has thrown me off my stride. This has been a private moment of reckoning and now I know I'm on CCTV—that's bloody appropriate come to think of it. It's so bad it has to be funny.

OK, enough brooding. I came here to go into the woods so that is what I'll do.

I walk down the steps, waiting for the tilt on the bottom one. It doesn't come. Someone has finally fixed it. I could take it as a good omen but I'm not superstitious. I cross the lawn and enter the wood by the little path I usually took. This too has been cleared by the crew—no brambles to cut my ankles. See, Merle, life moves on. This isn't the same wood as it was when you were nine. Many of the trees are different, saplings now mature, old ones felled or rotted away. The bark you once touched would long ago have been shed.

I head for the old bluebell clearing. This is where the filming would be taking place so it's easy enough to find. I stand in the middle of the flattened ground and listen. The wood is full of noises at night—rustling, rushing, the faint cry of an owl—that hasn't changed, but I don't find it disturbing. Nothing ever happened at night; the day was far more troubling.

So I let myself remember. I take out each memory and lay it out like a shell on a nature table. It's mine but separate. I can look at the twisted threads of shame, shyness, fear, powerlessness, desire to please for what they are. The poor kid had no say. She was doing what she was told, as she had been taught to do when asked by an adult, particularly someone holding a camera.

That's right, sweetie. As nature made you. Lie down. Now kneel. Look happy. You like this, don't you? Playing outside. Your pretty skin – your hair – no need to be shy. You're perfect. Show me how perfect you are. Exactly.

Fanning had probably thought it was art. It didn't seem to excite her any more than a life drawing class does a room of art students. Yet it was all so very wrong. She had to know that her customers weren't art connoisseurs but men with prurient fantasies. In a world of con artists, she conned herself. Had she even to this day questioned what she did, riding roughshod over my innocence?

A child's fantasy life is a fragile thing, a place of exploration of body and spirit. Am I a hero? Am I clever? Am I brave? Am I pretty? An adult entering that space tips the balance from being a voyage of discovery to a show for the onlooker. In a way, all that sharing of the funny sayings and cute pictures of kids on social media treads on this path, turning the child into a product for a proud parent to display—fine for friends and family, maybe, maybe not, but definitely not for the world to watch. I'll never post a single image of any of mine for strangers to see—not that I think I'd ever be in the right place to have kids. I'd want to leave their butterfly uniqueness a private matter, not crush their wings with my heavy-handed desire to capture and preserve it. It's not clever.

But neither is it the worst abuse of a child's trust, I know that. Lucinda lived through something much worse. But I allow myself the right to feel bad. It was my experience, my trauma, to have the most precious thing I had in my messed-up life—my escape into fantasy—taken from me, posed and sold over and over. She didn't touch me but the camera did. She taught me to feel odd about my body and my hair in particular. That she had a strange fascination with, getting me to curl it this way and that over my little shoulders, spreading it out on the ground like a fan. Butterfly pose, she called it. But she didn't just bruise my wings, she tore them off and left me trapped inside the squeezing hand of the woods.

And she should pay for that.

31

Then the law to him
Is like a foul, black cobweb to a spider—
He makes it his dwelling and a prison
To entangle those that shall feed him.

John Webster, 'The Duchess of Malfi'

I suppose it takes a certain courage to face your demons because they don't go away just because you acknowledge them while sitting at midnight in a wood. They hop and grin before you, spoiling the nicest views in daylight; or they edge in, tugging at your consciousness like needy children, begging you to 'look at me, look at me'. As soon as you do pay them attention, they spring on you and bite into your chest and rip out great chunks of your heart. I know I'm far from alone in travelling the world with my own pack of devils. Maybe most people have one or two? Travelling on the Underground on the way back from Paddington station, I look around the carriage. I can't diagnose who has them and how many but I'd wager that several of my fellow passengers will be pursued by ones brought about by grief and loss, others by loneliness, mental or physical trauma, and then there are those that are self-inflicted, the addictions and cruelties that bring their own penalties. If I could invent a camera that could capture these invisible presences, then this train would look like it was travelling in one of Dante's circles of hell, not the Bakerloo Line.

It's amazing any of us are still standing.

Gliding up the escalators at Charing Cross, I try to dissect my feelings to get down to the root that feeds these devils, but it so hard to do this on my own as I keep drowning in the emotions. Trying to make sense this way is like asking a person capsized from a life raft to analyse the sea so they can find a way back on board. They are too busy surviving to do more than flail and blow their emergency whistle.

I pass through the ticket barrier and take the stairs up to Trafalgar Square. The crowd is building behind me in the rush hour storm surge. After sleeping in the greenhouse at Dogberry, I travelled early in the morning. It's still early now —the square is owned at this time by commuters and pigeons. The flocks of tourists will come later. I'm in no hurry so I sit on the edge of one of the fountains and let the workers flood past. The sun is out, making the shallow water of the pool a Mediterranean turquoise. London sometimes does this on fine days: it suddenly forgets the rain and fog and pretends it is a city of exteriors in a warmer climate, a place to congregate and take in the pavement life. Two young men in hi-viz jackets stop and strip off their top layers to display freckled northern skin. Some girls have peeled off their tights; they sit on the ledge of the fountain, and wave painted toenails in the air, chatting how they got their clothing choice wrong when they left the house this morning in the distant cloudy suburbs.

I breathe, allowing myself full consciousness of what it is like to be alive.

This is now.

That was then.

There are philosophical questions as to how much of me is that girl from the past. My cells have nearly all changed by now so in a material sense the majority of me is something else. There are die-hard cells in brain and heart, but otherwise we are like a beach, swept clean every decade or so. Does that help?

No, not really. I look at the fountain, dancing in the sunshine. The droplets of water are different every second but the shape remains fairly constant. Me—we—are more like that, a pattern that is formed by our experience. I can't disown the little girl as a 'not me' just because I find her experiences hard to look at.

One of my demons bites my ankles. *Look in the camera, sweetheart. Look. Smile.*

This isn't about you, I think. *Go away.*

My phone vibrates. A message from George. I decide to call him rather than reply.

'Hey, George.'

'Merle, are you OK? June said you didn't come home last night.' Of course, they'd be worried after my last walkabout. I should've messaged her.

'I'm fine. I went to Dogberry Cottage and had a run-in with the security guard.'

'Seriously?'

'Yeah. It was great fun making him back down. I did the "do you know who I am?" routine on him.'

'And was everything, you know, all right?'

'Apart from the film people padlocking my gate, then yes.'

'They haven't?'

'Oh yes, they have.' I pause. 'That's the bit where you're supposed to say, "oh no, they haven't".'

He huffs. 'I hate pantomime.'

I grin. 'Had to climb over—not fun.'

He hesitates, wondering if he should ask me any more. A child, released from a pushchair, runs by me and reaches her hands towards the fountain. Her dad lifts her up so she can reach the pool and she laughs as she splashes the water. Beautiful. I move away to give them privacy.

George comes down on the side of leaving sensitive subjects alone on a phone call. 'So, Merle, are you going to work?'

'Yes, later. I need a shower first.' I rub at a green stain on my jeans.

'Shall I come by at lunchtime?'

'I'm seeing the lawyers again. They sent me an email saying they had news.' I'd picked this message up on the train.

'I could come with you—if you want me to.'

'Thanks. Yes, that would be nice.' I move into the shadow of St Martin's-in-the-fields.

'Any idea what the news might be?'

'None. Not a clue.'

'OK then. Let's hope for the best and prepare for the worst.'

'Good philosophy. See you at one?'

'One o'clock. Love you.' He ends the call before I can tell him off for going there. Does he really love me? Doubtful. Not only because the origins of our relationship are hopelessly twisted up in his passion-project on Sligo, but also because, to be frank, there's not very much that's loveable about me. I participated in the mental torture and extortion of Sylvester from the age of eleven to twenty-one—or as I now know from my birth certificate, ten to twenty. I might've been forgiven at the start due to my age but, once I reached adulthood, I should've put a stop to it — or walked out earlier. I have unresolved issues because someone exploited my innocence and put my image on display without my consent. Fanning left me with a hatred and fear of my own body that surface when I feel low. I was mentally abused by my father—yes, I can say that now, for that was what his hall of mirrors personality resulted in. I'm a survivor. I'm not kind—not like Bette, Viv and June. George really can do much better than me.

MR COX HAS SENT out for a sandwich lunch for us so our meeting happens in a little dining room they have for entertaining clients. I take this as a good sign. If he were delivering bad news, he'd probably not want me to have my mouth full of mozzarella and basil focaccia.

He pours me some sparkling water as Luke offers around a selection of savouries.

'Miss Carlisle...' says Mr Cox.

'Please, call me Merle.'

He smiles. 'In that case, I'm Francis. Merle, your...I mean, Evan Carlisle has come to us with an offer to settle the case.'

'I thought this was now in the hands of the police?'

'It is. But if he can tell them he's making restitution and coming to a private agreement with you, then they might reduce or even drop the charges against him. He won't want a criminal conviction.'

'And what's his offer?'

'Repayment of the money taken out of your share of the estate, to be made in instalments over fifteen years. He can't afford to repay the total amount, most of it's long gone, but he's suggesting he pay fifty percent and you forgive him the rest.'

'I see. And what do you think?'

'I think, if your aim is the return of the money, then this is the best offer you're going to get. I believe his wife is behind the suggestion as she is the one with the assets in the relationship. Mr Carlisle appears not to be in regular employment.'

'In other words, Rima is paying for his mistakes and he walks away without a record?'

'You could put it that way.'

'She would probably prefer the father of her child isn't saddled with a criminal record,' says George. 'That's got to be worth a lot to her.'

I don't disagree but it is infuriating that my father walks off once more, like the action hero chucking the grenade over his shoulder and emerging from the explosion with just the merest ruffling of his hair as he strides coolly away. My gut instinct—and it's an ugly one—is to say 'suffer, Evan, suffer' but what about Orson and Rima?

I take a deep breath. Then another.

'I need a will.'

'I'm sorry?' My sudden statement takes Mr Cox by surprise.

'Evan pointed out the other day that if I die then my estate goes to him as my closest relative. I can't have that.'

'Do you think you're in danger?' asks George.

'Not really—not like that. Though I wouldn't stand near the edge of the platform if I was with him and a train approaching.' I say it as if I'm joking, but actually, I'm not. 'I just need to know he won't benefit.'

Mr Cox makes a note. 'We'll get on that right away. Who do you want the estate to go to?'

'It should go back to Sligo's children. Fold it back into their inheritance in equal shares.'

He nods. 'That's simple enough. You have no dependants at the moment, so I can't see any legal problems.'

'You mean children? No.'

'I'll get that done.' He catches Luke's attention, who is caught mid samosa.

Luke swallows quickly. 'I'll send you a draft by close of play.'

'Thank you.'

'And the offer?' asks Mr Cox.

'What's your advice?'

He rubs the bridge of his nose in thought. 'Well, you might be able to get an improved offer if we go back to them.'

'Squeeze them for more money?'

'Yes.'

That's what my father would do in my shoes so it's probably the wrong course of action.

I turn to George. 'What do you think?'

'It depends if you want your day in court. What would that do for you?'

He's right. I need to think about how this will affect me, rather than my father. Do I need that catharsis? My father is a bad man and I want society to punish him? And with Evan's ability to squirm even on the hook, he might find a way of turning it back on me. I can imagine him putting my character on trial as an excuse for making the financial decisions he did. Did I want all that grief played out in public?

'You don't need to give me your answer right now,' says Mr Cox. 'Evan Carlisle's lawyers have given us a week to answer their letter.'

I decide to take that time. Even if my answer is forming, in this time of doubt, my father will be suffering. Briefly, I'll hold the upper hand, so I should enjoy it. I'm really not that nice a person.

'OK, I'll tell you by Friday.' I get up to leave. 'Do you know where the paintings are?'

He pulls a face. 'Unfortunately, we think they left the country.'

Another question answered. I'm not getting them back. In fact, this experience is teaching me that life only moves forward. Looking back down the trail you've come is only helpful in so far as it shows you where to go next. Move on.

I HAVE a lot to think about and June's flat is often too busy for quiet reflection. Bette and Viv let me stay behind in the shop after hours with Brutus for company. I say I'm dusting the shelves but not much of that gets done. I spend most of the time with my arms curled around Brutus as we huddle in the children's corner.

'What did you feel like when you were abandoned?' I murmur. 'I bet that sucked.'

He licks my face, which is not a very pleasant experience as he has bad breath, but I take it in the spirit in which it is offered. Knowing Brutus, he probably sat on the corner on which he had been left with his injured paw in the expectation that things would look up. And they had: Bette had found him.

I have a little more agency than a dog, of course. Sitting here on the floor, I'm looking directly across the shop at Sylvester's shelf, which is also low down. I circle back to *A Walk in Bluebell Woods* and the decision Anna makes not to shoot. It is much easier to hold off squeezing the trigger when the person who has wronged you is remorseful. You can tell yourself they in some way are ready to be forgiven. Maybe that wasn't what Sylvester believed though? Edmund in the play is riven with guilt but that is exposed mercilessly by the writer as another part of his selfishness. Sylvester was aware of his own contradictions. Edmund still sees what he did as his wrong, his drama. He hands the responsibility for his punishment to his victim, making her a victim again in another way as she has to take charge of the burden of his fate. When she refuses to fall into the role of score-settler, that's when she is truly free of him at last. It's not so much that she forgives him as she says that she no longer needs to live out her life through his.

Forgiveness, or perhaps more accurately, letting go of past wrongs, is more about healing the victim than helping the victimiser.

Maybe this is the hard-won wisdom of forgive us our sins as we forgive those who sin against us?

Catching myself in the middle of this serious thought, I have to laugh. Oh my word, had I just reduced centuries of religious and philosophical thought to a Disney 'Let it Go'? I rub my nose into Brutus' ruff of fur.

OK, I can live with taking the deal. What I'll do, though, is put the money—which I realise is really Rima's money at this point—into a fund for Orson. I don't need it, thanks to the continued popularity of the play. The pictures I'll just have to give up for lost, but as I hadn't been as attached to them as the John Piper I can shrug that off.

But I'm not going to tell anyone my decision until a minute before the deadline. Evan needs to squirm a little longer.

There's an insistent knocking at the front door. Checking the clock, I see that it's nine so it can't be a late customer. Whoever it is must've seen the light on inside.

I get up, pins and needles in my calves. I give them a quick rub to get the circulation flowing. 'Brutus?'

He heaves himself up too and follows me to the door.

A man I don't recognise is standing in the funnel shaped opening where I once slept. He looks in his late sixties, but still handsome, a bit too rough to be called a gentleman. Short grey hair, scruff of a beard framing a square jaw, clear blue eyes—I feel as though I might've met him before. I don't rush to open the door, however, because he looks angry, something I can tell thanks to the scowl lines at the top of his nose.

'I'm afraid we're closed,' I say through the glass.

He bangs on the doorframe again. 'I'm here to see Bette. Let me in!'

'She's not in the shop right now. Come back tomorrow during opening hours.' I happen to know Bette is upstairs but something tells me she wouldn't thank me for letting this man inside.

'Open the fucking door, love.' He bangs again.

'Shut the fuck up, mate,' I fire back, losing patience with him.

Brutus growls.

The man glares at me, then to my surprise he gives up and strides off.

'What the heck was that about?' I murmur, giving Brutus a calming scratch. I'd better go and warn Bette that someone is looking for her so she can take steps to protect herself.

But I'd underestimated the persistence of the man. Brutus' bark comes a second before I hear the crunch of the backdoor being kicked in. I haven't yet armed the alarm so the sisters don't know that their perimeter has been breached unless they've heard the noise we're making. I have to get to the stairs before he does.

Dashing across the shop, I yell:

'Viv, Bette!'

Brutus barks but fails to live up to his job description of guard dog when he doesn't go for the man as he comes out of the stockroom. He runs up and barks, then backs off, scared rather than aggressive. I don't blame him for looking afraid: the man is wielding what looks the umbrella my father abandoned after the book launch. Bloody typical for Evan to arm my enemies. He's holding it the wrong way round so he can use the wooden knob as a club. Despite this, I straddle the staircase.

'Get out of here! You're trespassing!'

'Bette! Bette!' the man shouts, ignoring me. 'You'll fucking pay for what you did!'

Viv's voice comes from behind me. Thank God, I'm not alone. 'William, you've gone too far this time. Get out at once!'

'No I won't, bitch.'

'I've called the police.' This comes from Bette who is out of sight. She sounds terrified which makes me even angrier. He's not getting through me to hurt her.

The man—William—Bette's ex I now realise—completely loses it on hearing her voice. He takes a swing at me with the umbrella. I turn my back so the blow falls there rather than on head as he'd aimed. Pain shoots up my spine.

'Leave her alone!' bellows Viv. 'She's nothing to do with this!'

Bette screams.

The strikes finally makes Brutus attack but he goes for the umbrella rather than the man. William gives it up, disconcerting the dog who was prepared for a tug-o'-war. He seizes me around the neck.

'Get Bette down here, or I'll break the girl's neck!'

I stamp on his foot, but his arm has me clamped tightly to his chest. Hefting me off my feet, he pushes me up the stairs like a shield wall used to storm a castle. I scratch his hands, try to pry his fingers off, but I'm also gasping for breath, my counter-attacks losing power.

'Bette, you bitch, what did you say to her?'

Bette is hovering on the landing at the top of the stairs in great distress as she sees us come towards her. Viv hasn't unblocked the way but is slowly backing up before us.

'Let Merle go, William. She can't breathe!' says Viv.

Black spots are swirling in my vision. I hurt all over—lungs, neck, back...

William barely registers me or Viv. His gaze is fixed on Bette. 'What did you do?'

'I warned that poor woman that you were violent, that you put me in hospital three times, and that she should know this before she married you!' Bette manages to sound both defiant and terrified at the same time.

'She left me!' His howl is one of agony.

'Good. Then she's safe,' Bette hisses back.

'Let Merle go!' Viv now has a weapon of her own: a heavy book. She looks ready to swing it at his head. We've almost reached the top.

'I'll let her go.' Then tossing me behind him, he throws me down the stairs and lunges towards Viv.

32

I can't go on, I'll go on.
Samuel Beckett

Consciousness is a funny thing. Floating, not-quite-there, but strong enough to connect me to the here and now. Like a cobweb. I register that my head is on a pillow, my neck in a brace, and my arm strapped across my chest.

Then I float away.

WHEN I COME BACK, I'm still feeling strangely light. Must be drugs as my brain is telling me that I'm really not all right. I'm in hospital for one thing and I haven't been in one since I had pneumonia. I can tell this from the noises around me, the clatter and conversation of a public building. My bed space is in twilight with curtains drawn but I think it might be day outside. I can't turn my head but I do manage to shift my gaze to my right. George is sitting in a chair beside me, reading.

Reading? That's OK then. If I were at death's door I hope he would at least be hovering over me and clutching my hand while he sobbed over my inert form.

'George?' I rasp.

'Merle!' He dumps the book on the bed and brings a cup with a straw to my lips. 'The nurse said you would be thirsty. They had to do a general anaesthetic to operate.'

I am. I obediently take a drink while I wonder quite what they operated on.

'You'll want to know what happened?'

I pull away from the straw. 'Yes.'

'You were pushed down the stairs.'

I roll my eyes as I have a limited range of movement. 'I know that part.'

'You landed on Brutus.'

'No! Is he all right?'

'He's being checked out but we think he did better than you. You smashed your arm against the wall as you went down. Broken wrist.'

'Neck?'

'Just a precaution. They think you banged your head too but they've not spotted any sign of anything serious beyond bruising and a bump. They'll be keeping an eye on you in case of concussion but the dog saved your life, we think.'

I shut my eyes. It'd been that close. There was I all wrapped up in my own drama when it was someone else's life crisis that blew me up. Experience isn't neat like stories suggest but full of random events that end up reshaping it unexpectedly.

Or maybe not so random? If I'd been paying more attention, I should've picked up on the hints that Bette had a difficult past and still carried the burden of it. She'd not become a single mum because she thought it a fun thing to do. I wonder if she is OK? I missed out on how that all ended. I'd come to in the ambulance but there had been no chance for questions.

'Bette? Viv?'

'They're fine. Viv threw a big book at William and held him off with a kitchen chair, then the police arrived. He's been arrested. They'll want to see you later.'

'Who? Bette and Viv or the police?'

'Both. All of the above.' George takes my hand. 'Don't do that to me again.'

'What? Fall down the stairs and land on a hairy crash mat?'

'No. Don't be a hero. Viv would've protected Bette. She has before, she says.'

'So there was no need for me to rush in and try and stop him going upstairs? That's rubbish, George. I don't have that in me. You had to be there. William looked like he'd take her apart with his bare hands.'

'And instead, our little caped crusader took him on.'

'I don't wear a cape.'

He brushes his thumb over the back of my hand. 'No, you don't need one.'

'I'd only trip on it. Or strangle myself.'

He raises my hand to his lips and kisses it. 'You were very brave. I don't mean to take that away from you. I just don't want you hurt.'

'I'm not exactly over the moon about that myself. And there was I just thinking I'd have a quiet evening of contemplation.'

George offers me the drink again but I lock my lips against the bump of the straw. He moves it away.

'Can I sit up?'

'I'll ask.' He goes to the nurses' station and gets the go-ahead. We work out how the bed works with the electric control and I feel a lot better to be facing the world rather than staring at the ceiling. I'm in a four bed ward. Two of the beds are empty and the other is occupied by a girl who looks in a worse plight than me with her leg hoisted in one of those rigs for compound injuries. She has headphones on so George and I have privacy for our conversation.

'Where am I?'

'St Thomas'. You've actually got a great view. Do you want me to move back the curtain?'

'Please.'

He's right: I have a view across the river to parliament and Westminster.

'Worth every penny of your tax payer contributions,' he says.

I grimace. 'I don't think I've paid tax yet. Not yet been part of the system.' That is another thing I have to sort out.

'What about your inheritance?'

True—the lawyers had probably been keeping on top of that. One more surprising aspect of my life that I have to thank Sligo for: my part as a responsible citizen contributing to worthy things like the NHS. 'Do they say when I'll be let out?'

'The doctor will see you on his round and boot you out if you're OK.' He taps my nose. 'No malingerers. We've all said we'll make sure you're not left alone.'

'Oh no, I'm going to be cosseted, aren't I?'

'I think that's a certainty.'

There's nothing I can do but submit to the process that began with the push down the stairs. A day later, I'm assessed and declared out of danger, bundled up by George in a wheelchair I don't need, and pushed to my taxi ride home. I realise that this is more about him finding a way to vent his fear and concern than the true state of my health. He has the compulsion to look after me, so I let him.

June, Viv and Bette are all waiting for me at the flat. George carries me upstairs—again refusing to let me walk—and places me on my bed. Cushions are immediately found to prop me up and I then have to face my worried chorus of surrogate mothers. Fortunately, it is Viv who starts with her usual bracing tough love.

'You look grim, dear. That bruise is going to turn into a black eye.'

'Oh, I don't think so, Viv,' says Bette, getting confused as she offers me tea, tissues and biscuits, all in a flurry of concern to make me comfortable. I take the tissues, and refuse the tea and biscuits.

'I've got makeup that will cover the worst,' says June. 'And a bright scarf will cover the neck cushion. How long did they say you were to wear that?'

'At least twenty-four hours,' says George.

But it is itchy and my neck feels fine. I've never been one for rules, even if coming from a doctor. I reach up with my uninjured hand, unfasten it and toss it aside. Immediately I feel much better.

'Merle!' gasps Bette.

'It's fine. If I get a headache, or if my neck hurts, I'll put it back on. But I can't see it's doing much good while I'm lying down.'

'What if…?'

Viv puts a hand on her arm. 'Bette, it's Merle's decision.'

'But I got her hurt!' Bette wails.

'You did no such thing!' snaps June. 'It was that monster you married.'

'Bette, you had nothing to do with it,' I say. 'How's Rupert taking it?'

Bette sits at the end of the bed. 'He's upset but he knew what William was like long before today. He said to tell you how sorry he was.'

'Not his fault either.'

'Will you tell him that yourself? I think he needs to hear it.'

So Bette, to worry about saving others. 'Of course I will, and you need to hear it too. Bette, I repeat, this is not your fault. Can I see Brutus? Where is he?'

'He's with Lillian at the shop. Of course you can see him. I'll get Rupert to bring him over this afternoon.'

'He's the real hero of the hour.' I smile at the thought of Brutus in his cape and mask. 'I bet you didn't guess that would happen when you rescued him?'

Rupert, like his mother, is undeservedly shame-faced when he arrives with Brutus. The dog bears me no grudge for landing on him, gives me a sniff, then curls up for a sleep at my foot. Rupert sits gingerly on my visitor's chair at my bedside. I'm struck again how extravagantly handsome Rupert it—not how I imagined Julius as a child though. My vision then was more boy band cute than adult actor gorgeous.

'How's the play going?' I ask him to shift him from apologies about his monster of a father.

'Merle, I…' His tawny head is lowered like a young lion at bay.

OK so that hadn't worked. 'Look, Rupert, your father sucks. So does mine. We have that in common.'

'Oh.'

'Mine never pushed me down a flight of stairs, but he

did hang me out to dry by revealing my secret on national TV.'

'God, yes, he's a bloody psycho. I'd forgotten.' His head goes up, showing his profile that would make sculptors swoon.

'He's not worth the emotional energy so I try not to think about him. You might like to do the same for yours.'

Rupert pats his thigh twice, in a quick motion of decision taken. 'Yes, you're right. The play? We've got ninety percent advance ticket sales and usually end up with a full house with last-minuters. Reviews have been good.'

I smile. 'Liar. They've been stellar.'

He smiles sheepishly. 'OK. Extremely good.'

'I saw you mentioned as every woman's fantasy.'

He laughs, then stops. 'I've not really thought of this before, but since the story about your writing relationship with Sligo came out, I suppose I have you to thank for my character?'

'In a way—but in a way not.' I explain how I'd seen the story in fairy tale form, not fleshed out, how the playwright had taken it and fashioned it for his own ends. 'I'm learning to think of it like a riff played on an idea I once had.'

'Meaning you haven't always seen it like that?' Rupert is more than just a pretty face.

'Has George been talking to you?'

He shakes his head. 'Not about this. I promise.'

'I wasn't always at peace with Sylvester's use of my material.' Understatement of the year. 'But I think I can see that he's done something much more interesting with it than I ever imagined. After all, I was only nine at the time.'

'So he did steal it from you.' Rupert nods as if I've confirmed something for him. 'We've discussed this in the cast. None of us think it right that he took this and kept it so close to your original idea. If he needed a source, why not see the outline, the style that belonged to you, and come up with his own version?'

After all these years, I'd never thought of that. 'You're right. The bastard.'

'Perhaps he was too lazy, or maybe as an artist he had a ruthless magpie nature.'

I can buy the ruthless side. Whatever my mixed feeling about Sligo I never forgot that tough core that kept going under a treatment from my father than would've broken weaker men much earlier. In fact, it wasn't my father who broke him, was it? It was me. It was me he listened to, not Evan, when he finally gave up.

'Merle? You look...well, you look like you've seen a ghost or something.' Rupert touches my hand. 'Do you need anything?'

I squeeze his fingers. 'No, just realised something. Not important.'

'I don't believe that.'

'OK, I meant it's something that only means anything to me.'

'Hmm, right.' He still sounds doubtful. 'The cast wondered...when you feel better, that is...if you'd like to be the guest of honour at one of our shows?'

Would I? Now the truth, most of it, is out there, do I want to go?

'I've never seen the play, you know?'

'Really? Maybe I'm not surprised. I don't rush to shows when someone else is given the role I auditioned for.'

I smile. 'Yes, that's it exactly.'

'Think about it. We'll find a seat for you any time you feel ready for it. We're doing a gala performance for Keira Fanning to mark the opening of her exhibition. Perhaps you'd like to come to that one. You know her a little, don't you?'

'General Ariek?' Part of me wants to run screaming, but the other is feeling it's time to face down my enemy.

'*She's* General Ariek?'

'Keira backwards.'

'God, I'm slow!' He slaps his forehead.

'Yeah, and so are the critics. I've never seen anyone make the connection.'

'The clicking noise and bug-eyes, bloody obvious now I see it.'

I shrug. 'Well, I wasn't going to tell anyone, was I?' I flex my toes. Am I up to this? 'When's the gala?'

'Week Saturday.'

'OK, I'll be there. And...and do you think I could say a few words before the performance starts, a kind of introduction?'

'Oh, er, I think...I'll have to ask of course but I'm thinking the cast will love that. More press attention as you speak in public for the first time since you came out of the shadows.'

ALL I NEED NOW IS a gun. Fortunately, there's a rich business man with a collection and I know the person with access to a key.

33

Now she's playing with pistols again.
Henrik Ibsen, 'Hedda Gabler'

I avoid Keira Fanning at the reception held between the opening of her exhibition and the gala performance despite Larry's best efforts to bring us together. I have George to thank for running interference. He is the only one who has any inkling what I've got planned and even he doesn't know the full story. The gun he fetched down from a display case at his parents' home for me is a duelling pistol from the eighteenth century. What he doesn't realise is that while he switched off the alarms, I slipped a little mother-of-pearl ladies handgun from the case while his back was turned, the kind of piece a lady might carry today when venturing into the wilder parts of a plutocrat's business empire. This one has ammunition, while the duelling pistol is unloaded and, in any case, I don't have access to the old-style shot and power it would take. The duelling pistol is safely on my bed in a box with George's name on it so he can return it before it is missed, while the handgun is nestled at the bottom of my sequinned evening bag, a comforting weight.

Soon, Keira, soon.

When I'm sure the photographer is occupied with the arts reviewers, I stroll around the show on my own. Damn, the woman can take a good photo. As with Sylvester, there is no denying that the morally corrupt person has talent. What are we supposed to make of that? Looking at them as dispassionately as I can manage, I can see how she captures the character in all of her subjects. Harold Pinter, for example, is looking down the lens with a barely concealed anger. Alan Bennett seems ready to run for the hills, perhaps smelling out her corruption. But the image of Sligo and me, that's probably the best of them all: she's caught his manipulation in the tilt of his head, his cunning in his expression, so that even though we pair are sharing a secret, he is holding on to yet deeper secrets. The glow of summer day does not hide the clouds that obscured his true nature. Was he a monster in life? To his own children, yes. To me? Well, that's far more complicated, isn't it? I'm wondering now if we didn't come out somehow even?

A settling of scores. This is what this night is about.

Lost in contemplating the image, I don't see the danger until almost too late. George rushes over and grabs my elbow. 'Incoming.'

The last thing I want is a premature entrance on the scene I have in mind. I let him lead me out of Keira's path to the cloakroom. Having had enough of the crowd, I hand over the ticket for my coat.

'I'd better get to the theatre,' I say.

'I'll come with you.'

I pat his arm. 'No need. I prefer you to keep Larry and Keira away from me. Bag my seat for me?' I've told him I'm going to make a speech before the play begins. He thinks the pistol is for me to explain how Sylvester told me of the opening of the piece that morning nineteen years ago, his first audience. 'A prop to illustrate' is what I told him.

'You're very brave, speaking out like this.' He kisses me, surprised that I don't pull away as I have done recently.

'Just...just forgive me, OK?' I meet his eyes. He's not going to like this.

'Merle, what are you planning?' He's not as gullible as I hoped.

I press my lips together. I can't tell anyone.

'If you...' He shakes his head, rejecting all the things that had sprung to his mind. 'OK, just don't do anything that'll get you arrested.'

And then I realise that he had seen me slip the handgun into my bag; he'd not bought my flimsy story about the pistol, but he has my back even when he doesn't think he should. Love him for that, as I realise I do, I can't say anything because not knowing exactly what's about to happen will be his best defence.

'You know, you really are quite...' I search for a word. 'Adorable. For a geek.'

He closes his eyes, battling his desire to stop me from whatever I've got planned. 'I'll remind you of that later. Just don't go all Hedda Gabler on us, OK?'

He fears I'm going to do something dramatic, like turn the gun on myself after getting my revenge. I go up on tiptoes and kiss his lips. 'See you after the show.' Our fingers link as I pull away. He doesn't want to let go.

'Won't you be sitting with me?' he asks.

I free my right hand from his. The left is still bound in a sling and plaster. 'See you later.'

THERE ARE no security checks to get backstage. I pass through easily with my handgun, to be welcomed by the director and the cast. They are flattering with their attention, praising my imagination as a child, thanking me for the inspiration I gave Sylvester. Rupert stands at my side protectively; I tease him for playing the arch priest defending his queen.

'I should've imagined someone like you when I conducted your funeral in the bluebell woods the first time,' I tell him seriously, though the cast laughs as if I've made a good joke.

'Thank you. I think,' he says.

The audience is gathering, a rumble like a distant storm heading our way. Charles Collins, who has been tasked with chaperoning me on and off stage, asks how I would like to be introduced.

'How about Sylvester's muse?' I say. I might as well claim the title as it's true, isn't it? According to legend, the muses always exact crushing punishments on those artists that challenge them, silencing or turning them into magpies. I'd silenced Sylvester in his last years; I'm going to give magpies a try tonight.

Yet it's hard to keep my nerve. As seven-thirty approaches, I'm seriously reconsidering my commitment to this course of action. I'm already in trouble, having stolen a handgun, but the next few minutes are going to see me break many other laws. Is revenge worth this? I have a nice life at Last Chance. Do I really want to shoot it all to pieces?

I close my eyes and ask myself what my father would do

in my shoes. The answer is clear: he'd run for it. OK, that decides me. I'm sticking. The truth will be told, no matter the cost.

Charles goes on in front of the curtain and receives his own round of applause.

'Ladies and gentleman, thank you for coming to this gala performance of *A Walk in Bluebell Woods*. We're here celebrating the life of one of our greatest playwrights, Sylvester Sligo, and the work of those that he inspired, such as tonight's special guest, Keira Fanning.' Applause breaks out and I bite the inside of my cheek to stop a rush of nerves. 'But there's another person here tonight who tops even Keira's contribution. We—actors, directors, photographers—have been inspired by Sligo, but this woman was his inspiration. May I give you, Merle Carlisle, Sylvester's muse?'

The applause is greater for me than it is for the photographer, something I take to heart and helps me cross to the centre of the stage. I hold the gun in the folds of my evening dress skirt. I've chosen a black number from June's stores as it will look suitably dramatic against the red velvet curtains. I meet Charles' eyes. He reads something in my expression and retreats to the wings, leaving me alone centre stage.

I can do this. Can't I?

I turn to face the audience. The lights are still up, as I requested. Keira is sitting in the centre of the front row. Memory flashes. Click-click-click. Black lens looking at me, pining me like a bug to a card. I raise the gun and point it at her.

'Revisiting the scene of your old crimes, *Keira*?' There's a confused murmur in the auditorium as I use the opening line of the play. Only the photographer—and George—understands. She grips the arms of her seat, white knuckled.

George half rises. He's going to leap in the way if I fire, stupid hero. I smile, knowing I probably look crazed. No one yet knows if this is drama or real. The theatre, the easiest place in the world to get away with murder.

'Now, you might all be wondering why I am holding our very important guest, our VIP, at gunpoint? I assure you this is a real gun, not a stage one like Anna will be holding in a little while. My answer? It's the best way to get your attention, isn't it, Keira?' I leave a pause for her to reply but she can only manage a whimper. 'You see, ladies and gentlemen, Miss Fanning is not all she seems. When I was nine, ten, eleven, in fact for many years before I was old enough to escape Dogberry Cottage, she took my picture. These weren't the ones you've all seen in the exhibition. These were what I think the polite term for is erotica. I call it child abuse. I did not give permission. I was not asked. I was told though to sit still and smile. So I thought it only fair that I got to make Keira sit still for me. Not so fun on the other side of the power relationship, is it, Keira?'

The audience is deathly quiet. Larry is gasping for breath like a fish on dry land. His partner, Greg, discreetly hands him an inhaler. Funny how I catch all this even while I'm setting my plan in action. Out of the corner of my eye, I can see cast members and stage crew gathering, wondering what to do. Rupert pushes forward.

'Merle?' he asks, hands out imploring.

'It's OK, Rupert—Julius. I just need you to stand by me.'

'We can't let you shoot her.'

The tip of the gun wavers a little. 'Really? Not even if she deserves it for killing my childhood?'

He draws in a quick breath. 'Not even then.'

I laugh and pull the trigger. Keira screams, hands up to her face. George lunges in front of her, ending up on the carpet. He would've been too late, I think with some satisfaction. The click of an empty barrel is hardly heard among the shouts of the audience. I laugh again, just about holding hysteria at bay. 'Guys, have none of you read the play? The power is in *not* firing.' I stuff the gun back in my pocket. 'That's what Sylvester learnt about crimes and their victims.'

Rupert waves the stagehands back. I think they were planning to carry me off but fortunately they obey him. It would've spoiled my big exit.

I hold up a hand and the audience, well trained for the theatre, falls silent. 'Keira Fanning, what you did was not art; it was sick. I hope the press now follow this up and show the world what you are. Your own images will condemn you, not my words. Maybe I'm the first domino in the chain that leads to that. I hope so. You see, to me, you were nothing but a magpie thieving the brightest moments of my childhood. I hope you get what you deserve, but I won't be the one to deliver it. I'll flick the domino but I will not shoot.' And then, because the moment seems to call for it, I bow.

There's silence. Then George, on his knees, starts clapping, Rupert joins him, as does Greg, Larry, Charles, Viv, Bette, Lillian, June, Regan and Lady Netta. By that time, the entire audience has joined them on their feet. Keira is the only one sitting. I can't find the words to describe her expression. Horror is close. I don't think until this moment she's ever thought of her subjects as fellow human beings. The front of house manager, more alert than the rest of us, comes to her side and takes her arm. He bends over, whispering something in her ear. In a daze she lets herself be led out.

I doubt there are police cars waiting for her—this isn't the movies. I expect she'll get on a plane and fight this out in

America. But as they say, my job here is done. George climbs up the stage stairs and hugs me, which prolongs the cheering. With his mouth close to my face, he whispers:

'Let's get out before someone thinks to ask about the gun.'

He's right. I was prepared to be arrested, but I shouldn't seek it out if it can be avoided. He leads me away. I catch Rupert's arm in passing.

'Sorry, I think I'm going to miss the show.'

'Show? You think we can top that?' His eyes are bright with tears. He embraces me. 'Merle, get out of here.'

I nod. 'I've broken a lot of laws tonight but there's one I can't see ignored.'

'What's that?' He asks.

'The show must go on.'

He laughs and pushes me towards the wings. 'Fly, you fools!'

George and I run, leaving Charles, Rupert and the cast to clear up the mess.

EPILOGUE

We had tapped into one of the theatre's primal functions: to give dignity to the stories of our lives by performing them for each other.

Nicholas Hytner, 'Balancing Acts'

I put the script down in front of George. He looks up, reading glasses catching my reflection and I lean in to kiss him so I don't have to see me.

'What's this?' He pulls me onto his knee.

'My play.'

'Your play?'

I'm feeling awkward now, fingers knotting in the bottom of my blouse. 'Yeah. I've been writing. Will you read it while I'm at the shop? I'd prefer not to be here.'

'I thought you were writing your college essays and all this time you were doing this?' He looks down at the manuscript and up at me.

'If you don't want to read it, don't worry. I'll ask Rupert.'

He catches me before I can run off and hide. 'I'm reading it. Not bloody Rupert.'

I hug him tight. 'Thank you.' We've been living together now for six months in our little flat in Camden and I still haven't scared him away. He must be made of strong stuff.

'It's my pleasure. What's it called?'

'Working title only.' I point to the front.

He flicks through the two acts, seeing the familiar names whisk by.

'I'll change those. Eventually,' I explain.

He grins. 'So I don't get to be famous? What time will you get off from work today?'

'Cristofor is taking over at five.' The wandering Romanian had surprised everyone by returning from Bucharest with his lovely bride last month. The wedding in question had turned out to be his. He repaid the money (with interest), apologised for his sudden departure, and rapidly charmed his way back into Bette's good books with the promise of a baby on the way. He is in the 'not yet quite trusted' book of everyone else, but he is a great help now Lillian has landed herself a role in *Mama Mia*, the touring company. Before she left, I was reassured to find that she had heard of ABBA.

'How about I read this now, meet you and take you out to supper to celebrate? I'm seeing Larry at four to go through Noel Coward. He'll be interested to hear about your writing.'

I groan. I'm giving it to George partly because I want him to do this—share it with a professional—but it still feels horribly exposing to put anything I've written out there for others to judge.

'Don't worry. I'm sure it'll be great.' He kisses my fingertips. 'Be good.'

'I'll try.' I click my fingers to Brutus who gets up with a put-upon sigh. It's just playacting. We all know his favourite part of the day is when he gets to go with me to the shop to meet his adoring public. The old ham.

We trot down the stairs, Brutus with his lead in his mouth. Bette's two strays have joined forces and thrown in their lot with George, so the shop is now free of foundlings. For the moment.

Upstairs, George is turning to the first page. The narrator, a broken woman washed up on the doorstep of the last theatrical bookshop, speaks:

This is the story I don't want to tell.

ABOUT THE AUTHOR

Eve Edwards is a writer of contemporary novels for adults, as well as historical YA fiction.

Eve loves bookshops so this series celebrates love and books. *Summer at the Last Chance Bookshop* is a companion to *Christmas at Sweet Notes Bookshop.*

In *The Summer of Wishful Thinking*, she explores the world of the registrar of births, deaths and marriages—think a modern version of Four Weddings but with a just-managing single mum twist.

She has a doctorate in literature from Oxford University and finds researching a large part of the fun for writing historical fiction. *Dusk* and *Dawn* deal with the events of World War I from the point of view of two teenagers caught up in the first day of the battle of the Somme. For the Lacey Chronicles, she visited Tudor houses, attended jousts and ate Elizabethan banquets to get the sights, sounds and tastes right for the books.

She lives near Oxford, UK, a city full of history, and is married with three children. She also writes under the pen names Julia Golding and Joss Stirling.

ALSO BY EVE EDWARDS

Contemporary

Christmas at Sweet Notes Bookshop

The Summer of Wishful Thinking

Historical Fiction

Dusk

Dawn

The Other Countess

The Queen's Lady

The Rogue's Princess

Printed in Great Britain
by Amazon

23237449R00189